SLAYING YOU

ALSO BY MICHELLE GAGNON

KILLING ME

KIDNAP & RANSOM

THE GATEKEEPER

BONEYARD

THE TUNNELS

YOUNG ADULT NOVELS

UNEARTHLY THINGS

DON'T LET GO

DON'T LOOK NOW

DON'T TURN AROUND

STRANGELETS

SLAYING YOU

Michelle Gagnon

G. P. PUTNAM'S SONS
NEW YORK

PUTNAM
— EST. 1838 —

G. P. Putnam's Sons
Publishers Since 1838
An imprint of Penguin Random House LLC
penguinrandomhouse.com

Library of Congress Cataloging-in-Publication Data

Names: Gagnon, Michelle, author.
Title: Slaying you / Michelle Gagnon.
Description: New York: G.P. Putnam's Sons, 2025.
Identifiers: LCCN 2024044060 (print) | LCCN 2024044061 (ebook) |
ISBN 9780593540770 (hardcover) | ISBN 9780593540787 (epub)
Subjects: LCGFT: Thrillers (Fiction). | Humorous fiction. | Novels.
Classification: LCC PS3607.A35862 S53 2025 (print) | LCC PS3607.A35862 (ebook) |
DDC 813/.6—dc23/eng/20241021
LC record available at https://lccn.loc.gov/2024044060
LC ebook record available at https://lccn.loc.gov/2024044061

Printed in the United States of America
1st Printing

Title page art: Knife © Haali/Shutterstock

BOOK DESIGN BY KRISTIN DEL ROSARIO

To Stephanie Rostan

What the hell is going on?

—IMOGEN HEAP

SLAYING YOU

PROLOGUE

ODDS AGAINST TOMORROW

LAS VEGAS, NEVADA

I've heard that most people go through life without encountering a serial killer. In fact, the vast majority make it through without ever experiencing serious peril. They just saunter along, whistling jauntily to themselves (at least, that's how I imagine them), and then, after a relatively peaceful spin atop this green-and-blue marble, they expire in their sleep, a gentle smile on their lips.

Gee, I wonder what that's like.

Because here I am, halfway through my twenty-fourth year, about to confront my second murderous psychopath. Wait, no—this is the third. When you forget one? That's a bad sign.

At this point, maybe I should just acknowledge that a nice, normal life was never in the cards for me. Chasing down a freak? *Yawn* . . . must be Tuesday. Some combination of fate and DNA resulted in me being launched into the void like a pinball, destined to bang into all the dark shit out there.

"You ready, toots?" Dot asks in a low voice.

I nod, tightening my grip on the gun. She holds up a finger and counts:

One . . .

Two . . .

On *three*, she throws open the door and I charge out.

CHAPTER ONE

CROSSFIRE

FOUR DAYS EARLIER IN PENROSE, COLORADO

Wright leaned over his shoulder, peering out at the road ahead. "Shit, man. Can you even see?"

Peterson didn't answer, intent on driving. The prison bus was a beast in the best of times, and this was definitely not that. The wiper blades were basically just moving ash back and forth, smearing it across the windshield in dark streaks. Visibility was down to a few yards, the entire sky blotted out by smoke. It wasn't much past noon but looked like twilight, the only sign of daylight an apocryphal red sun.

It's like driving into hell, Peterson thought, repressing a shudder.

Wright wasn't helping. Every few minutes he'd let out a low whistle and say something stupid, like, "You sure this road is still clear?"

No, dumbass, Peterson wanted to snap. *I'm not sure of anything anymore.* The road *had* been clear when they'd left the supermax an hour earlier, but how in the hell was he supposed to know now? Cell service was down, and they were supposed to stay off the radio unless there was an emergency.

It hadn't been like this when he drove to work that morning. The only sign of a wildfire then had been a slight tickle in the back of his throat as he belted out "Jolene," evoking memories of camping with his dad when he was a kid. Aside from what looked like morning fog, you'd barely have known a fire was raging nearby.

Well, it sure as shit looked like it now. On this section of Route 24, you usually could see for miles, low, scrub grass–covered hills stretching into the distance. But now, all that dry brush was aflame. The wildfire was eighty acres wide and growing by the minute. The smoke to his right was tinted red, and he would've sworn heat was coming off it. *Should I call in?* Their bus had already been diverted once because I-25 was overtaken. If this road had become impassable, too, wouldn't someone have let them know?

Peterson swore under his breath. It was the warden's fault for waiting so long to start the evacuation. Granted, shifting more than three hundred of the nation's most dangerous criminals to different prisons probably wasn't easy. He'd heard rumors that Colorado State Penitentiary had flat out refused to take any, claiming they didn't have beds to spare. Which was why he was driving these assholes to Sterling Correctional instead, nearly two hundred and fifty goddamn miles away. And at the rate they were going, they wouldn't get there until nightfall.

Peterson really didn't want to be dealing with these creeps after dark. He was a year into this gig and already hated it. Lifers like Wright got off on the power trips, but that wasn't his scene. If it weren't for the benefits, he would have left after a month; now, he was just waiting on a transfer to minimum security. At least there you were dealing with human beings. A glance in the rearview mirror showed two dozen figures in dusky orange scrubs, each shackled in a bus seat. As the last guy hired, Peterson had been assigned the worst of the worst: cartel bosses, serial killers, even a couple of goddamn terrorists. They were, to a man, eerily silent and expressionless. He wondered if that meant they were as freaked out as he was.

Either that, or they were plotting something. One of them was a notorious escape artist, and when he'd gotten the assignment, Peterson's first thought had been, *Shit. I bet we end up getting mowed down by a bunch of narcos with AR-15s.*

But even they wouldn't be crazy enough to drive through this, he thought grimly.

"Shit!" Wright cried out.

Reflexively, Peterson hit the brakes. The rear of the bus skidded as the tires fought for purchase. Wright was thrown against the wire gate separating them from the prisoners, his yelp matched by shouting from the back. There were a scary few seconds as Peterson rode the tipping point; he could feel the back of the bus wanting to cant sideways, dragging them with it. But the beast righted herself at the last moment, and he heaved a sigh of relief.

It was short lived.

"Ho-ly Christ," Wright breathed, leaning forward.

The fire had jumped the highway, leaving Peterson staring at a solid wall of flames. It looked how he'd always pictured the Red Sea when Moses parted it, red stretching up on either side and smoke swirling in between. Tendrils started to leach into the bus despite the closed windows, and a few of the assholes in the back started coughing. One swore in Spanish, yelling for them to turn around. Within seconds the cry was taken up by the others, a cacophony of men screaming for him to head forward, or back, *Just go, you bastard!*, *Drive, asshole!*, along with a lot of choice comments about his mother.

"Peterson," Wright said from his shoulder. "Hate to say it but they're right, man. I think we gotta go back."

Peterson realized he'd frozen. He shook it off and checked the side mirror. It didn't look much better behind them, but at least that section of road was familiar. He cautiously shifted into reverse and slowly started to back up the beast. Route 24 was just two lanes, barely deserving of the title "State Highway." He cursed under his breath; this was going to require a twenty-point turn.

He was halfway through it, the bus perpendicular to the road and straddling both lanes, when Wright shouted again. Higher pitched this time, really more of a scream.

Intent on making sure the unwieldy bus didn't slide into the trench lining the berm, Peterson chanced a look where Wright was pointing.

A semi was coming straight at them, screaming out of the smoke at a hundred miles an hour. Through the windshield, Peterson could see two men in cowboy hats, their eyes wide and mouths open. The truck braked hard, stuttering into a skid. The back swung out as it started to jackknife, but it was too late. There wasn't even time to pray before the semi slammed into them.

CHAPTER TWO

TWO SMART PEOPLE

FORTY MILES OUTSIDE LAS VEGAS, NEVADA

I shuffled through the bills in my hand again, then said, "Um, I actually gave you a hundred."

The mini-mart cashier narrowed his eyes. "You sure 'bout that?"

I nodded earnestly, trying my darndest to look truthful.

He hesitated, then lifted the drawer and chuckled. "Well, hell. Sorry, miss. You wouldn't believe how many folks try to pull a fast one."

"Really?" I ruefully shook my head, reflexively mirroring him. "Terrible. Who would do such a thing?" *Me*, I thought. *Up until a couple months ago, most definitely me.* But I'd finally put my life as a grifter firmly behind me, once and for all. Hell, these past few months I'd practically become a poster child for law-abiding citizens.

"Here you go. Change for a hundred." As the cashier passed me a stack of bills, I caught movement in the security mirror mounted behind him. Glancing at it, I saw a teenager slip a bag of chips in his jacket and tsked internally. Sloppy. Kid was definitely going to get caught.

The cashier's eyes started to shift toward him. Impulsively, I tucked a five in the tip jar to distract him. "That's for you."

He threw me a puzzled look. "Well, thanks. Just so you know, that's mainly for when I get someone coffee."

I shrugged. "Good karma. Pay it forward, right?"

As I left, the kid darted through the door right ahead of me. In a low voice, I said, "You should be more careful. Juvie's not worth a bag of chips."

The kid startled, then muttered, "Fuck off, Grandma."

As he loped away, I called out, "I'm twenty-four, shithead!" So much for being a Good Samaritan. It would serve him right if he got caught next time. Carefully balancing my stack of snacks and drinks, I cautiously navigated back to my parked Audi.

When I got to the car, a pair of hands reached out of the passenger window. "Wow! You went crazy in there."

"Just grabbed the basics. Take these," I said, passing over the Icees.

Relieved of the worst of my burden, I circled the car and climbed in, tossing the snacks on the center console. Kat was frowning into one of the Icee cups. "Is it supposed to be brown?"

"Oh yeah," I said, nodding firmly. "We got lucky. They had pineapple *and* Coke."

"So this is Coke-flavored?"

"Of course not," I scoffed. "It's both. Classic mix, trust me."

Dubiously she took a sip, then wrinkled her nose. "It tastes appalling."

"It'll grow on you," I promised.

"I sincerely doubt that," Kat said. "So why zombies?"

"Why not?" I shrugged. One of the best things about my relationship with Kat was that since day one, we'd been engaged in an ongoing conversation with no clear start or end point. I would pick up the thread of something we'd talked about a week earlier, and without my having to provide any context, Kat was right back in it with me. I'd never experienced that with anyone before. For example, we'd spent most of the drive from San Francisco debating which type of fictional apocalypse would be preferable if given a choice. "I mean, slow zombies, obviously."

Kat shuddered. "I hate the fast zombies."

"Yeah, the ones in *World War Z* were terrifying."

"*I Am Legend* were worse," she said. "I still have terrible nightmares about those."

"Same. But slow zombies are manageable. You just shore up your compound and wear long-sleeved leathers whenever you leave it."

She was already shaking her head. "The zombies always break in."

"Impossible," I said. "Because my compound has a half mile of defenses on all sides. The outermost ring has a moat, then pointy sticks, then a fence, then another moat, and more sticks . . ."

"Impressive," she said.

"Thanks. I've put some thought into it." I shot her a grin. "What about you?"

"Aliens," she said decisively.

"Seriously?" I threw her a look.

"Yes. I believe they will most likely be friendly and solve all our problems."

"Or they'll terraform our planet while enslaving and eating us."

Jutting up her chin she said, "I accept the risk."

I burst out laughing; the gravity her German accent lent her words always cracked me up. "You're a nut, you know that?"

"Yes. And you love that about me."

"Yeah, I do," I said, reaching over and squeezing her hand.

Taking another sip of her drink, she winced and said, "Oh no."

"What?"

"It is growing on me," she said, faux terror in her voice.

"See?" I said triumphantly.

"It's oddly reminiscent of lebkuchen, even though it has none of the flavors," she said, cocking her head to the side.

"Mmm, lebkuchen. Totally my favorite," I joked weakly. That sort of statement always highlighted the gaping chasm between our upbringings. Katarina von Rotberg (which was actually the abbreviated version of her name; on her birth certificate, she had at least a dozen more tucked in between) was an actual baroness, raised in luxury and "finished" by Swiss boarding schools and what she referred to as her "stint at Oxford."

Let's just say that my life path had been markedly different. Six months ago, I couldn't afford a tank of gas, never mind an Audi to put it in. Being gifted three million dollars in cryptocurrency had changed all that. But even though I had money now, I wasn't fluent in the language that wealthy people like Kat spoke. Sometimes I bridled at that; other times it made me jealous.

"It's a kind of cookie," Kat explained. "Filled with fruit and nuts. Very popular around *Weihnachten*. Um, Christmas," she amended quickly.

"It's okay, Kat."

"I am not showing off," she said defensively.

"I know you're not." I sighed heavily and said, "I mean, neither of us can help how fancy we are, right?"

"So fancy," she agreed, cracking a grin.

"And hot, too."

"So hot." She shook her head. "It is a travesty, really."

"Hmm, I think *travesty* might be too fancy a word, even for us."

I waggled a finger at her. “Get it under control, otherwise people won’t be able to stand us. It’d be like staring into the sun.”

She threw a chip at me. Nonchalantly, I scooped it off my lap and popped it in my mouth.

“Ew.”

“Just trying to take the hotness down a few notches.”

“Very effective,” she agreed. “And yet you still remain very, very hot.”

“Thank you.”

“Perhaps we could stop off somewhere?” she asked, cocking an eyebrow while trailing her fingers up my thigh. “And arrive tomorrow instead?”

“That’s tempting,” I agreed. We’d spent quite a bit of time in bed over the past three months. Better still were the moments in between: nights on the couch watching movies and laughing together or fine dining at some of San Francisco’s foodie destinations—places I never could’ve afforded a year ago (or even gotten into; it’s amazing how being a millionaire literally opened doors). We had even spent one magical weekend touring Napa’s vineyards.

For the first time in my life, I was in what felt like a normal, happy relationship. I was crazy about Kat. She seemed to feel the same way about me. All I wanted was to spend every minute with her for the indefinite future. Maybe even the rest of my life.

And if I was being honest, that scared the crap out of me. “Sorry,” I said, clearing my throat. “I promised Dot we’d be there by dinner.”

“Who are these friends again?” she asked around the Icee straw.

“Oh, just some people I met in Vegas when I stayed there last spring,” I said vaguely.

“Well, I cannot wait to meet them. And to see Las Vegas. I have heard wonderful things!”

"Just so you know, it's not going to be anything like *Ocean's 11*," I warned. I'd discovered the hard way that Kat tended toward an overly rosy portrait of American tourist destinations, largely thanks to their heavily filtered appearances in movies.

"I bet it will be even better!" She grinned at me.

I smiled back wanly, wondering again if I should have booked a room at one of the fancier hotels on the Strip. But Dot had threatened to draw and quarter me if I did. And after all, we were going for her wedding; the least I could do was check us into one of her motels. Still, I was more than a little trepidatious about how Kat would react to staying somewhere that Tripadvisor described as "kitschy-cute, but watch out for bedbugs."

And that wasn't my only concern. Maybe it was finally time to come clean with Kat about everything that had happened last spring. In my defense, it wasn't easy to explain that while completing my college education, I'd been abducted by a Pokémon-obsessed serial killer in Tennessee who shaved my entire body and painted me blue, only to be saved at the eleventh hour by a weird lady named Grace. I'd found out later that Grace had spent decades tracking serial killers in hopes of catching a specific one: her psychopathic twin brother. And in a truly delightful twist of fate, that psychopathic twin had latched on to *me* as his next victim. He lured me to Vegas, killed one of my new friends, and kidnapped another, all of which led to a showdown in a motel room, where Grace shot him dead. And here's the real kicker: My newfound fortune came from that psychopath. In a move that seemed wildly out of character, Grace gifted it to me because she was already set financially.

See? Complicated. Not exactly conversation fodder for a first date, or even a third. At least, that's what I'd kept telling myself.

But that excuse was wearing thin three months into our relationship. Kat would be meeting Dot in Vegas, along with Marcella and everyone else who had been involved (well, mostly everyone else; I very much doubted that Grace would be making an appearance). There were bound to be some awkward moments if people started reminiscing about our escape from a serial killer and Kat had no clue what they were talking about.

But selfishly, I wanted to keep my secrets for just a little longer. Partly, I worried that sharing too much might taint what we'd built together. Or maybe I was just afraid to let her see that I was damaged goods. Because so far, I'd largely managed to keep my shit together around her. As far as Kat was concerned, I was an independently wealthy future clinical psychologist who hoped to start grad school next year. I'd become very adept at dodging any and all questions about my past, including my "stint" in Vegas.

But later today, those two worlds were going to come together. I just had to hope they didn't collide.

"Everything okay?" Kat asked, snapping me back to the present. A sign ahead read **LAS VEGAS, 30 MILES**.

"Yeah, great. I was just thinking that maybe you're right. Aliens over zombies."

"I don't know, you might have convinced me with your fancy defense plan." Her eyes widened, and simultaneously we yelled, "Alien zombies!"

We both collapsed in giggles. Wiping her eyes, Kat said, "I feel so lucky to have found you."

"Same," I said sincerely. "Now let's go do some stuff we'll regret."

CHAPTER THREE

ESCAPE

PENROSE, COLORADO

Peterson woke up in hell. The air was filled with smoke, screams, and the smell of roasting flesh. He tried to get up, but as soon as he shifted, his body shrieked at him. Everything hurt, and when he swallowed he tasted blood.

Okay, he thought from a distance. *This is bad. Take it slow.*

The smoke-filled landscape outside his windshield was disorienting. As he coughed, he stared at it, trying to make sense of what he was seeing. The bus was on its side, he realized, and the windshield had shattered. Which also explained the shard of glass sticking out of his chest.

Seeing it, he started to hyperventilate. Blood pulsed out with each breath, joining the thick slick already coating his uniform. Peterson squeezed his eyes shut tight. He was still alive, and he'd taken first aid back when he'd considered becoming an EMT. *Stay calm*, he told himself sternly. *And no matter what, don't touch that shard.*

He carefully shifted his hands and wiggled his fingers—they were free, at least, and seemed unharmed. His legs were pinned, though. Raising his head, he could see that they were trapped by something solid and heavy. He tried to shift it off his feet, but it was wedged in the footwell. And it was disconcertingly squishy.

He looked around for something to use to free himself. The screams from the back were getting louder, but he couldn't be bothered with that right now. Anything happening outside his body no longer mattered. In this state of detachment, he noted Wright lying a few feet away, gazing blankly at him. Part of Wright, at least. The window must have sliced him in half, and Peterson had a bad feeling that the other half might be what was pinning down his legs.

Don't think about it.

It was getting hotter. The smoke was so thick he could see only a few feet in any direction, which honestly was a bit of a relief. Peterson blinked sweat out of his eyes. He fumbled around with his hands, trying to shift the weight on his legs . . . and then something moved in his peripheral vision.

Peterson turned his head. A guy in orange scrubs was balancing on the gate that used to separate them from the prisoners; it must've been dislodged in the crash.

Shit.

"Please," Peterson said plaintively. "Please help me?"

The guy looked at him. He was older, tall and slim. The guy's eyes flickered, reflecting the flames outside and something else . . .

Peterson heaved a sigh of relief. Maybe they weren't all assholes. In a real crisis, humanity shone through, right?

Or maybe not, he thought as the guy leaned in and deftly plucked the shard from his chest.

"My apologies," the guy said in a low, oddly formal tone. "But I have a pressing matter to attend to."

"No," Peterson protested, but it came out as more of a sigh. He experienced an overwhelming sense of lightness as the life flowed from his body. When the guy drew the shard across his throat, he barely even felt it.

– – –

"Um, Dot? I can't breathe."

"Sorry, toots. I'm just so chuffed to see you!" Dot held me at arm's length, beaming.

"You look incredible," I said appreciatively. Dot was dressed in a brilliantly patterned housedress with a leopard-print scarf wrapped around curlers. Her cat-eye glasses matched her outfit, and her makeup was perfectly applied.

When we'd parted last May, Dot had spent weeks in hiding (thanks to me) and then Grace's brother had murdered her best friend, Jessie (also largely thanks to me, since I'd turned out to be a magnet for serial killers). Fear and grief are exhausting; they had taken a lot out of all of us, especially Dot. But clearly she'd bounced back. She was glowing and looked every inch the blissful bride-to-be.

"Look at me, running around in my unmentionables!" she said, tapping my arm. "But I just had to welcome you in person."

"The place looks great, too." I cast a glance around. We were staying at the Mayhem, the nicer of the two motels that Dot owned. Still not as fancy as what Kat was probably accustomed to but decorated with lots of mid-century elements meant to attract a hipster crowd.

"Thanks, toots. And this must be Kat!" Dot said, pulling her into an embrace. "My, aren't you a knockout!"

"That is awfully kind of you!" Kat kissed her on both cheeks, smiling. "Lovely to make your acquaintance."

Dot's eyebrows shot up. "Yours too, toots. I hope you're treating our Amber well, she's a catch."

Kat nodded firmly. "Yes, she most certainly is."

I allowed myself to feel a rush of pride. This gorgeous blond goddess who could have pretty much anyone she wanted had chosen me. Sometimes, it still didn't feel real. "Y'all are making me blush."

"Well, you deserve every last bit of happiness, Amber. Now, let's get you squared away." Dot tucked my hand under her arm as she led us toward the office. "I've got you booked in number twenty, it's the best in the joint."

"Thanks, Dot," I said with genuine relief. I knew it was silly to worry, but as we'd turned into the parking lot I'd gone cold, wondering if she'd accidentally put me in number five. Not that there was anything wrong with that room, unless—like me—you knew that Grace's brother had strangled one of his final victims there, leaving her body in the bathtub.

I shuddered involuntarily. Dot gave my arm a reassuring squeeze and said in a low voice, "You sure this is okay, kiddo? I can always get you a suite at the Nugget instead, just say the word."

"I'm good, but thanks." I was trying to treat this week as a sort of exposure therapy; staying at the Mayhem meant I'd be forced to confront some pretty terrible memories, and maybe that would help me process them. At least, that's what I was hoping. Besides, I wanted to be close by in case Dot needed anything.

After all, I was one of her bridesmaids.

I'd been genuinely shocked when she asked. Dot was the unofficial Queen of Vegas, universally beloved, with a vast network of people who either owed her a favor or liked her enough to help out for free. When I'd said as much, she explained, "I know we didn't have a lot of time together, hon, but it meant a lot to me."

"So do I have any official bridesmaid duties?" I asked.

"Just the dress fitting! Other than that, we're all set."

"Really?" I said, slightly disappointed. "Aren't I supposed to get you something blue?"

"Only if you want." Dot patted my hand. "I got a friend who's kitting us all out. You'll love her." Off my expression, she added, "I just want you to enjoy yourself. Didn't want to put you to work after you came all this way."

"Thanks," I said, mollified.

As we followed her toward the staircase, Kat said, "I smell smoke. Are there fireplaces in the rooms?"

Dot burst out laughing. "Don't I wish! That's from the wildfire in Colorado. The winds shifted, and it's smelled like a cookout all day."

"I heard about that," I said. "It's pretty big, right?"

"A hundred acres and counting. Damn global warming." Dot shook her head. "It's messing with everything, isn't it?"

"Yeah. It's chillier than I expected, too," I said. "Thought a desert was supposed to be warm."

"Ain't that the truth! Cold front blew in last night," Dot said. "Hope you brought warm clothes."

"Oh, yeah. Turns out in San Francisco, you gotta bundle up." That old Mark Twain saw, "the coldest winter I ever spent was a summer in San Francisco," had proven to be accurate. If I hadn't met Kat, I might've already bailed for warmer climes.

Similarly, this was a very different Vegas from the one I'd left in late spring. The sky was slate gray, the air crisp. It didn't look like there'd be much opportunity for the swimsuits we'd packed.

We climbed the stairs to the second floor, passing a veranda complete with a firepit surrounded by Adirondack chairs. "So is Jim still out of town?" I asked.

"For a couple more days," Dot said. "I'm missing the hell out of him."

"Is that the groom?" Kat asked.

"Yup. Instead of a bachelor party, he and some of his Marine buddies are riding motorcycles cross-country to raise money for injured vets."

"That is very cool," Kat said.

"That's my Jim," Dot said proudly. "He's flying back the day before the wedding, so I'm on my own and ready for some quality gal time! Now c'mon inside."

We followed Dot into the office tucked behind the firepit. I watched Kat take in the space as Dot ducked behind the desk to grab a key. The office was charming, filled with polished wood and Coachella posters. Still, I worried that Kat was secretly finding it wanting.

"Got it!" Dot popped up, brandishing a key. "Now, I want to hear all about how you two met." The desk phone rang, and she frowned at it. "Ah hell, that's probably number three complaining about the ice machine again. Why don't you go get ready? Limo'll be here in twenty."

"I'm so excited!" Kat chirped. "I have never been to an American bachelorette party before!"

"Me either," I muttered.

"Well, you two are in for a treat!" Dot exclaimed. "Now excuse me while I grab this." Picking up the receiver, she chirped, "Mayhem Motel, so close but so far out, can I help you?"

She waved us out. Kat stopped on the balcony and shaded her eyes, scanning the motel's exterior with what I hoped was delight. Turning to me, she gleefully exclaimed, "It is just like in the movies!"

"Kind of," I said, hoping a tiny bathroom without spa amenities would hold the same appeal. We trotted down the stairs together, and I popped the trunk on my Audi. After wrestling the bags out, I turned to find her looking perplexed.

Kat frowned. "Where's the bellhop?"

"You're looking at her," I said grimly, wheeling the suitcases. "I warned you it wouldn't be as fancy as Napa."

Gamely, she took the handle of her suitcase. "Right. No problem! Where's the elevator?"

Sighing, I motioned toward the stairs. "On the plus side, we get some cardio, right?"

CHAPTER FOUR

LADY IN THE DEATH HOUSE

JEFFERSON COUNTY, COLORADO

Deputy Sheriff Cynthia Veracruz guided her SUV up the long drive to the last house on Platte River Road, trying to repress her irritation.

She was going to be late for dinner again, and all because some weekenders had freaked out when a random guy strolled onto their precious vacation property. Probably just a hunter who accidentally wandered out of the national forest. But it was an election year, and some of those weekenders voted, so her boss had her out here knocking on doors, warning people there might be a "shady character" in the area.

At least the wildfire had veered away. It had been touch and go this morning, and there'd been a scary half hour when it looked like they might have to evacuate the entire area. But the wind had ticked up, thankfully, pushing the fire east and clearing away the worst of the smoke and ash.

Cynthia parked in front of a small red house with blue trim that had seen better days. She'd been meaning to check on Mrs. Abbott anyway, especially with the fire coming so close. Two birds, one stone and all that.

Walking up to the front door, Cynthia noted that the gutters needed a good cleaning. Best to handle that before the snows came, and they were already overdue. Maybe she'd send Bill out this weekend, have him muck them out as a favor.

Developers had been sniffing around this property for years, but Mrs. Abbott was one of the last holdouts. She refused to sell and move into the retirement community her kids wanted to stick her in. Said she'd been born on this land and would die on it. There weren't a lot of folks like her left.

I'll get Bill to check the steps, too, Cynthia thought as she carefully made her way onto the porch. Some of the boards looked almost rotted through. If Mrs. Abbott fell and hurt herself, all the way out here on her own . . . Cynthia shook her head. Maybe those Abbott kids weren't wrong. Winters were tough up here in the mountains.

"Mrs. Abbott?" she called out, rapping her knuckles against the door. "It's Cynthia Veracruz." She waited a few beats, then knocked again. "Hello?"

Frowning, she cupped her hands and peered through the window. It was dim inside; all she could make out was the narrow hallway. There didn't seem to be any lights on, even though twilight was falling. Cynthia felt a prickle of concern. Turning, she scanned the yard more carefully. *No car*, she realized belatedly. Millicent Abbott tooled around in an ancient Subaru Outback, and she made a point of never driving after dark due to her cataracts.

Perhaps she'd had car trouble? Or gone to the store and was arriving home later than expected? She could even have evacuated, although Cynthia had a hard time imagining Mrs. Abbott leaving unless the fire was on her doorstep.

Should she call it in?

Cynthia bit her lip. It seemed silly to raise the alarm just because an old lady was out driving past dark. She'd take a lap around the property just to ease her own mind. Then she'd wait in the car for Mrs. Abbott to return. Bill would be less irritated about her lateness if it was for a good reason.

Picking her way carefully through the high grass—it was late in the season for ticks, but you never knew—Cynthia rounded the corner of the house. Old statues peeked out of the overgrown lawn: Cynthia reflexively crossed herself as she passed the Virgin Mary. Should she have Bill give the yard a mow when it would be covered in snow soon? Might as well. She added it to her mental to-do list.

The back door was wide open. Seeing that, Cynthia stopped dead. Someone had waded through the grass to the back porch, flattening a path that led all the way to the tree line. "Mrs. Abbott?" she called out, unclipping her belt holster. "Anyone in there?"

No answer. *Shady character*, Cynthia thought as she pulled out her sidearm and braced it in front of her, slowly approaching the open door. "Sheriff's department!"

Cynthia gave the door a wide berth, circling around until she could see inside. It opened into a mudroom, where stacks of old boots were piled below hanging parkas and wool scarves.

Cynthia drew a deep breath: Maybe Mrs. Abbott had left the door open by mistake?

Or someone else had.

Deciding, she clicked her radio and said, "This is Veracruz, I'm at the Abbott place on south Platte. Looks like someone might've broken in."

A pause, and then the dispatcher responded, "Got it, Cynthia. You need backup?"

"I'm gonna take a look inside," Cynthia said. "But yeah, probably not a bad idea to send another car."

"Cole's close. He'll be there in five."

"Thanks, Reina. I'll keep an open channel."

"Roger that."

Cynthia eased inside, swiping her boots clean on the mat. An atavistic tremor stirred at the base of her spine: Something felt off. The house was too quiet, the air weighted—

She nearly stepped in a dark pool that extended into the hallway from the kitchen. Cynthia drew a deep breath, bracing herself, and then edged around it to peer inside.

It took a few seconds for her brain to make sense of what she was seeing. A few more to get a grip on herself—she was a professional, and this wasn't her first dead body, not even the first time she'd seen the corpse of someone she knew.

But it was the first time she'd seen anyone completely eviscerated. Crossing herself again, Cynthia muttered a prayer for poor Mrs. Abbott.

"Sorry Cynthia, I didn't copy that. Everything okay? You find Mrs. Abbott?"

She'd forgotten she was on an open channel. "I found her. And we're going to need more than Cole. She's been murdered, Reina, and it's bad. Real bad. You better tell the boss. And put out an APB for her car, okay?"

A beat, then Reina gravely confirmed, "Roger that."

Cynthia went back outside to wait in her patrol car. She sat there for a minute, her mind oddly blank. Whatever had done that to Mrs. Abbott wasn't human. Couldn't be.

Sirens in the distance. Cynthia drew a deep breath and checked herself in the rearview mirror. She barely recognized the person staring back with terror in her eyes. The truth was, whatever had done this, she never wanted to come face-to-face with it. Deep down, she hoped it had driven Mrs. Abbott's Subaru far away from her and everyone she cared about.

Shit. Bill. Cynthia dialed her cell phone, absently noting that her hands were shaking. "Hey, honey?" she said, trying to keep her voice steady. "I'm gonna be late. And, um, could you make sure the doors and windows are locked? I'll explain later. Just do it."

CHAPTER FIVE

LADIES IN RETIREMENT

LAS VEGAS, NEVADA

Fortunately, after we'd lugged our bags upstairs, Kat had exclaimed with delight over the room. It wasn't as bad as I'd feared. In fact, a year ago I would've been floored by the retro light fixtures and high-thread-count bedding; funny how quickly my standards had changed. I was becoming a bit of a snob about stuff like that, which wasn't something I was proud of.

As promised, when Kat and I came back downstairs a half hour later, a stretch limo awaited. Dot was already ensconced inside, looking gorgeous in a vintage gown that Grace Kelly could've worn to the Oscars, topped by a fur stole in a nod to the chill outside. She held a champagne coupe and looked positively giddy. "Welcome, ladies! Can I pour you a glass?"

"Sure," I said. "I promise not to throw up on your shoes this time."

"Oh, that was some night, wasn't it?" Dot tilted her head back to laugh while Kat looked puzzled.

Turning to Kat, I explained, "Last time Dot took me for a big night out, I was overserved."

"And that's not the half of it," Dot said.

"Yeah, I might've made a bit of an ass of myself," I interjected hastily. "Ruined a koi pond, too."

Dot cocked an eyebrow at me, probably wondering why I wasn't saying more. Smart cookie that she was, though, she smoothly added, "Don't you worry, hon. No scorpion bowls on the menu this time."

"That's a shame. I wouldn't mind another trip to the Tiki Hut since I barely remember the last one."

"Another time. Tonight is strictly top shelf." Dot winked at us. "Hope you're ready to experience high-roller Vegas, Kat."

"Oh, I cannot wait!" Kat said.

"And can I say, the two of you look stunning. Kat, hon, that dress is just the nines."

Kat beamed. Dot was right: She looked phenomenal. Her long blond hair was swept up into a complicated knot, and her makeup was perfect. She wore a strapless dress that brought out her green eyes and high heels that raised her up to at least five-foot-ten, which to me was basically Amazonian.

"I swear, you're the spitting image of Rita Hayworth in *The Lady from Shanghai*," she added approvingly.

"Yes? I have not seen this film."

"Oh, it's fabulous. You'd love it," Dot gushed. "Orson Welles directed it. He and Rita had been married, but they were estranged by the time it started shooting . . ."

As Dot prattled on about the film, I gazed out the window. We were driving through the section of Vegas known as "Naked City," which, according to Dot, was not generally the safest. The Mayhem did well in spite of that, though. As we cruised past pawn shops and bail bonds offices, I felt an unexpected pang of nostalgia. Six months ago, I couldn't get away from Vegas fast enough. But even though I liked San Francisco, something about this garish neon landscape oddly felt more like home. That was probably largely thanks to Dot.

As we turned into the parking lot of an apartment complex and two more woman climbed in, Dot clapped her hands with glee. Exchanging air kisses with them, she exclaimed, "Portia and Raquel, you look just gorgeous! Amber and Kat, these are two of my favorite Fatal Femmes!"

I nodded and said hi as the two of them slid in next to me. They exchanged a look, and then Portia said, "Wait, *the* Amber? As in, Pikachu Amber?"

"Um . . ." I shifted uncomfortably and threw Dot a look. The "Fatal Femmes" was a group of citizen sleuths who collaborated on unsolved crimes. Dot was one of the cofounders, and clearly, she'd shared more than I would've liked. She made a face and mouthed, "Sorry."

"Yeah, I guess," I muttered.

"What is Pikachu Amber?" Kat asked, eyes wide.

"Long story," I said evasively. "I'll tell you later. So, um, are you folks working on any cool cases right now?"

Weirdly, it was the Femmes' turn to look discomfited. Avoiding my eyes, Portia said, "Oh, we're not working on anything right now. Are we, Dot?"

"Too busy, I'm afraid," Dot said airily. I frowned; she was wringing her hands, which she only did when she was stressed. "But I guess that's for the best, right?"

"I guess," I said as we pulled into another parking lot. Before I could press them on it, another round of people crammed inside, squealing and gushing.

It was a good thing Dot had sprung for the stretch option, because by the time we arrived at our destination, the limo more closely resembled a clown car. As we piled out under the portico at the Wynn resort, everyone adjusted hemlines and heels.

"Thanks, Maury, you're a prince," Dot said, going up on her toes to give our driver a peck on the cheek.

"Anytime, Dottie." He tipped his cap.

Kat slipped her hand into mine. As I gave it a squeeze, I looked up at her and smiled, hoping that the tension I felt wasn't showing in my face. Every time we'd approached another destination to pick up passengers, I'd caught my breath. I hadn't said anything, and Dot hadn't mentioned it, but I'd assumed that Marcella would be picked up at one of our many stops. I wasn't sure how to interpret the fact that she hadn't been. Was she avoiding me?

And did I care?

Nope, I thought, taking in my stunning girlfriend. Nothing was going to ruin this. Not even a hot, sort-of ex-girlfriend.

"Well, hello," a honeyed voice said in my ear.

I jumped and spun to find Marcella grinning at me.

And just like that, I vaulted back six months to the time we'd spent holed up in a hotel room. The memory set my pulse racing, and a flush spread over my entire body. I swallowed hard.

Marcella was wearing stilettos and a slinky red dress that clung to every curve. She had on less makeup than usual, and long, dark curls framed her face.

In short, she looked amazing. I barely managed to croak out, "Oh, uh, hi, Marcella."

We stared at each other for a long beat, which was interrupted by Kat leaning in and planting a double kiss on Marcella's cheeks. "Lovely to meet you. I am Kat." She pulled me close to her side and added, "Amber's girlfriend."

"Lucky you," Marcella said. I couldn't tell if she was being snide or not.

"Inside, everyone!" Dot ordered from the front of the pack. "Our reservation awaits!"

As she led us through an opulent lobby, I tried to recover. I'd thought I was mentally prepared for Marcella to be here, but seeing her in person had thrown me. Even though we'd only had a few days together, they'd been incredibly intense. And things hadn't ended well.

The day that we'd set a trap for Gunnar Grimes, Marcella had known that she was supposed to lie low, safe in her room at the Mayhem. But her heroin addiction had proven stronger than her common sense. She'd gone back to the Getaway to score a dime bag from her dealer, even though she knew it was dangerous. And Dot's friend Jessie went after her, an act of goodwill that she paid for with her life. By the time I arrived, Jessie had been killed by Gunnar and Marcella was his captive.

The last time I'd seen Marcella, she'd been standing beside me in the bathroom of room eleven, staring down at Jessie's body. It wasn't a happy memory.

Yet oddly, that wasn't the worst experience I'd had with a girlfriend. As the memories flashed through my mind, I stumbled and nearly went flying into a potted fern; Kat braced me with her hand. "Are you okay, Amber?" she asked with concern. Lowering her voice and glancing back, she asked, "Is it that woman?"

"Yeah, it's just . . . we've got history," I said lamely. *How can I even begin to explain without telling her everything?* I swallowed hard. Maybe bringing her had been a mistake. I should have come alone, or begged off and stayed in San Francisco. "It's complicated."

Kat's brow was furrowed with concern. Maybe it was time to come clean. I drew a deep breath and got ready to blurt out the whole, horrible story . . .

"Why are you waiting in the hallway? Is something wrong with the food?"

I froze. It couldn't be.

Slowly, I turned to find Grace Cabot Grimes frowning at me. I gaped at her and then finally managed to sputter, "What are you doing here?"

She cocked an eyebrow and said, "I'm an invited guest. Frankly, Amber, I'd hoped your manners would improve. Aren't you going to introduce me to your friend?"

— — —

Gina was seriously over it. She'd been walking the track for hours with no luck, and it was fucking freezing. She drew the sleeves of her bolero more tightly around her arms—not that the thin fabric did shit to keep her warm—and took another hit off her vape pen.

The air was thick with smoke from the wildfire; it gave her a sudden, unexpected pang of nostalgia for Tempe. Back before they'd lost the house, there was a firepit in their backyard. On cold, clear nights like this one, her mom would stoke it and let them make s'mores. Gina would always burn her marshmallows. Her brother Mark gave her shit for it, but she loved biting into the charred exterior until the sweetness gushed through . . .

A car turned the corner and approached. As the headlights caught her, the vehicle slowed. Gina quickly dropped the sleeves of her bolero and thrust her chest forward while cocking a hip to the side and grinning broadly. As the driver eased to the curb, she bent over and pursed her lips seductively. The passenger window lowered a crack. Fighting to keep her teeth from chattering, she asked, "Hey, you looking for a date?"

Gina couldn't see the driver; his face was cast in shadow. There was a long beat—too long, to the point where something felt off. A shiver shimmied up her spine that had nothing to do with the weather. She was about to straighten and walk away, cutting her losses, when a deep voice said, "Climb in."

Gina hesitated. Marcella always said you had to listen to your gut. But her own gut was notoriously unreliable—just look at all the losers she'd dated—and besides, it was currently rumbling with hunger. Turning down a date definitely wouldn't fix that.

"You coming?" the driver rumbled.

Fuck it. Opening the door, she chirped, "Sure, honey. I got a room just down the street."

CHAPTER SIX

GASLIGHT

So dinner was awkward, to say the least. We were seated at a long table in the garden of a Michelin-starred restaurant. I really shouldn't have been surprised by the lengths that people went to for Dot; hell, I'd certainly done it myself on occasion. But the fact that someone had reserved the entire outdoor patio of a top Vegas eatery exclusively for her and her friends was impressive. At one point during dinner, a legendary Vegas crooner stopped by to serenade Dot with "Strangers in the Night." I wouldn't have been all that surprised to see the real Elvis waltz in.

I'm sure the food was delicious, but I barely even registered it. I was distracted by Marcella loudly regaling one end of the table with stories about all the bizarre things that had happened since she started managing the Getaway, Dot's other motel. And at the other end, Grace was delicately picking at each course, her manners impeccable.

Meanwhile, I was having a hard time scraping my jaw off the floor. It felt like one of those bizarre dreams. At any moment, I expected someone to jump up and announce that we were being pranked. The fact that Grace was even here was staggering enough. But to see her in a normal environment, interacting with regular people, not a cattle prod in sight?

That was hard to wrap my head around.

So I made stilted conversation with Portia, the Fatal Femme who nattered away at my elbow throughout the meal. Apparently she was some sort of fancy lawyer who kept alluding to her "extracurricular activities," as if I'd know what she was talking about.

"Love the Rolex," she said, pointing to my wrist. "Is it real?"

I reflexively covered it with my hand. Kat was always giving me extravagant things I never would have bought for myself; wearing it still made me self-conscious. "Um, yeah. My girlfriend gave it to me."

Portia's eyebrows shot up and she issued a low whistle. "Damn. Well, she's a keeper. But back to the big stuff: I still can't believe you were captured by an actual goddamn serial killer!" The wine had stained her teeth red. She polished off the glass and waved to the waiter for a refill. "And then got chased by another one? I mean, how many people can say that? You are going to tell me *all* about it."

"Um . . ." I shifted uncomfortably. "There's not a lot to tell."

"That's not what Dottie said." Portia leaned in conspiratorially. "She told the Femmes you were *in the room* when Gunnar Grimes was shot. And you saved Marcella's life, right?"

"Kind of, I guess."

"Poor Jessie, though. Terrible tragedy. We all loved her." Portia raised her glass in a salute.

"Yeah, that was terrible," I agreed, squirming. Talking about all this was kicking up my nerves, and between that and the alcohol, I was starting to feel nauseous and faint. I'd gotten the sense that the Fatal Femmes was a pretty big group; did they *all* know the details of that night? Because that would be downright alarming. *Breathe*, I told myself. "Honestly, Portia, I really don't like talking about it."

"Shouldn't say that," she said, downing another half a glass.

"Say what?"

"Honestly." Leaning in too close again, she said, "Makes people think you're usually lying. They teach us that in law school."

"I'll bear that in mind," I muttered.

Across the table, Kat was eyeing me questioningly, so I clearly wasn't doing a fantastic job of concealing my agitation. I couldn't help it, though. All this was just too stressful and weird. When I saw Grace get up to use the bathroom, I tossed down my napkin and followed.

"What are you doing here?" I asked as the door closed behind us.

Grace regarded me coolly in the mirror. "What do you mean? Dot invited me."

"And you came?"

"Of course I came. It would have been rude to refuse." Grace leaned in and reapplied her lipstick. "And how are you, Amber?"

I goggled at her. Grace Cabot Grimes was standing in the bathroom with me, (apparently) unarmed, wearing a dress, and putting on makeup? It felt like my head might explode. "I, uh, I'm okay, I guess."

"Enjoying San Francisco?"

"Are you seriously making small talk right now?"

Grace looked bemused. "Is there something you'd prefer to discuss?"

"So many things, it's hard to know where to begin," I said. "For starters, how did Dot even get in touch with you?"

"I sent a thank you note for her assistance last spring. She responded with a wedding invitation."

"Wait, so . . . she has your address?"

Grace scoffed. "I use a PO box and obviously take all necessary precautions."

"Obviously," I said, feeling somewhat mollified. Still. *They're pen pals now?*

"Congratulations on completing your degree, by the way."

"Oh, thanks." I'd managed to earn a BA in psychology from East Tennessee State University a few months ago. Which was a pretty big deal for me, especially since my final semester had been interrupted by multiple serial killers. But over the summer I'd finished the coursework online and received my diploma in the mail. I promptly went out to celebrate by buying a round for everyone at my local lesbian bar.

Coincidentally, that was also the night I'd met Kat. I flushed at the memory and cleared my throat. "So what have you been up to?"

Grace shrugged. "The usual."

"Really?" I felt a twinge of panic. Grace had spent her entire adult life pursuing serial killers; well, she was mainly chasing her twin brother and stumbled across the others along the way. And whenever that happened, she zapped them with a cattle prod and left them tied up with a bow for the cops to find.

Now that her brother was dead, I'd assumed she'd stopped her side hustle. The possibility that she might still be on the clock was worrisome. Lowering my voice, I asked, "You're not after someone here in Vegas, are you? I thought you were done with all that."

Grace clicked shut her clutch and said, "We should get back."

"That wasn't an answer," I said, hurrying to follow. As always, it was a challenge to match her long strides.

"I'm officially retired," Grace said. "Have you started applying to graduate programs yet?"

"Not yet. I'm thinking of going to a UC, but I have a better shot at getting in if I establish California residency first. And don't think I didn't notice that you said 'officially.' *Unofficially*, are you after someone here?"

Grace glanced over at me. "Why? Is another killer after you?"

"Not that I'm aware of," I said. "But based on past experience, I'm usually the last to find out."

Grace laughed. "Fair point. Well, as far as I know, your life isn't in danger at the moment. No more than anyone else's, existentially speaking."

"Well, that's a relief, I guess." At the restaurant's threshold I grabbed her arm, forcing her to stop. "You're *really* only here for the wedding?"

Grace sighed. "Why is that so hard to believe? I told you before, Amber, I have always had a life outside of chasing my brother. Now if you'll excuse me, I believe dessert is about to be served. The meal has been lovely so far, hasn't it? Much better than I was expecting."

Blithely, she headed back toward the patio. I watched her go, unable to shake the sense that she wasn't telling me everything. But of course she wasn't—it was Grace, after all.

My real fear was that whatever she was *actually* here for had something to do with me.

— — —

The guy hadn't said a word during the two-minute drive to the motel, which made Gina even more anxious. She prattled away to fill the silence, going on about the wildfire and the cold and anything else that popped into her mind. She hardly even knew what she was saying; the whole time she was doing her damnedest to ignore the small voice that was shrieking at her to *Get the fuck out! This guy is creepy, it's not worth the money . . .*

Easy for the voice to say. It didn't have to pony up another week's rent tomorrow.

Still, she was wary. A couple girls had had bad experiences recently, and she definitely didn't want to join them. *Don't let him get between you and the exit*, Marcella was always saying. So after unlocking the motel room door, Gina waved him past. "After you, sexy."

He grumbled something that might've been "thank you"; it was hard to tell. She flicked the light switch, finally providing her with a good look at him, and he winced in the glare. He was an older white dude with a bit of a paunch. Beard, mustache, and a ball cap pulled low over his eyes. He had on a giant parka and sunglasses even though it was dark outside, which was odd, but she'd seen weirder. He looked clean, at least, and didn't seem to have a weapon.

"So what do you want, sugar?" she asked, the quaver in her voice betraying the fact that she was still freaking freezing and the room wasn't much warmer than outside.

"Drink?" he asked, pulling a split of champagne from his parka.

Gina hesitated. She wouldn't mind a nip, but as a rule she didn't take food or drink from a john. Too many freaks out there, it wasn't worth the risk. "That's so sweet! But I'm good," she said. "So it's twenty-five for a hand job, fifty if I go down on you, a hundred for sex, but I'm on top. Which do you want?"

He frowned at her and waved the bottle, growling, "I *want* you to take a drink."

Shit. There was something in his tone that she definitely didn't like. Feebly, she said, "I don't really drink, but thanks. So how about—"

Before she could finish the sentence, he slammed her back against the door, knocking the wind out of her. Gina struggled, clawing at his arms and face and kicking at his knees . . . but he was strong, much stronger than he'd looked. He'd produced a cloth out of nowhere and pressed it to her nose. It smelled off, sickly sweet, like it had been doused with something.

Colored dots crowded the edges of Gina's vision, and her eyes drifted shut. She wanted to keep fighting, but it was as if something had shut down the part of her brain that sent messages to her hands and feet. *Well, crap,* Gina thought. Her gut had been right after all.

It proved impossible to shake my suspicions. While everyone else was having a grand old time during the rest of dinner, and afterward at the burlesque show (okay, I might have found that a little distracting), I was watching Grace like a hawk.

We were ending the night at the Bellagio, indulging in Vegas's number-one pastime: gambling. At least, the rest of the bachelorette party was. I didn't gamble. As a former grifter, I'd never understand the appeal of handing over your money to the house; it just made me feel like a mark. So Kat and I had grabbed seats at the bar instead. As I sipped my drink, I scanned the room.

"Should I be jealous?" Kat asked.

"What?" I asked with a frown, turning to face her.

Kat was perched on the next barstool, brandishing a martini and a look of annoyance. She nodded toward the craps table, where Grace was sipping what looked like seltzer while the rest of the bachelorette party chortled and took turns throwing dice.

"You cannot take your eyes off that woman," Kat complained. "And you followed her to the bathroom. Is she another former girlfriend?"

"Grace?" I laughed out loud. "God, no. She's just—" I hesitated. How to explain our relationship without going into all the gritty details? "Um, she's sort of a frenemy, I guess. That's, like—"

"I know what a frenemy is," Kat said, cutting me off. I raised an eyebrow at her. "Sorry," she continued. "I just was not prepared to meet so many people from your life. It's been a bit overwhelming."

"Hey, c'mere." I pulled her in for a kiss. "I'm crazy about you, you know that?"

Some of the tension left her body as I nuzzled her. "I am crazy about you, too."

"You better be." I leaned my forehead against hers and said, "Otter or dolphin?"

"Dolphin, definitely. Otters cannot surf."

"Wait, what? Dolphins can surf?"

"Absolutely. We should drive to Carmel after this," she purred in my ear. "I know a darling little bed-and-breakfast near a white sand beach where the dolphins ride the waves this time of year."

"That sounds amazing," I agreed with a sigh. Why was I letting Grace get under my skin? I was here to enjoy myself with my amazing girlfriend and to celebrate with Dot. Everything else was superfluous.

"I was wondering if you gave it any more thought," Kat murmured.

"What, the alien zombie thing?"

She cracked a smile. "That too, obviously, but I meant the money thing. I was speaking to my financial adviser the other day, and he offered a free consultation."

"Yeah, sure. Maybe when we get back."

"We should book it soon, though. He only works with people referred by current clients," she said. "I was lucky he agreed. Last time I referred someone, he was too busy to take them on."

"Uh-huh. That is lucky." Over Kat's shoulder, I saw that Dot and Marcella had joined Grace. They huddled together, engaged in what looked like an intense discussion. Then, abruptly, all three turned and hurried toward the exit.

"Huh," I said. "That's weird."

"Seriously?" Kat protested, following my gaze. "Are you even listening?"

"I'm sorry. It's just, all night I've had this weird feeling that my friends are keeping something from me. And it's driving me a little crazy."

Kat shook her head and sighed. "Then I guess we had better find out if it is true."

"Yeah?" I asked hopefully.

Kat drained the rest of her martini and made a show of pulling on her jacket. "Will it make you less distracted?"

"Definitely," I said. "And it's probably nothing. I just want to know for sure."

"Then let us go." She grabbed hold of my hand. "Which way?"

"They headed toward the main entrance," I said, pointing.

"All right. *Auf geht's!*" Kat marched toward the door, blazing a path.

"I don't deserve you, you know that?" I said, hustling to keep up.

Over her shoulder, Kat said, "Yes, you are very fortunate. Now maybe take off your heels so we can run."

— — —

We arrived at the front entrance out of breath and barefoot, toting our heels by their straps.

"There they are!" Kat gasped, pointing to the valet stand, where Grace was handing over her ticket.

"Okay, let's grab a cab." I motioned toward the taxi stand at the other end of the portico; thankfully, there was no line. We slipped our shoes back on and hobbled toward the cab idling at the curb, keeping our heads down. I glanced back; a valet had just pulled up with Grace's car (a sensible, nondescript sedan, natch), and the three of them climbed in.

"Where to, ladies?" our driver asked.

"We need you to follow that car!" Kat said excitedly.

The driver raised an eyebrow. "Seriously?"

"Yeah," I said apologetically. "It's kind of a prank. I'll give you an extra fifty on top of the fare."

"What kind of prank?" he asked suspiciously. "I won't do nothin' illegal."

"It's okay," I said weakly. "They're friends of mine."

He threw me a look in the rearview mirror. I couldn't blame him. Most people didn't tail their friends through the streets of Vegas in the middle of the night.

"It is a scavenger hunt for our friend's bachelorette party," Kat piped up. "We do not know where one of the items is, but that team does because they are from here, so they have an unfair advantage. We are just trying to level the playing field."

I raised an eyebrow at her. The driver chuckled and said, "Sure, I got you. What's the prize?"

"Tickets to the *O* show," Kat said without missing a beat. "I have always wanted to see that one."

"It's the best for sure," the driver agreed, finally putting the car in gear and easing out at what felt like a glacial pace.

I chewed my lower lip, worried that we'd lost them, but at the next light I spotted them two cars ahead. "There they are!"

"Got 'em," he said. "So where are you ladies from?"

"San Francisco," Kat said, leaning forward.

"Yeah? One of my kids lives there."

"Oh, what a lovely coincidence!" Kat exclaimed. As she and the driver chatted about the Bay Area, I tuned them out. Thankfully, Grace didn't seem to realize we were tailing them because she drove sedately.

Where could they possibly be going? Were they doing something for the wedding? At two a.m.? I couldn't help but feel a little left out. After all, I was the one who had brought all of them together; well, at least I'd unintentionally introduced Dot and Marcella to Grace. As we followed them off the Strip and into a more dilapidated area, I wondered what the hell was going on.

"Quite the hunt they got you on," the driver said. "I gotta say, this ain't the best part of town. You sure about all this?"

"Um, yeah," I said. "I think it's fine."

The sedan abruptly turned into the parking lot of a motel. I frowned; this wasn't one of Dot's places. It was definitely one of the sketchier-looking establishments I'd ever seen, and that was saying something. The only letter in the neon sign that remained illuminated was a crooked *X*, and the lot was nearly empty. Our cab slowed as Grace parked in front of one of the rooms. When the three of them climbed out, I said, "Right here is great, thanks."

The driver hesitated. "Maybe I should stick around, this isn't really safe for a couple young ladies. Could your friends have the wrong place? What are you looking for, anyhow?"

"An ashtray from the worst motel in Vegas," Kat said exuberantly. "So this is perfect!"

I threw her a look; it was truly impressive how she kept coming up with this stuff on the fly. "Do you mind waiting, actually?" I asked. "You can keep the meter running."

"I was gonna take a break anyway," he said, shifting into park. "Go get your ashtray. I'll be right here."

"Thank you so much, Frank." Kat leaned forward and patted his shoulder. "You are a lovely man. I hope things work out with your son."

He flushed deep red and mumbled a thanks. As we hurried across the lot, I pulled my jacket tighter around me. Tomorrow I was investing in a parka for sure. "What's up with his son?"

"Frank did not handle it well when he came out. Hopefully, he can make amends."

I smiled in spite of myself; Kat had a real gift for seeing the best in people. "An ashtray, huh? That was slick," I said approvingly. "Where'd you come up with that?"

"It was on the list for our senior scavenger hunt at boarding school," Kat said. "Now, what next?"

"That's a great question." Now that we were here, the cold was cutting through my buzz and suddenly this didn't seem like such a brilliant plan. Whatever was going on wasn't really any of my business, right? And obviously they didn't want me involved.

"We could just return to the Mayhem," Kat suggested, reading me. "If you have changed your mind."

"No," I said, squaring my shoulders. "We've come this far. Let's find out what's up."

Kat waved toward the battered row of doors facing the parking lot. "They went into number eight."

We tiptoed forward and leaned against the plywood door, listening. I frowned; it sounded like someone inside was sobbing. I hesitated, but before I could share my reservations, Kat turned the knob and pushed the door open.

As we gaped at the tableau before us, Grace said, "As always, Amber, your timing is appalling."

CHAPTER SEVEN

MAN IN THE SHADOW

The room was tiny, barely large enough to contain a listing queen-sized bed and rickety side table, never mind the five other people crammed inside. It stank, too, emanating a distinctive "something died in here" aroma.

"Good God," Kat choked, covering her nose with one hand.

Marcella and Dot were beside the bed, looking down at a woman—a girl, really—who was lying in the center of it. She seemed out of it; her eyes were having a hard time staying open. Dr. Aboud, the wig store owner/surgeon who had helped us out the previous spring when Grace was stabbed, knelt beside the bed, checking the girl's pulse.

But what really threw me was that the girl was totally, completely bald. I swallowed hard and staggered back a few steps.

"Amber? Are you okay?"

It sounded like Kat's voice was coming at me from a distance. The walls of the room receded and then sprung back, pulsing like a heart. Dot hurried over and took my arm, saying, "Let's get you some air, hon. You look a little peaky."

I only vaguely registered what she was saying, could barely even see the room around me. Instead, I was back in a dank basement, shaved bald and painted blue, staring up at a bare bulb, the steel table cold under my naked skin . . .

I staggered to the parking lot and put a hand on Grace's car hood to brace myself. Eyes closed, I silently repeated my mantra: *You're okay now. It's over, and you're okay.*

"You all right there, miss?" I heard Frank call out.

"She'll be fine, I've got her," Dot called back. Distantly, I felt the weight of her hand on my back as she murmured, "Easy, kiddo. Breathe with me."

I nodded, but it was taking everything I had to keep from throwing up. Drawing in deep breaths on top of that seemed impossible. But I tried to follow along as Dot said, "Four counts in . . . that's a good girl, you're doing just peachy. Now breathe out for six. Nice. Okay, let's do it again."

"What is wrong with her?" Kat asked.

And that shook me right out of it. Before any of my friends could explain why the sight of a bald woman sent me into panic mode, I straightened and said, "It's cool. I'm fine now."

"Probably a bad oyster," Marcella said from where she leaned against the doorframe.

I threw her a grateful look, and she responded with a knowing nod. Kat wrapped an arm around my shoulders and pulled me close, asking in a low voice, "Are you sure you are okay?"

"Yeah, totally. Sorry I freaked you out. It was just the smell," I said weakly.

"Yes, it is truly ghastly," Kat agreed.

"What are you doing here, hon?" Dot asked wearily.

"We were, um—"

"Following us in a cab," Grace called from the room. "Poorly, too. I spotted her almost immediately. I told you she was constitutionally incapable of staying out of it."

Before I could respond, Dr. Aboud appeared in the doorway. Eyeing me, he said, "Your color is a bit off. Do you need me to prescribe something for food poisoning? Unfortunately, I did not bring an extra IV drip."

"I'm cool, thanks. Um, nice to see you again."

"Yes, well. Someday it will hopefully occur under happier circumstances." Wearily turning to Dot, he said, "Physically, Gina is fine. She just needs to sleep it off."

"So we can move her?" Dot asked.

Dr. Aboud nodded. "Absolutely. In fact, I would recommend getting her out of here as quickly as possible. Anyone who entered that room should bathe thoroughly as soon as you get home. And put your clothing in plastic." He shuddered. "This might be the filthiest place I have ever seen in my life."

"Thanks so much again for coming on short notice, doc," Dot said, laying a hand on his arm.

"Of course. See you at the wedding." As he turned toward his car, I overheard him say, "And not before then, if I am lucky."

A groan from inside the room. Dot made a face and said, "Oh, dear. I should get back to Gina."

"Who's Gina, exactly?" I asked.

"One of the girls from the Getaway." Marcella took a hit off her vape pen as she stepped aside to let Dot back into the room. "Nice kid."

"And someone drugged her?" I asked, feeling a wave of nausea swell again.

Kat gave me a funny look. Marcella glanced at her, then said, "Yeah. Been happening a lot lately."

Turning, she went back inside. I hesitated, then started to follow. Kat laid a hand on my arm to stop me and said in a grave tone, "Amber. This seems like something we should not involve ourselves with."

"Well, they're involved," I said weakly. "And they're my friends, so let's just get a little more information, then we can go back, okay?"

A beat and then Kat nodded. "I will go wait in the cab."

"Thanks." I squeezed her hand. "You're the best, dolphin."

She smiled thinly but didn't respond, which was probably not a great sign, but I was too tired and nauseous to care. I stopped on the threshold where the smell was less pungent and said, "So what the fuck is all this?"

"Oh, dollface," Dot said, shaking her head. "I really wish you hadn't come."

"It's genuinely remarkable how adept you are at interfering," Grace said.

"Interfering?" I bridled. "Seriously?"

"There's no time for bickering," Dot said sternly. "We need to get Gina out of here—this place really gives new meaning to the word 'dump.' Once I get her squared away, we can meet at the Stardust diner. 'Kay?"

We all mumbled agreement. From the bed, a weak voice said, "Are any of you fuckers gonna get me a hat? My head is fucking freezing."

Kat's new best friend Frank was relieved that we'd survived our experience with Vegas's skankiest motel unscathed, although he looked askance at our lack of an ashtray.

"It turns out they do not even have them," Kat explained with a shrug. "So we got matches instead."

"Should count," he agreed. Frank felt a lot better about dropping us at the Stardust diner and filled the silence en route with a long-winded story about how he'd met his third wife there.

I wouldn't call it romantic, but the Stardust certainly fit the bill of an old-school diner, with wide, circular booths and a revolving display case layered with pies. Despite it being nearly three a.m. on a weekday, it was hopping, with just about every table occupied. Kat and I managed to grab a large booth at the far end of the room.

The waitress set steaming mugs of coffee in front of us and hustled away. Kat took a sip and said, "So this is turning out to be a bit of an odd night."

"That has generally been my Vegas experience," I said, rubbing my eyes. "Sorry, babe. If I'd known, I would've just taken us back to the motel."

"Oh, it is not that." She shook her head vigorously. "I suppose I just was not aware of how . . . interesting your friends would turn out to be."

A bit taken aback, I cautiously asked, "What do you mean?"

"That bald woman seemed to be a prostitute," Kat said hesitantly. "Was she not?"

"Yeah, probably," I said. "Sex work counts as work, though, right?"

"Does it?" Kat cocked her head to the side. "I do not mean to offend; I simply never thought of it that way."

"Yes, it does. Here they come," I said, half-standing to wave them over. "Um, look. Probably don't talk about sex work around Marcella, okay?"

Kat's eyes widened. "Oh, is she—"

"She was. Retired now," I said. "But maybe just don't bring it up."

Kat pursed her lips and eyed me. I stared back, trying to repress the thought that had popped into my mind: Maybe people who came from completely different backgrounds—different worlds, really—weren't destined to work out.

You finish each other's sentences, I reminded myself. And no relationship was perfect, right? Maybe it was good that we were still discovering new things about each other. And Kat probably had never encountered a sex worker before, so it was understandable that she'd have some misconceptions. It didn't mean she was a bad person.

"I gotta tell you, toots, this is not how I pictured my bachelorette party ending," Dot said wearily, sliding into the booth. She was still wearing her vintage gown, but Marcella had changed into jeans, a sweater, and a motorcycle jacket, and Grace was in her standard all-black uniform. I frowned; did she keep a spare outfit in her trunk?

"Definitely not what I was expecting," I agreed. "How's Gina?"

"Better, I think. The IV drip seems to be helping. One of the other gals is keeping an eye on her."

"Great. So what's going on, exactly?"

Before anyone could answer, the waitress came over to take our orders. After she left, Dot ran a hand through her hair and sighed. "I hardly know where to begin. So a couple weeks ago, Marcella told me something upsetting."

"More than fucking upsetting," Marcella muttered. I couldn't help but notice that Kat was examining her closely. "Jade got so spooked she caught a bus back home."

"Hang on," I said, holding up a hand. "Who's Jade?"

"Another working girl. Poor thing says she's eighteen, but I think she's younger." Dot shook her head.

"She was staying at the Getaway," Marcella said.

"There's a bad john kicking around," Dot explained. "He's already attacked three girls that we know of."

"Four including Gina," Marcella said darkly.

"Oh." I swallowed. "A rapist?"

"Not that kind of attack," Dot said. "Luckily."

"Well, it's not much better," Marcella said.

"He drugs prostitutes and shaves their heads while they're unconscious," Grace stated bluntly. Nodding at me, she said, "You should find that particularly relatable."

"Why would Amber find that relatable?" Kat asked.

"No reason," I said quickly, glaring at Grace. "Um, is he painting them blue, too?"

Kat threw me a perplexed look. I really couldn't blame her.

"No, Amber," Grace said. "It doesn't appear to be a copycat."

"The creep doesn't even have sex with them," Marcella said.

"Which is why the cops won't get involved," Dot said. "They say unless we can prove the girls didn't consent to being shaved, there's nothing they can do."

"As if anyone would agree to that," Marcella snorted. "Fucking fetishists."

"Yeah, that's super creepy," I agreed. My chest still felt tight, but the panic was easing. Based on what they were saying, this wasn't related to what had happened to me. And selfishly, that was a relief.

"How does he drug them?" Kat interjected. "Perhaps these women could just not take anything from their . . . customers?"

Seeing Marcella's expression, I rushed to intervene, saying, "Not to be judgmental, but maybe Kat's right and there's an easy fix?"

"There's not," Marcella snapped. "Jade thinks he dosed the cheap bubbly he brought with him. Mystique had heard the rumors, so she turned it down when he offered and tried to leave."

"Then he grabbed her and held something over her mouth that made her pass out," Dot said grimly. "Did the same thing tonight to Gina. Cindy called me when she found her because she knew the kid was one of Marcella's."

"One of yours?" I asked, raising an eyebrow.

"I'm not pimping," Marcella said, rolling her eyes. "Just offering safety tips, that sort of thing."

"Kind of like harm reduction," Dot explained. "The girls really seem to appreciate it. And Lord knows, with this creep around, they need all the help they can get."

The conversation was interrupted by the arrival of our food. Silence fell while we waited for the waitress to pass around the plates. After she left, I asked, "So why didn't you tell me this was happening?"

"It's not personal, hon. We just thought it would be too much for you. After, well, y'know . . ." Dot cut her eyes meaningfully toward Kat, then continued, "everything you've been through, we thought it best to keep you out of it."

"Plus you don't add value," Grace said blithely, cutting her toast with a knife and fork.

"I don't 'add value'?" I glowered at her. "What about you?"

"I created an algorithm."

"Of course you did." Moodily, I scooped a bite of eggs into my mouth. They were surprisingly tasty.

Dot looked abashed. "I just figured Grace was coming to the wedding anyway. And she's so good with that computer stuff."

"It's my wedding present," Grace said, wiping the corner of her mouth with her napkin.

"Seriously?" I gaped at her.

Dot laughed nervously. "Well, yes. It's not on the registry, but it is kind of the perfect gift for me. Some of the Fatal Femmes are helping out, too."

Which explained their caginess in the limo earlier. "And here I only got the vintage candlesticks," I muttered.

"I am confused," Kat said. "Could you explain why the police will not help?"

I kept forgetting that Kat was there; I really needed to stop doing that. "Um, yeah, so . . . the police aren't always so helpful to people who work in the sex trade."

"They're fucking useless," Marcella scoffed.

"But that is terrible!" Kat said. "Is there no one to report them to?"

I sighed, not really up for explaining the injustices of the American legal system, especially when a hangover was already creeping over me. "It's complicated."

"Not really," Marcella said. "They don't give a shit about you unless you're white and rich."

"Really?" Kat asked, eyes wide.

"Basically, yeah." I pushed the last of the eggs onto my fork. "I still can't believe no one told me about this."

"Spoken like a true adult," Grace said.

Dot rapped her on the arm and said, "Sorry, kiddo. It sounded like things were going really well for you. I didn't want to rock the boat by dragging you into something messy."

"Yeah," Marcella said. "We'd hate to screw up your perfect little life."

I threw her a look. She met it, raising an eyebrow in a challenge. I shifted my gaze away, focusing back on my food.

"We would love to help," Kat said. She'd barely touched her plate.

"We would?" I asked, taken aback.

"Absolutely," she said firmly. "It sounds important. So what do we do?"

"Well," Dot said hesitantly. "Me and the other Femmes set up a sting operation for tomorrow night . . ."

"A sting!" Kat's eyes lit up. "That sounds exciting!"

"Oh, it is," Marcella said with a smirk. "And I've got an outfit you can borrow."

"Nope, she's not doing that," I said, jabbing a finger at Marcella.

"More of a stakeout, really," Dot said reassuringly. "I suppose it couldn't hurt to have another team available. But only if you're up for it, toots."

I mulled it over; a stakeout sounded relatively low risk. "Do you even know what this guy looks like?"

"Grace helped with that, too." Dot scrolled through her phone and then held it up to show me a series of images, all of a nondescript-looking white guy in his forties. In some he had a beard; in others, a ponytail or glasses.

"How many people are you looking for, exactly?"

"That's part of the problem. The girls all described someone slightly different, so we think he's wearing disguises," Dot said. "So the pictures aren't very helpful, I'm afraid."

"Which is precisely why I developed the algorithm," Grace said. "There's a ninety-five percent chance that he strikes again this week, sometime between midnight and three a.m."

"And we'll be waiting," Dot said firmly.

"We will, too," Kat said.

I leaned over to her and said in a low voice, "Are you sure? I know this isn't what we'd planned." Far from it. I'd promised her we'd rent a cabana at a fancy resort and spend the days poolside, gorging on fruity drinks and greasy food.

"But this sounds like more fun," Kat murmured back. "It will be an adventure!"

I sighed; she seemed determined. And Vegas was chillier than I'd expected. Since neither of us were gamblers, I wasn't a hundred percent sure how to occupy the rest of the week otherwise. "Exactly how dangerous is this guy?"

"Well, aside from the drugging and head-shaving, he hasn't technically injured anyone," Dot said.

"Yet," Grace said, striking her usual ominous tone.

"I guess that's something. So what's the plan if you catch him?"

"Oh!" Dot clapped her hands together. "That's the best part. The other half of my wedding present from Grace is a cattle prod."

"Carbon fiber, top of the line," Grace chimed in.

"Fabulous," I sighed.

"Can I get one of those, too?" Kat asked, eyes wide.

"I guess we're in," I said, already knowing that I'd regret it.

CHAPTER EIGHT

KNOCK ON ANY DOOR

KINGMAN, ARIZONA

Travis Hardin sighed as he took in the long row of parked camper vans and RVs. This was easily his least-favorite part of working at Walmart, and he wasn't a big fan of the rest of it either. He'd prefer taking inventory or restocking shelves any day of the week over this. At least he'd managed to sneak a joint in his car on the drive over, so his senses were, for the moment, pleasantly numbed.

Still, this sucked. Travis shivered in the early morning light, a stack of green stickers in his hands. The problem was, a lot of Walmarts let people camp in the parking lot overnight. Whole hordes of sunburned tourists fresh from the Grand Canyon or Vegas would wander through the aisles, buying food and whatever else they needed. Win-win. It had been the same at the Kingman superstore until recently. For some reason, the corporate policy had changed and overnight stays were now a big no-no. So for the past few weeks, right after clocking in, Travis had to come out here and affix bright green stickers to the RVs. Which pissed off the owners, and some of those folks were armed.

Consequently, Travis tried to treat it like a covert op, like this was a real-life *Call of Duty* mission.

He just hoped the folks boondocking in the back lot were still asleep. More than anything, he didn't want to spend the first hour of his shift running from tourists.

Moving as silently as possible, Travis sidled up to the line of RVs tucked along the lot's far perimeter. It smelled awful back here, a toxic mix of gasoline fumes mingled with rotting food from the dumpsters. Trying not to gag, he managed to plaster stickers on the first four RVs. Then he hesitated.

The fifth vehicle was a battered Subaru wagon, dwarfed by the RVs flanking it front and back. Travis frowned. Should he skip it? His boss would be pissed if he found out, but Travis really wasn't in the mood to face off against an angry asshole. And he probably wouldn't be able to get the sticker on without waking whoever was inside.

Screw it, he decided. They didn't pay him enough to risk an ass-whupping.

Travis eased forward, trying not to scuff his Vans against the pavement. He could see a dark silhouette through the Subaru's rear hatch window. Kind of a tight space to crash in, but whoever it was probably didn't have a choice. He'd been there himself when his mom kicked him out of the trailer, but at least he had a truck bed to lay a mattress in. It looked like the Subaru was leaking oil, too; there was a big pool of it spreading out from the rear . . .

He frowned and bent down to get a closer look. The liquid was thicker than oil and ruddier-looking. It wasn't coming from beneath the car either, but from the cargo area, a stream of it running under the hatch door and over the rear bumper.

Maybe something inside had spilled? Travis rubbed his goatee with one hand. Not really any of his business, but for some reason, an alarm bell was pinging in the depths of his consciousness.

He'd just take a better look, ninja-like.

Travis shifted closer to the car, tilting his head to see inside. The windows were slightly tinted, but he could make out a figure curled up in the small rear cargo area. They hadn't even bothered to put the back seats down to make more room, which was super weird. His breath fogged the outside of the window slightly as he peered in, seeing long hair, a hand—

An eyeball, open and staring right at him.

"Oh shit!" Travis exclaimed, jumping back. He was ready to bolt, but no one jumped out of the car and started cursing him out.

There was no movement at all, in fact.

Travis frowned. He was pretty stoned, so it was taking an extra beat for his mind to process. But something should've happened, right?

Emboldened, he lightly rapped on the window and asked, "Hey, you okay in there?"

While he waited for a response, his brain nudged him. Something was off. What was it?

The hand. There was something wrong with the hand.

Travis leaned in again and cupped his fingers around his eyes to get a better look.

He clapped a hand to his mouth and stumbled back, nearly falling.

"What the fuck?" a deep baritone rumbled behind him. The bang of an RV door as the voice said, "Hey, asshole, did you stick this on my RV?"

Travis couldn't answer. He was too busy puking his guts out.

CHAPTER NINE

YOU AND ME

LAS VEGAS, NEVADA

I spent what little remained of the night staring at the ceiling of our motel room while Kat dozed peacefully beside me. Returning to Vegas apparently had inspired my mind to compile a reel featuring all the terrible things that had happened six months ago. Every time I shut my eyes, I saw the Pikachu killer's dank basement kill room. Or Jessie, dead in a motel room bathtub. Or Grace, passed out and bleeding on a table in a wig store.

So, you know. The usual.

It's not as if I never had nights like that in San Francisco, but thankfully they'd become less frequent during the past few months. Meeting Kat had definitely helped, too.

And now, I was right back in it.

Around seven a.m., I finally gave up and got dressed as quietly as possible. I pulled my hair into a ponytail and tiptoed out of the room, carrying my sneakers. As I eased the door shut, I cast a last glance at my girlfriend, who never seemed to have her sleep interrupted by terrible flashbacks. Feeling an unreasonable surge of jealousy, I let the lock click and bent to put on my shoes. Then I set off.

Last night, I'd sussed out a good spot a few blocks away. It was a long stretch of sidewalk that flanked empty lots, warehouses, and body repair shops. When I reached it, I was relieved to see there wasn't a lot of foot traffic at this hour. Not that I really cared, but I'd learned from experience that my particular workout routine sometimes attracted unwanted attention.

Mind you, it wasn't a real exercise regimen. More my own sort of therapy. The previous spring, it had become glaringly apparent that maintaining a basic level of fitness was critical if you tended to attract a lot of serial killers. Even one serial killer, really. So a couple months ago, I decided to go out a few times a week to run. Literally run. I wasn't bothering to jog or engage in marathon training. This exercise was specifically intended to enable me to flee for my life if necessary. And I figured not even a super-committed serial killer would bother chasing me over long distances.

Was this the healthiest thing for my mental state? Tough to say. But it served the dual purpose of imparting a sense of control while also generally making me feel better about myself (at least, compared to my previous utter lack of conditioning).

Here's how it worked: I would start out walking very casually while I composed an image in my mind, usually Grace's twin, Gunnar, but sometimes the Pikachu killer in his leather apron. As soon as I developed enough of a mental picture to kick my pulse up a few notches, I ran. Full tilt. All out. The sort of running a person only did when a tsunami was bearing down on them. I sprinted for as long as I could, until it felt like my heart and lungs were on the verge of ripping free of my body. Then I stopped dead, panting and covered in sweat.

After I caught my breath, I did it again. And again.

Four or five rounds were usually enough, but I never decided in advance how many I was going to do or how long I would go. I just stopped when it felt impossible to continue. Probably because of all the feelings kicked up by returning to Vegas, that morning I set a personal record with eight full circuits. And aside from a few early shift workers I circumnavigated as they walked toward a bus stop, I managed to do it without freaking out anyone.

When I finally made my way back to the Mayhem, the streets were getting busier. It was still fairly early, and Kat always slept in. So I decided to stop by the buffet, figuring that at this hour, I'd probably have the dining room all to myself.

As I walked down the corridor to the motel's dining area, it became apparent that I was mistaken. The place was packed—thronging, even. I stopped on the threshold and gaped at the assembled crowd. The dining room seated twenty people comfortably but there were at least twice that number packed into the small space, and the mood seemed dark. People were scowling, grumbling; some were dressed in casino uniforms, others looked like they'd come straight from cruising. I spotted Dot and Marcella by the cereal dispensers, roughly in the center of the room. Marcella had her arms crossed over her chest and looked annoyed. Dot waved her arms and called for silence. "Hey! Pipe down, all of you! Let's get started!"

The din subsided to a low murmur. Recognizing Portia, I made my way over to her, muttering apologies as I squeezed past people. She was dressed in a finely tailored suit and towering heels. "What's going on?" I whispered.

"Dot's telling everyone what happened to Gina." Wrinkling her nose, she added, "Don't sweat on the suit. It's Armani."

Dot raised her voice to be heard. "Most of you already know there's a real creep out there. Last night, he went after Gina."

The murmuring kicked up a notch. "She's okay!" Dot said quickly. "Just recovering. And she won't be earning for a bit, so if anyone wants to pitch in to help her out, we're passing around a hat."

"So what are we doing about this?" a woman in a miniskirt and six-inch heels growled. "Is anyone going to stop this fucker?"

"That's why we're here, right?" Dot said, throwing her a look. "Same plan as before. We'll spread out as much as possible tonight to cover a lot of territory. And ladies, if you get a date and something seems off, get out of there right away and call or text me."

"Screw that," one of the other women said. "I'm not working 'til you get this guy."

"I have to work," someone else said plaintively. "I got kids to feed. What am I supposed to do?"

"Rest assured, we're doing all we can." Grace's voice was quiet, modulated, but it still cut through the crowd. I went up on my toes and spotted her in the far corner, partially concealed by a large fern.

"All you can?" someone snorted. "Hell, easy for you to say. I might shave my head just so I don't have to worry about this freak doing it for me."

Murmurs of agreement all around.

"That's up to you, doll. But better if we stop him, right? There's a sign-up sheet over by the juice," Dot said loudly. "If you want to help out, let us know which corner you're working and who you'll be with; we're thinking teams of three. I'll text more info later."

The hubbub picked up again as the crowd started to disperse. People formed a ragged line, shuffling past the juice machine to sign up and collect the paperwork Dot had left. Portia came back with a flyer: It was a copy of the facial composites Grace had produced. Noticing me staring at it, she said, "You want it? I've already got a digital copy."

"I'm good, thanks."

"Suit yourself." Tucking it into her Birkin bag, she said, "I have to get to a deposition. See you tonight, Pikachu Amber."

"Yeah, see you." As she joined the group trickling out, I approached Marcella. She was wearing jeans, a sweatshirt, motorcycle boots, and a furious expression. Hesitantly, I said, "Hey. Um, how's Gina doing?"

"Bald and hungover," Marcella said bluntly. "So not fucking great."

"But physically she's fine, toots," Dot interjected as she came over. "And Dr. Aboud is going to give her a wig; he's been doing that for all the girls. Such a prince."

"Cool. Well, Kat and me are happy to help," I said. "Just tell us where to go."

"You got it, kiddo." Dot peered around. "Now where did Grace get to? She was just here a minute ago."

I spotted Grace through the plate-glass window. She was standing by the firepit, having what looked like a heated conversation on her phone. Which struck me as odd, because unless things had changed dramatically, Grace didn't have a very active social life. Last spring I'd spent two full weeks under her roof, during which time she hadn't made or received a single phone call.

"What's going on with her?" Marcella asked.

"I don't know. It's strange, though. She seems . . . different."

"The two of you need to cut her a break," Dot said. "Poor thing looks exhausted."

I realized Dot was right; Grace did look tired. There were dark circles under her eyes, and in the daylight, her skin was pale and washed out.

What could have taken such a toll on her? I seriously doubted that trying to track a guy who shaved women's heads was having this sort of effect; she'd spent literal decades chasing serial killers and always managed to look fresh as a daisy.

Which only served to rekindle my suspicions: Grace was up to something, and whatever it was must be pretty serious.

"I just hope we get lucky tonight," Dot said, wringing her hands. "I overheard some of the girls talking about arming themselves with more than pepper spray. I'm afraid someone's gonna end up getting really hurt."

"Hopefully the asshole," Marcella growled.

"Yeah," I agreed, only half-listening as I watched Grace tuck the phone back in her pocket. Turning, she noticed me watching and cocked an eyebrow. I threw her a little wave, at which she rolled her eyes and stalked back toward us. Nearly everyone else had left, barring a few motel guests who were scattered around the café tables having breakfast. My stomach grumbled, reminding me that I should do the same.

Without preamble, Grace said, "I've adjusted the algorithm based on the data points from last night's attack."

"What data points?"

"Information on the car the attacker is driving, the street corners and motels he's targeted, the day and date, and the time of day." She shook her head. "Unfortunately, there still don't appear to be any commonalities."

"Aside from the fact that he's going after working girls," Dot said.

"Aside from that, yes," Grace acknowledged.

"There has to be something else linking them," I said skeptically. "What about the victims?"

"What about them?" Grace asked.

"Well, I mean . . . all the stuff you listed is mostly about the guy, right? So what do the victims have in common?"

"I considered that. They're all different races," Grace said dismissively. "A fairly wide age range, too, considering. Although obviously there are not many older prostitutes."

"Well, not on the corners, at least," Dot said. "And they usually prefer to be called sex workers, hon. Maybe it's just random?"

"That would explain it," Grace said crisply. "In which case, there's not much more I can do."

"Oh shit," Marcella said slowly. "Blond."

"What?"

"They're all blondes," Marcella said.

"Oh my goodness, you're right! I can't believe it didn't occur to us!" Dot clapped her hands together.

"The fact that he's choosing blond women as targets is not necessarily helpful," Grace said. "For me to incorporate that into my algorithm, I'd have to know the hair color of every sex worker in Las Vegas and which corners they've worked during the past few weeks."

Trust Grace to immediately shoot down anyone else's contribution. "Maybe we don't need the algorithm," I said slowly. "If the blond women who need to work tonight wear a different color wig, and the people volunteering as bait go out as blondes—"

"That's brilliant!" Dot said enthusiastically. "I'll call Dr. Aboud to see if he's got some cheap wigs he won't mind lending us."

"I can cover the cost if we need to buy them," I offered. "I mean, I kind of owe him anyway."

Grace was eyeing me. "What?" I demanded.

"It's not a terrible idea," she conceded.

"Well, you know how I love to add value." Out of the corner of my eye, I saw Kat coming into the dining room. Her hair was wet from the shower, and she looked dewy and well rested. She threw me a little wave and trotted over, wrapping her arm around my waist and leaning in to kiss me. "Hey, baby. I had that dream again last night."

"Yeah?" I asked distractedly. "What did the octopus do this time?"

"It was amazing. He told me the secret to life."

"That sounds important. What is it?"

"No idea. I forgot as soon as I woke up." She gestured to my outfit and asked, "Did you already work out?"

"Yeah, I couldn't sleep," I said apologetically. "Sorry if I stink."

"Do not worry about it. This buffet looks amazing!" Kat gushed, as always erring on the side of exuberance. "It reminds me of my time at Rosey!"

Grace cocked an eyebrow. "You went to Le Rosey?"

"I did," Kat said, looking abashed. "Sorry, I realize that makes me sound like a dreadful snob."

"I went to Choate," Grace said.

"Oh, a fellow boardie!" Kat clapped her hands together. "We will have to swap boarding school horror stories."

Grace's features were hard to read, but I knew her well enough to assume that snarkiness was sure to follow. Heading it off, I said, "We should probably grab a table, baby."

"Of course. Grace, will you be dining with us?"

"I've already eaten," Grace said curtly. "And I really must be going."

"By the way, who were you talking to earlier?" I asked.

"No one," Grace said.

"Really? Because you looked pretty upset."

Appearing discomfited, Grace replied, "It was nothing that concerns you, Amber. Now please excuse me, I'm late for an appointment."

"Lovely chatting with you," Kat said formally. She squeezed my hand and then said, "I am going to see if I can get an omelet."

"Sounds good," I said, watching as Grace hurried out of the room. "I'm gonna take a quick shower."

"Are you sure?" Kat said skeptically. "You must be hungry after your run."

"Yeah." I pecked her on the cheek and said, "It's cool. I'll be back in a few."

— — —

I rushed back to our room and grabbed my keys, then dashed to the parking lot and dove into my car. For a minute, I thought I'd lost her, but then I spotted Grace's nondescript sedan idling at the red light a block down on the left. I eased out of the parking lot and followed, taking care to keep a few cars in between us.

It had not escaped my attention that I was becoming someone who stalked her friends. But I didn't particularly care. If I'd learned anything, it was that having as much information as possible went a long way toward keeping me safe. So I was tailing someone through Vegas for the second time in less than twenty-four hours. Because last night had proven I should always trust my gut, and right now it was screaming that Grace was acting even shadier than usual.

We drove for about fifteen minutes, the area becoming increasingly familiar as we went. I frowned. *Is Grace staying at the Getaway?* Maybe she'd taken Dot up on the discounted rate for wedding guests? Which would be weird, because she could afford somewhere much fancier.

But no, she passed the motel entrance without slowing. I heaved a sigh of relief. At least whatever nefarious business she was tied up in didn't involve one of Dot's motels.

I never could have predicted where she went next. My jaw dropped as Grace's car turned into the driveway of the Buggy Suites, a dive that made the Getaway look like the Four Seasons. This was the motel where her brother had stayed, and where Grace had planted evidence of his crimes for the authorities to find. It was L-shaped, with two levels wrapped around an empty parking lot. The covered wagon neon sign was dimmed, and a banner in front of the office read **CLOSED FOR RENOVATIONS**. Yet there was no evidence of work underway; the exterior was the same drab brown I remembered. It looked completely abandoned and desolate.

What the hell was Grace doing here?

My confusion only grew as Grace parked her car in front of the bank of rooms at the far end of the lot. I pulled to the curb and watched as she waved her wrist in front of a motel room door and then went inside. I sat there for ten minutes, waiting for her to come out. There was no movement, and no one else pulled into the lot. Finally, I muttered, "Screw it." Throwing the car in reverse, I backed up and pulled into the lot. I parked beside her car and went to the door of the room she'd vanished into. It had a crooked number *6* dangling from one nail, and the curtains on the window were drawn so there was no way to see inside. I hesitated. *Grace decided to check in here, of all places?* Repressing a shudder, I knocked.

No answer.

I banged again and called out, "Hey! I know you're in there!"

"Go away, Amber." Grace's voice crackled from somewhere above my head.

Startled, I flinched, then turned until I spotted the video camera aimed down at me from the eave of the building. I cupped my hands around my mouth and shouted, "Not until I get some answers!"

"The camera has a microphone, there's no need to shout," she said. "This is not a good time."

"Well, I'm not leaving," I said, lowering my voice slightly. "So you might as well let me in!"

I heard a noise—it sounded like someone in distress. *Shit.* Was I interrupting one of Grace's rescue attempts?

And worse yet, was I putting myself in danger?

I stepped back, debating whether or not to just jump in my car and make a run for it. Then I heard a loud *bang!*

And like an idiot, I went to see what it was.

The noise had come from a room a few doors down. I hurried over and started banging on the door with both fists.

Inside, it sounded like some kind of struggle was underway. I heard muffled protests and a loud wail. The hairs on the back of my neck stood up. I tried the knob and then threw myself against the door—unsurprisingly, it didn't budge, but my shoulder screeched in protest.

And suddenly, it got quiet. Footsteps approached the door from the other side: They sounded loud, heavy. Whoever was coming was definitely not Grace. I stepped back, dread in my heart, and looked around wildly. I had no weapon, not even my phone, which I'd stupidly left on the seat of my car. *What the hell was I thinking?*

As the door cracked open, I braced to run. An enormous man in scrubs glowered down at me. He was probably six-five, two hundred fifty pounds. Shaved head, tattoos, and a full beard. Beefy hands that could easily squeeze the life out of me.

The smart thing would've been to bolt. But no one ever said I was a genius. Swallowing hard, I said, "I've called the cops, so you better not have hurt her."

His brow furrowed. "What? Who the hell are you?"

"Where's Grace?" I demanded, cocking my chin. "What did you do to her?"

"Ms. Cabot?" If anything, he looked more confused.

From behind him, Grace called out wearily, "Let her in, Chuy. It's fine."

Chuy? The guy stepped aside and motioned for me to enter. I edged past him carefully, keeping him in my sight line the entire time. Then I shifted my gaze to the room and stopped dead in my tracks.

I'd never actually set foot in the Buggy before, but I had been expecting something along the lines of the Getaway or the Mayhem, except much more run-down and filthy.

This . . . was not that.

The room was small but immaculately decorated. The size was deceptive; it looked like a wall had been knocked down to combine two motel rooms, because it was easily two hundred square feet. My eyes swept over the plush carpet, the small sitting area with a love seat and an armchair, and the gas fireplace installed in the wall. Aside from the hospital bed, it could've passed for a luxury hotel room, easily as nice as the grand-a-night resort Kat and I had visited in Napa.

An old woman lay on the bed, seemingly asleep. Grace sat in a chair pulled up to the bedside, giving me one of her trademark death glares. Chuy, meanwhile, hadn't moved from the doorway, where he stood with his arms crossed like some sort of medical bouncer.

"What the actual fuck?" I said.

"Hello to you, too." Grace sounded drained, her voice lacking its usual acerbic quality. I noted that she was holding the woman's hand. "What are you doing here?"

"I followed you. Again."

"That's obvious, Amber. Why?"

"Well, you were acting kind of sketchy, and, uh," I shrugged. "I don't know, I guess I got suspicious. Then I heard noises and thought maybe you were being attacked."

Grace rubbed her eyes with her free hand. "I see. Well, then. Has your curiosity been satisfied?"

"Not entirely, no. Who's that?" I pointed to the bed.

The older woman stirred and let out a moan. Grace's lips pursed and she hissed, "Please keep your voice down, Amber. Mother has been sedated, but it's best not to agitate her."

"Wait. *Mother*?" I goggled at her. "That's your mom?"

"Yes, Amber."

"She should sleep," Chuy chimed in from the doorway, his voice a low rumble. He was also eyeing me with sharp disapproval, my usual charm apparently failing with him as well. "If you don't mind, Ms. Cabot."

"Of course, Chuy. My apologies." Grace leaned forward and tucked her mother's hand under the comforter and then murmured something to her.

Watching, Chuy said, "Sorry I had to call you in, Ms. Cabot. She just wouldn't settle down. Thought she saw him again."

"I know. It's all right." Grace threw him a reassuring smile, which was almost more astonishing than our surroundings.

"Might be time to have that conversation," he said hesitantly.

Grace's smile vanished. "Not now Chuy, okay?"

"Sure, Ms. Cabot. I'm just saying—"

"I know what you're saying," Grace interjected, cutting him off. She seemed to compose herself and then said, "I apologize. That came out harsher than intended."

"It's fine, Ms. Cabot. I get it. Why don't you take a break? We're cool here for now."

"Thanks, I will." She smiled at him again. "Someday, I'm going to get you to call me Grace."

"Not gonna happen, Ms. Cabot," Chuy said slyly, grinning back at her.

As she turned toward me, Grace's smile vanished. She nodded briskly and said, "This way."

Without checking to see if I followed, she strode toward a doorway on the right. It led into another room, which was identically tricked out, except everything was white and in place of the hospital bed stood a queen-sized bed with a white headboard. Weirder still, I could swear it was the one from Grace's Los Angeles home.

Hustling to keep up, I said, "I'm so confused. So do you, like, live here now?"

Without looking back at me, Grace cocked her head to the side. "I suppose I live here as much as I live anywhere."

"But, I mean, the owner is okay with that?"

As Grace opened a door at the far end of the room, she said with a sigh, "I'm the owner. Try to keep up, Amber."

My snarky response died in my throat as we entered the third room. Grace had knocked down walls here, too, and extended the ceiling to the top of the second level. The room was twice the size of the others, occupying an entire wing of the motel. It was also eerily familiar. The main section was almost an exact replica of what I'd dubbed Grace's "Serial Killer Suite" (SKS for short) in Los Angeles: white walls, thick black floor matting, a rolling whiteboard, and an expensive wheeled desk chair facing an entire row of computer towers and monitors. The only thing missing was the giant map of the United States filled with pushpins.

The SKS was flanked on one side by a sleek, modern kitchen with top-of-the-line appliances and a marble waterfall island. The opposite end of the room sported a seating area with a large sectional sofa facing a giant wall-mounted television. Basically, Grace had replaced squalor with a luxury open-floorplan apartment.

I shook my head and held up a finger. "Nope. Uh-uh."

"What seems to be the problem?" Grace asked.

"Seriously?" I made a sweeping gesture that encompassed the room. "Just give me a second to process this. So last May, you came here to set up the stuff in your brother's room—"

"The evidence of his crimes, when we were framing him." Grace went over to the kitchen and started filling an electric teakettle.

"Right, his creepy trophies. And while you were doing that, you looked around this complete shithole and thought, 'Y'know what?

This would be a great place to live. Right here in this vermin-infested, disgusting motel.'"

"The exterminator was very thorough, I assure you," Grace sniffed. "Besides, the benefits were clear. There's a busy international airport close by and several major highways. This section of Las Vegas is primarily commercial, so there are no neighbors to speak of. It offers considerable privacy."

"So, no guests?"

"Absolutely not." Grace wrinkled her nose. "This establishment will be 'under renovation' indefinitely."

"You live here now." I shook my head. "Holy crap. Does Dot know?"

"As I said, I value my privacy. So, no. Would you care for some tea?"

"Yeah, sure." I stalked over to the sectional couch and plopped down on it, suddenly exhausted. "And your mom is here, too."

"Yes."

I watched as Grace carefully filled a small teapot with loose tea and then poured the steaming water into it. She brought it over on a small tray, along with two matching china cups on saucers with a full tea service on the side. "Fancy."

"Yes, well. My boarding school featured an entire class on tea preparation."

"Really?"

"No," she said, filling my cup. "Choate was more of an academically focused institution. Your girlfriend's school, however, might offer that as part of its curriculum."

"Probably." I blew on the tea to cool it and then took a sip. It was delicious. Awkwardly, I asked, "Um, is your mom okay?"

"Mother has Lewy body dementia." Grace sipped her tea without meeting my eyes.

"Oh, sorry. That sucks."

"Yes, it does suck," she said dryly.

"Nice of you to take care of her," I offered. This was rapidly shaping up to be the most awkward conversation we'd ever had, and there had been one where I'd thought *she* might be a serial killer.

"Yes, well. Last spring there was an incident at the facility where she was staying. Mother is a bit of an escape artist, and they did a highly inadequate job of ensuring her safety."

"Wait," I said, suddenly realizing something. "Is *that* where you disappeared to when we were in L.A.?" When I had been hiding out at her house, Grace had vanished without explanation for nearly twenty-four hours and returned looking the same sort of drained that she did now.

"Yes." She cocked an eyebrow at me. "After that, I decided she would be better off with family. And with Gunnar taken care of, there was no longer a risk to her safety."

I frowned. "You were hiding her from Gunnar?"

Grace sipped her tea. "Gunnar was particularly loyal to Father. It seemed prudent to take precautions, considering the fact that Mother turned him in to the FBI."

"Wow, really?" I nearly choked on my tea. "Good for her. Did she tell you that, back when—"

Grace shook her head. "Mother was never one for confiding. Father's capture was attributed to an anonymous tip, but I realized later that only one person could have possibly known about his activities."

"Dang." I shook my head. "So hunting serial killers runs in the family."

"As do serial killers," Grace said.

I blinked at her. "Holy crap. Did you just make a joke?"

Grace smiled thinly at me. "Some people find me quite funny."

"Sure they do. Hell, I always found you hilarious." Taking another sip, I said, "I can't believe you're living right next to Dot and she doesn't know about it."

She looked discomfited. "In general, I prefer to protect my privacy. In light of which, if you wouldn't mind—"

"Oh, don't worry. I'm certainly not going to be the one to tell her."

"Thank you, Amber. I appreciate that."

I finished my tea as we sat in an oddly companionable silence. Almost as if we were friends. It was weird, but nice.

Grace set down her cup. "Speaking of which, I thought it over on the way here. It was smart of you to consider the victims' profiles."

"Thanks," I said cautiously. Grace was caretaking, cracking jokes, and complimenting me? Clearly we'd entered some sort of *Invasion of the Body Snatchers* situation.

"Of course, it will likely prove to be an enormous waste of time," she added.

"That's more like it," I said.

She threw me a look. "Pardon?"

"Never mind. Thanks for the tea." I carefully set my saucer back on the tray and got up. "Fifty bucks says we get him tonight."

Grace reached out her hand. "You never tire of wasting money, do you?"

"Nope, never," I said as we shook. Looking her in the eye, I said, "So this is it, then? No other deep, dark secrets you're hiding?"

She smiled thinly at me and extricated her hand. "No, Amber." There was more than a hint of sadness in her voice as she added, "This is my life now."

As I climbed back in my car, I tried to shake off an overwhelming sense of melancholy. It was funny; I never thought Grace was capable of regular human emotions, especially sadness. I was starting to realize that maybe I didn't really know her at all.

One thing was for sure: I was done following people. I planned on spending the rest of the trip appreciating the fact that my life was going great. I had money, a hot girlfriend, and friends who liked me enough to include me in their weddings.

All in all, I was killing it. Rapping my knuckles on the console, I muttered, "Knock wood."

Because it's never a good idea to tempt fate.

CHAPTER TEN

CRY OF THE HUNTED

Grace, age nine

SHAKER HEIGHTS, OHIO

Grace threw herself on her bed and buried her face in the pillow. "It's not fair," she said, carefully muffling her voice because *young ladies do* not *scream*. "Not fair not fair not fair . . ."

A *click* from behind her. Grace shifted to see her twin standing in the doorway, pointing a hunting rifle at her. She glowered at Gunnar as he pulled the trigger and said, "Bang. You're dead."

Father stepped into view and grabbed the barrel, raising it as he said, "Now, now. We never point guns at someone unless we plan to shoot them."

"It's not loaded," Gunnar grumbled.

Father went very still.

Grace caught her breath, and Gunnar's face fell as he realized his mistake. "I—I'm sorry, sir."

Father carefully extricated the rifle from Gunnar's grasp. Evenly, he said, "Are you talking back to me, son?"

"No sir." Gunnar shook his head vigorously. "Absolutely not, sir."

"Then you're implying that I am mistaken?"

Gunnar gulped and shook his head. Grace felt conflicted—part of her thrilled to see her brother in trouble, the rest abjectly terrified for him. But she knew that the worst possible thing she could do was intervene.

"And now you're not answering when spoken to." Their father's voice had gone softer, always a bad sign. If there was one thing she and Gunnar knew, it was that when Father became quiet, he was at his most dangerous.

Gunnar's voice pitched up to a high squeak as he said, "Father, I apologize. I did not mean to offend—"

"Get the wheat." Father said in a voice barely above a whisper.

Gunnar blanched but said, "Ye—yes, sir."

Grace had to repress a shudder. "The wheat" was the worst of all possible punishments. Father kept a container of uncooked wheat kernels in the pantry for this express purpose. She could hear Gunnar sniffling as he shuffled down the hall to collect it. He'd have to pour the wheat into the bathtub and then kneel on it until Father decided the punishment was over. Then Gunnar would clean up every kernel by hand or risk a repeat.

Grace had only had to do it once, and she'd limped for a full week after. For Gunnar, it was becoming a regular occurrence.

"Now, then," Father said, coming over to her bed. He was wearing his hunting camouflage and a thin smile. "What were you saying earlier, about it not being fair?"

"I wasn't thinking," Grace said meekly. "I was being a selfish, naughty girl. I'm sorry, Father."

Grace had to resist the urge to flinch as he laid a hand on her head. "I know it's frustrating for you, Gracie. But Mother feels strongly that hunting is not appropriate for young ladies."

Grace was having a hard time gauging whether or not she was in trouble, too. Hesitantly, she said, "I know, Father. I just think I would be really good at it."

Father smiled at that. "I believe you would. Probably even superior to your brother. Perhaps Mother can be persuaded to change her mind."

"Really?" Grace said hopefully.

"Not today, obviously," Father said. "But I will see what we can do about next time."

"That would be wonderful, Father. Thank you." Grace wrapped her arms gently around him and gave a quick squeeze.

"You're my best girl," Father said, pressing his dry lips to her cheek. "Never grow up."

As always, the way he said it gave her the creeps. But she nodded and said, "I won't."

She spent the rest of the day helping Mother with chores around the house. Mother had a way of drifting from task to task, eyes vacant, barely responding even when spoken to. It would have struck Grace as odd if it weren't for the fact that she'd always been that way, and since Grace had no friends aside from Gunnar, she also had no real experience of what other moms did. Her best guide was what she saw on television, the few times a year they were allowed to watch it. And obviously, those moms were made up.

Their chores were very specific. Father had composed a list of what had to be cleaned daily, weekly, and monthly. Grace found the routine comforting. Today, the extra work entailed wiping down the baseboards, polishing the silver, and cleaning the inside of the oven hood. Grace hummed to herself as they worked. As usual, Mother didn't say a word.

It was late when Father and Gunnar returned, well past dinnertime. Grace was absolutely starving, but the rules were clear: No one was allowed to eat if Father was expected. So she and Mother sat across from each other at the dinner table, sipping water while dinner was kept warm in the oven. The aromas wafting from the kitchen were enough to make Grace swoon. When she finally heard the sound of the back door closing, she could have cried with relief. Mother immediately sprang into action, hustling into the kitchen to assemble the plates. Grace double-checked to make sure that Father's place setting was perfectly straight, the tips of the fork tines lined up perfectly with the top of the knife blade. Then she sat back down and chewed on the inside of her cheek to distract herself from how hungry she was.

She heard the sound of water running in the powder room off the hall and then Gunnar limped in. He was still wearing his hunting clothes and had a glassy look in his eyes.

Father, on the other hand, was in one of his garrulous moods. "That pot roast smells amazing, Marjorie. I just hope you didn't burn the potatoes this time."

Mother froze on the threshold. "I—I think they're fine. But I can always make more."

"Well, why don't we just see how they are first," Father said jovially, tucking his napkin onto his lap.

Grace cut her eyes at Gunnar, but he was avoiding her gaze, staring down at his plate. Which was unlike him; she'd been fully prepared for him to come home gloating about what a great time he'd had, rubbing her face in it (not at the table, of course, at least not with words; those would be saved for after dinner, when they were alone). But instead, he looked . . . off. She frowned. Had something gone wrong on the hunting trip?

Father delicately sliced off a hunk of meat and forked it into his mouth, the signal that the rest of them could begin. Ravenous, Grace had to force herself to be equally dainty, lest her plate be snatched away without warning. A few bites in, with the worst of her hunger satiated, she tentatively asked, "How was hunting, Father?"

"Excellent!" he boomed. "Really a five-star day, wasn't it, son?"

Gunnar nodded without looking up and whispered, "Yes, Father."

"Did you kill anything?" Grace asked, thinking maybe that was what was wrong with Gunnar. He'd been bragging for weeks about all the deer he was going to bag, but when the time came, maybe it hadn't been as "awesome" as he'd expected.

"Did we ever!" Father said with a wide grin. There was a smear of blood on his front teeth from the roast. Seeing it made Grace shudder, although she'd be hard pressed to explain why. "Maybe we'll go back tomorrow and see what else we can find, eh, kiddo? Finish the job, as it were!"

Gunnar made a small noise in the back of his throat. Mother stiffened but didn't say anything.

"Where is it?" Grace asked.

"Where is what?" Father replied.

"The deer?"

"Oh." Father wiped his mouth, then returned the napkin to his lap. "I only took a small steak; it's in the freezer for a special occasion. The rest was dropped off at the meat processor."

Mother winced. Father smiled at her, but it was one of those that never reached his eyes. "Did you want to say something, Marjorie?"

"No," Mother said quietly. "I'm glad you had a good day."

"The best!" Father clapped his hands together. "And I'll tell you what, this young man has the makings of a great hunter. Mark my words."

"Thank you, Father," Gunnar said woodenly.

Father sat back and pushed away his plate. Even though she was only half finished, Mother leapt up to collect it. Father grabbed her wrist as she reached for it and said, "I was thinking, Marjorie, the hyacinths are looking a little limp. Perhaps I should switch them out for some rosemary this weekend. And then we could have rosemary chicken. That's your favorite, isn't it, Gracie?"

Grace nodded. "Yes, Father."

"Well, it's settled then." He tossed his napkin onto the table, pushed back his chair, and left the room. Mother followed, bringing his plate to the sink.

Grace noticed that Gunnar had barely eaten. "What's wrong?" she whispered, too quietly for either parent to hear.

He slowly lifted his head, meeting her eyes. Grace almost recoiled. She knew his face as well as her own; maybe even better. And she'd never seen this particular expression before. "What?" she pressed.

Gunnar glanced furtively toward the kitchen, checking to make sure their parents weren't in hearing range. Then he leaned forward and said in a low, earnest voice, "It wasn't a deer, Grace."

Grace frowned. "So what was—"

"Well!" Father said, coming back in. "I'm in the mood for a nightcap. I'll have a Manhattan, Marjorie."

As they were getting ready for bed that night, Grace asked Gunnar what he'd meant. But he refused to say anything more about it. And later, he acted as though it had never happened.

She never did end up going hunting with her dad.

CHAPTER ELEVEN

DESTINY

LAS VEGAS, NEVADA

"How about this one?" Kat asked, holding a shirt up for me to examine.

"Love it," I said absently. We were in one of the price-gouging stores that lurked in every casino, eager to separate gamblers from whatever cash the house had grudgingly let them keep. The showroom we stood in was cavernous but contained only two discreetly placed racks on either side with a sofa in the middle. They'd actually offered us champagne when we walked in.

Admittedly, I was a fan of the free booze. Halfway through my second glass, I was weighing whether or not it would be tacky to ask for a third.

I'd spent most of the morning thinking about the side of Grace I'd seen at the Buggy; it was still kind of wigging me out. I felt awful about invading her privacy and was wondering if I should apologize the next time I saw her.

Anyway, I was distracted. Which was clearly starting to piss off my girlfriend.

She pouted. "You didn't even look at it."

I sighed. "Kat, honey, it's a black turtleneck. I can only muster so much excitement." I checked the price tag and tried not to openly gag.

"Where did you disappear to this morning, anyway?" she asked.

I could tell she was trying to keep her voice casual. Avoiding her eyes, I shrugged. "Just helping out with wedding stuff."

"Oh?" She made a face. "That's odd. Dot didn't mention it."

"Yeah, well, it's kind of a surprise for her." Why was I lying? It wasn't like I'd done anything wrong. But part of me didn't feel okay about sharing my glimpse into Grace's life.

"Do you think I should get it?" Kat asked, turning toward the mirror.

I sighed. A love of shopping was one of the few things Kat and I didn't have in common. Twenty minutes in, and I was already getting twitchy. "For four hundred dollars, it better have an eight ball tucked up one of those sleeves."

She went rigid. "Oh."

"I'm sorry," I said, immediately realizing my mistake. "That came out wrong."

"No, it's fine." Kat made a big show of marching over to hang the turtleneck back on the rack.

I hurried after her, trying to repair the damage. "I meant to say I love it, and it will look amazing on you. Let's get it."

"No thank you, Amber." Kat was already walking to the door, head held high. "Please excuse me, I need to use the restroom."

I grabbed the shirt and went to the register to pay for it, muttering under my breath. As I waited in line, I drained the rest of the champagne in one gulp. During the past few months, I'd learned something about serious relationships: You always had the same fight, over and over. There were seemingly endless variations on the specifics, but the bottom line never changed. And this was our particular battle.

Kat was loaded. Probably worth a lot more than me, and that was saying something. But what differentiated "old money" from the kind I had was that it wasn't "liquid." I'd spent the past few months undergoing a crash course in how rich people lived, and it wasn't at all what I'd expected. Kat told stories about flying to an island on someone's private jet and then getting kicked out of a bar there because none of her rich pals had thought to bring cash. "I mean, who doesn't take Apple Pay?" she'd asked, eyes wide.

"Shocking," I'd agreed at the time, still trying to get past the whole "private jet" part.

Anyway, that meant that I frequently footed the bill for things. And I didn't care. I'd have to buy overpriced turtlenecks by the truckload to even make a dent in the money Grace had given me. But considering the fact that not so long ago I was barely able to scrape together enough cash for a thirty-bucks-a-night motel room, sometimes the prices in the world I now inhabited made my head spin.

Whenever I commented on it, though, Kat always got weird. I wasn't sure if that was because mentioning how much something cost was considered tacky, or if she was embarrassed about not having the cash on hand to cover it herself.

I had learned one valuable lesson: Whatever it was, just buy it for her. That made my life a lot easier. And yes, I was fully aware that this made me sound like a problematic husband from the Eisenhower era. She reciprocated with pricey gifts like my Rolex and by covering our Napa weekend. All in all, it felt pretty even.

I was standing behind a middle-aged woman in a headscarf and sunglasses whose transaction seemed to be taking an awfully long time. I watched as the salesclerk swiped the woman's credit card over and over, a slight frown marring her perfect features. The customer, meanwhile, was prattling away about how disappointed she was that the sweater she was trying to return hadn't fit her sister, and she was so sad that they didn't have a smaller size in stock . . .

Tuning in to what was really going on, I bit my lip to contain my bemusement. The customer was pulling what my grifter mother had coined a "boomerang Alice" (not that she'd invented it, mind you, but Mom was constantly taking credit for cons that had been around since the Dark Ages). The way it worked was that someone shoplifted an item and then they (or ideally, a partner) came back later to "return" it. The con handed over a nonfunctioning credit card to put the refund on. Retailers had caught on to this sort of thing, so they usually insisted on issuing store credit. The trick was to persuade them that you were never going to be able to use it, you lived nowhere near one of their stores, nothing currently in stock fit you, etc., etc., etc. And nine times out of ten, the store would eventually cave and hand over cash for stolen goods.

I'd never used this con, mainly because it involved shoplifting, which was really stealing. I also knew that some jerky managers would subtract the loss from a hapless employee's paycheck. And back when I used to run scams, I'd always been careful not to target anyone who couldn't afford to take the hit. All of my marks could handle having their wallet lightened a little; a lot of them probably never even noticed.

Clearly, the woman currently holding up the line had no such qualms. She was arguing with the poor salesclerk now, her voice rising as she became agitated.

I frowned. There was something unsettlingly familiar about her. I leaned to the side, trying to get a better look.

"I apologize, ma'am, but I really can't give you cash for this," the salesclerk was explaining frostily. "The manager isn't here, and I—"

The older woman suddenly clutched her chest, grabbed at the counter, and slid to the floor. I resisted the urge to slow-clap at this obvious charade. The shocked clerk froze with alarm as the woman gasped and twitched, delivering a truly Oscar-worthy performance . . .

. . . and providing my first clear view of her face. As the clerk hurriedly punched digits into the desk phone, likely calling 911 (I could have told her not to bother because this character would be long gone by the time help arrived), I stood above the woman, hands on my hips.

Finally spotting me, her contortions stilled. She lowered her sunglasses and said, "*Emily*?"

"Hi, Mom," I said, offering a hand to help her up.

— — —

"Don't worry, I've got this," I said to the salesclerk as I pulled my mother to her feet.

"Are you sure?" the clerk asked uncertainly. "If you'd like, I can have an ambulance—"

"No!" my mother and I barked simultaneously. I glared at her and then told the clerk, "I'll help Mom back to her room. She's just a little, y'know . . ." I mimed tipping a bottle into my mouth.

My mother frowned at me. "Emily, that is absolutely not—"

"C'mon, Mom," I said loudly, grabbing her elbow and steering her toward the door. "Time to sleep it off. Again."

"Oh! I almost forgot!" the clerk called out when we were nearly at the door. "Ma'am, here's your refund."

She hurried over and offered my mother a few crisp hundreds. My mom smiled weakly at her. "Oh, aren't you a dear. I'm going to write a letter, make sure they name you employee of the month."

"I better hold that for you, Mom," I said, deftly plucking the bills from her hand. "Until you've sobered up. Thanks again!"

I nodded at the bewildered salesgirl and frog-marched my mother into the hallway that led back to the casino. Guiding her toward the exit, I hissed, "So. Where's Dad?"

"Where do you think?" my mom scoffed, her voice back to normal. She'd added a dramatic little quaver in the store, which explained why I hadn't recognized her immediately. "Losing at blackjack. That's why I needed to stop at the ATM."

"Right." I released her and sighed. "Well, great seeing you. Have a nice life."

She opened her mouth to say something, but I'd already turned away. I'd had no contact with my parents in nine years, not since they'd bailed on a con that went wrong (which was kind of a pattern for them). Fifteen-year-old me came home from high school to nothing but a wrinkled twenty-dollar bill and a note that read *Sorry kiddo, timed this one wrong.*

So yeah, they weren't in the running for any "parent of the year" plaques. I caught sight of Kat twenty feet away, scanning the hall for me, and quickened my pace. If there was one thing I definitely did *not* want, it was to introduce Kat to my erstwhile parents.

"Emily, wait!" my mom called after me.

I ignored her. Just a few more steps, and I'd be free and clear. *Sorry Mom*, I thought with a smirk. *I haven't been Emily for a long time now.* Part of starting over a few years ago had involved paying for a new ID, which is how "Emily Austin" became "Amber Jamison."

Kat looked perplexed as I approached her at a near run. "Is everything okay?"

"Yup, fine!" I wrapped my arm around her waist and guided her back toward the casino, mentally reviewing the layout. We'd passed the blackjack tables on our way in, so I'd have to exit by the slots instead . . .

"I bought you a present," Kat said, holding up a bag from an insanely expensive jewelry store. "Sorry I became so upset before."

"Don't worry about it," I said, picking up the pace until we were practically jogging. Trying to ignore the inner voice that was muttering, *Great. Another necklace you'll never wear,* I said, "That's so sweet, you didn't have to do that."

"Do you want to open it?" she asked, sounding breathless. "Amber? Can we walk more slowly, please?"

"Um, I just want to get back to the room and open it there. That way I'll really be able to give it my full attention, you know?"

"Okay." Kat was checking back over her shoulder. "Do you know that woman?"

"Who?" I said, feigning innocence.

"The one running after us?"

I heard my mom yell, "Emily, wait!"

"Never seen her before in my life. Let's grab a cab."

A surprisingly strong hand on my shoulder jerked me to a stop. I whipped around, ready for anything.

My mother and I stared at each other for a beat. Perplexed, Kat looked back and forth between us.

"I thought it was you!" my mother exclaimed, clapping her hands together in a decent approximation of unbridled joy. "Darling, what a lovely surprise!"

I gritted my teeth, but it was useless to pretend this was a case of mistaken identity. I looked eerily like a more petite version of my mother—her "mini-me," as one of my parents' derelict friends used to say. The jig was up.

Doubly annoyed by the victory in her eyes, I gestured at her and said with resignation, "Kat, this is my mom. Mom, Kat."

"Your mother!" Kat's eyes widened. "Oh, how amazing! What a coincidence!"

"Yup," I agreed, eyes narrowing as my mother enveloped Kat in an embrace. "Kind of unbelievable, really." Could my parents have orchestrated this "chance encounter"? But how would they have found me?

And why would they bother? They certainly hadn't made an effort at any other point during the past nine years. Of course, I hadn't had money back then . . .

My mother winked at me, which only heightened my suspicions. Then she drew back and held Kat at arm's length. "My, aren't you pretty as a picture."

Kat beamed in response. "Thank you."

"So what are you girls doing in town?" Mom asked.

"Gambling," I said at the same time that Kat offered, "A wedding."

"A wedding! Not yours, is it?"

"No!" I barked, a little too sharply. Seeing Kat frown, I threw her an apologetic look.

"Still," cooed Mom, not missing a beat, "how lovely!" She was channeling her best ideal-mom routine. If I hadn't grown up with her, I might even have believed it myself. "Well, your father and I would love to take you both out to dinner if you have time."

"We don't," I said firmly, grabbing Kat's hand and starting to move away. "But thanks. Have fun."

Sounding wounded, my mother called after me, "Wouldn't you like to say hello to your father? He'll be so disappointed to have missed you!"

"Give him my best!" I called back, maneuvering Kat double-time toward the door.

"Amber," Kat protested. "What's wrong?"

"Long story. I don't have a great relationship with my folks," I said in a low voice. "So let's just go, okay?"

We rounded the corner and nearly collided with my father. Seeing me, he startled. "Honey?"

"Fuck." I dropped my head, conceding defeat. "Hi, Dad."

"Hello, sweetheart." My dad beamed at me. He was dressed in khakis, a golf shirt, a Members Only jacket, and sneakers—the perfect uniform if you were trying to blend in with a typical casino crowd. Which was probably the point. "Wow, what a surprise!"

"Is it?" I asked skeptically. "I didn't think you ever came this far west for . . . work."

His eyes flicked to Kat and then back to me. He shrugged. "Well, your mom thought we could use a vacation. Gamble a little, see a show—"

"Right," I nodded. "So how far down are you?"

"Oh, don't worry about that."

"Oh, I definitely won't." My mother had caught up. She eased around us and tucked her arm through my dad's. "Anyway, we were just leaving."

"Now, don't be like that," my mom said. "We're family!"

I goggled at her. My initial reaction had been shock, followed by a strong urge to flee. But the way they were acting, as if they even had the right to refer to themselves as my parents . . . that was starting to piss me off. I mean, sure, I liked to think of myself as being pretty tough, even unshakable. But my parents had basically abandoned me when I was still a kid.

I'd imagined versions of this reunion for years. Usually, those fantasies centered around berating them for their selfishness. In every one of these scenarios I was rich and happy. I threw in their faces the fact that I'd survived—along with a twenty-dollar bill, which would be the icing on the proverbial cake. I'd show them everything I'd achieved and sneer, "See? I didn't need you anyway."

I realized, looking at them now, that this might actually *be* that moment. I was definitely rich, I was pretty happy, I'd graduated from college . . . and I hadn't conned anyone to gain any of those things. I'd done it all on my own (well, mostly). I'd won.

But as I opened my mouth to unleash the speech I'd mentally prepared, I noticed that in the fluorescent light, they appeared old and washed out. Diminished. The sleeves of my dad's jacket were frayed, and his glasses were held together with a safety pin. My mom's outfit was dated, her shoes worn. Maybe that was just costuming for whatever scam they were pulling, but something in me doubted it.

And just like that, my rage ebbed. Kat squeezed my hand reassuringly, and I reciprocated. Drawing a deep breath, I said, "If you're free now, maybe we could grab a coffee."

CHAPTER TWELVE

BABY FACE

Amber, age fourteen

CINCINNATI, OHIO

I'm too old for this," I protested again, tugging on the hem of the dress. Last year it had grazed my knees, but thanks to a recent growth spurt, it had more of a baby-doll fit now. "No one is going to believe I'm ten years old."

"With that face?" my mother said, grabbing my chin and turning my head from side to side to inspect her handiwork. "You can still pull it off, kiddo. Thanks to my genes, you'll be able to play young for a long, long time."

I scratched at the Ace bandage binding my chest under the dress; it was pulled so taut I could hardly breathe. "I don't get why I can't just be my own age."

"Because people hate teenagers," my mother said. Off my expression, she sat back and said, "What? I'm just telling you how it is. A teenager, they might feel a little sorry for. But a ten-year-old with a bad heart? Now *that's* tragic."

"Almost ready?" my dad asked, poking his head into the bedroom. The only thing in it besides us was a twin mattress on the floor and a suitcase whose contents spilled out the top. Which rendered it indistinguishable from every other bedroom I'd had, of which there had literally been too many to count.

"Daddy, this dress is too small for me," I said, appealing to him with my best little girl voice. "Can I please not do this?"

"Never try to bullshit a bullshitter, sweetheart," he said, tweaking his nose at me.

"That voice is perfect!" my mom exclaimed. "Say the lines just like that."

"What, now?"

"No time like the present!" my dad agreed.

I crossed my arms over my chest. Glowering at them, I mewled, "The doctors say that with one more surgery, I might be able to go back to school. But it's *so* expensive."

"Perfect!" my dad said, clapping his hands.

In spite of everything, I felt a rush of pride at his approval.

"Leukemia would still be better," my mom said.

"I am *not* shaving my head again!" I shouted, stamping my foot.

"Fine," she sighed. "Oof, what did I ever do to deserve such an ungrateful child? At least let me put another layer of powder on your cheeks, they're still just too damn pink."

"Maybe a little more shadow under the eyes, too?" my father offered, eyeing me critically.

"Definitely," my mother agreed.

I stood mutely while she finished working on me, a wave of rage thundering through my head. Someday, they'd be sorry they put me through all this. I'd grow up and do something amazing, and when they asked me for help, I'd tell them to go to hell.

"Ready, princess?" my dad said. "We pull this off, I promise we'll finally go to Disney World, okay?"

"I'm too old for that now," I grumbled. Pulling on the stringy wig and adjusting it by feel, I said, "Let's just get it over with."

CHAPTER THIRTEEN

THE DARK PAST

LAS VEGAS, NEVADA

"Well, this is just so lovely." My mom delicately wiped her mouth with the corner of her napkin. "Such a treat running into you girls!"

I suppressed the urge to gag, instead picking moodily at my croissant. No sooner had I agreed to coffee than my mother basically dragged us to a café at the far end of the casino, gushing about how it served the best croissants outside of Paris.

I knew for a fact that it would be a miracle if my parents had managed to visit Paris in the past decade, and they'd definitely never been before that. My mom was really playing up her "wealthy Midwestern lady" character; if I hadn't known better, even I might've been convinced. Kat just sat there nodding. (As always, it was nearly impossible to get a word in edgewise with my mother.)

Still, the croissant was pretty damn good. I polished mine off and took another gulp of coffee, then checked my watch. I could stand about five more minutes of this before it became impossible to suppress the primal scream burbling in my gut. My dad just sat there grinning like an idiot, which was his usual role in their scams; he played the quiet guy who just seemed so gosh-darned normal. You'd never suspect that while my mom was distracting you, he'd snagged your watch and wallet. Which was why I kept an eye on my wrist; no way was he walking off with my Rolex.

Meanwhile, Kat was lapping up everything they were serving. "Tell me more about what Amber was like growing up."

"Amber?" My mom's eyes slid across to me. I threw her a warning look but needn't have bothered. My mom was too much of a pro to screw up someone else's alias. "Oh, you know Amber. She was always a firecracker. But how about you? A real live baroness!" My mom clapped her hands together.

That's what they must think, I suddenly realized. Between the fake name, my nice clothes, and Kat's clearly impressive background, of course my parents would assume that she was my latest mark. As my mother prattled on, I could practically see her mentally tallying up what I could squeeze out of Kat.

The thought made me sick. And yet, I knew how easy it was to fall back into pulling cons. After all, I'd been forced to do it myself just a few months ago. I frowned, a feeling of dread blossoming in my stomach.

"Well, the title does not really mean much these days," Kat said modestly.

"But still!" The sinking sensation in my gut worsened at the familiar glimmer in my mother's eyes. *Shit.* This was a mistake. I should have dragged Kat away from them when I had the chance. My mom leaned forward and put her chin in her hands, saying, "Tell me *all* about it!"

As Kat launched into her family history, which apparently went back far enough that they qualified as "primeval nobility" (I'd googled it), I kicked my mother under the table. Her lips tightened, but other than that she didn't react. I tried for my dad next, but he anticipated the move and shifted his feet away so I encountered nothing but air.

Glowering, I finished my coffee and pushed back my chair. "Well, this really has been something. But we've gotta go."

Following my cue, Kat stood and said, "So lovely meeting you both."

Through tight lips, my mother said, "Oh, that's such a shame! I was really hoping to hear more."

"Yeah, well, guess we timed this one wrong." Unable to resist, I dropped a twenty-dollar bill on the table and added, "This is on me. Just paying you back."

I grabbed Kat's hand and prepared to make a break for it, only to nearly crash into Grace, who was standing silently behind me. Because of course she was.

"Hello again!" Kat said, looking delighted. "We just keep running into people today!"

Grace cocked her eyebrow in a way that I was all too familiar with and said, "It's not a coincidence. I deliberately came to find Amber."

I knew better than to ask how she knew where we'd be. Grace looked even more serious than usual, which was never a great sign. "Um, Kat? Can you give us a minute?"

"Why don't we visit the little girls' room together?" my mom said, seizing the opportunity to reinsert herself into the situation by taking Kat's arm.

Kat threw me a panicked look, but I nodded. "It'll just take a minute," I called reassuringly as my mom dragged her away. My dad had already disappeared, probably to cash in my twenty for chips.

"Who is that woman?" Grace asked.

"My mom." Off her look, I said, "I know, it's been a weird day. Very parent-forward. What's up?"

"Nothing pressing," Grace said. "I simply wanted to reiterate that I'd prefer you not mention my current living situation to anyone."

I examined her. She looked uncomfortable, a little shaky beneath her usual icy reserve. "Shit. Are you saying I shouldn't have rented that billboard?"

Grace issued an exaggerated sigh. "Must you joke about everything?"

"Sorry. I already promised not to tell Dot."

"Or your girlfriend?" Grace said, crossing her arms.

"Not that she'd care, but no, I haven't told her and wasn't planning to."

Grace held my gaze for a moment, as if trying to discern if I was lying. Then she nodded sharply. "Thank you, Amber. I appreciate your discretion."

"Sure, no biggie." Over her shoulder, I spotted Kat and my mother coming back. Kat looked tired and aggravated. I could empathize. "Is that it?"

Following my gaze, she said, "It must be unsettling, running into your parents like this."

"You can say that again," I muttered. Grace wore an odd look, like she was debating saying something. "What?"

"Nothing." She nodded stiffly. "I'll see you later tonight."

"Can't wait," I said, rubbing my eyes. "Make sure to bring enough cash to cover our bet. I take fives or tens, no singles."

Grace smirked. "I admire your optimism."

"Oh, we're getting him," I said, repressing a yawn. "Mark my words." I'd had a half dozen coffees today, but none had made a dent in my fatigue. I desperately needed a power nap. And to rescue my girlfriend. Leaving Grace, I marched across the café to where my mother had Kat backed into a corner. As I approached, I overheard my mother say, "Really, I shouldn't even be telling you this—"

I grabbed Kat's arm and said, "Time to go. For real, this time."

Kat smiled weakly at me. "Your mother was just telling me about an amazing business opportunity."

"Oh, she was, was she?" I narrowed my eyes at my mom, who tucked a stray hair behind her ear, deliberately avoiding my gaze.

"I should probably make sure your father hasn't gotten into any trouble," my mom said, backing up.

"Is everything all right with Grace?" Kat asked.

"She's fine," I said, waving a hand dismissively. "Honey, why don't you go get the car from the valet? I'll meet you out there. I just want a quick word with my mom."

"That's sweet, dear," my mom said, still edging away. "But I wouldn't want to hold you up."

"Oh, I insist," I said grimly, handing Kat the valet ticket and a five and grabbing my mother firmly by the elbow. I waited until Kat was out of sight around the bend and then growled at my mom, "Stay away from her. Do you understand?"

"Really, Emily," my mother sighed. "Still so dramatic."

My eyes narrowed, and I snapped, "I don't know what you're doing here, and I don't care. This is the last time we see each other."

"Is it?" my mother said, raising an eyebrow. "Because I have to say, that poor girl seems to know so little about you. Honestly, Emily, you know better. Always tell them enough to not raise questions, otherwise, it just looks like you have—"

"—some deep, dark secret," I said, finishing for her. I'd heard that little nugget more times than I could count. It was easily in the top ten list of "Sarah Austin's Guide to Cons." "She's not a mark. She's my girlfriend."

A long beat. My mother blinked at me. "Really?"

"Yes, Mom, really." I rubbed my eyes, irritated. "I'm not involved in that sort of thing anymore. So seriously, just back off."

"Well," my mother said. "That does change things."

I definitely did not like the look in her eye. "No, it doesn't."

"Because while you might have lucked into a relationship with an heiress, your father and I are barely scraping by." A tear slipped out from her lashes, and she dug a tissue out of her purse and dabbed at it.

I crossed my arms over my chest. "Crying on cue. Impressive."

"Yes, well. It's a shame you never mastered that particular life skill." The tears stopped as abruptly as they'd started. My mom sighed and said, "The truth is, Emily, your father has managed to get us in debt to some rather frightening people."

I shook my head. That wasn't surprising. When I was ten, we'd burned through three cities in as many months, trying to stay ahead of someone named "The Collector." I felt a reflexive twinge of panic, remembering my mother throwing things into bags as my father nursed a broken arm.

But that was a long time ago. And their troubles definitely weren't my problem anymore. "Welp, good luck with that," I said, turning away.

"I'll tell her."

"What?" I spun back around, fists balled.

My mom calmly picked a piece of lint off her sweater and said, "You heard me."

I guffawed. "You're seriously trying to blackmail me?"

"If the shoe fits."

I used to be terrified of my mother, with her mood swings and unpredictable fits of rage. But staring at her now, this middle-aged woman with crow's feet and gray roots showing through her dye job, I realized that she didn't have the power to make me cower anymore.

I'd faced much scarier people than her and walked away. Her trying to frighten me now was almost comical.

But it still pissed me off. I came right up to her and said in a low voice, "Knock yourself out, Mom. Because I'm going to tell her everything myself, tonight."

I'd already walked ten feet when she called out, "Everything? I seriously doubt it."

I whipped back around and spat, "You know what, Mom? You have no idea what I went through. What I survived. So do your worst. I fucking dare you."

And with that, I stormed away.

— — —

Kat stared at me. "I don't understand."

"Which part?" I asked, plucking at the comforter. I was feeling groggy and parched, but after everything I'd just dumped on Kat, it seemed like poor form to get up for a glass of water. Outside our room, I could hear the usual soundtrack of night in Las Vegas—well, at least this particular section of Vegas, which admittedly was not the fanciest. Car horns blaring, a siren whipping past, and what sounded like a domestic dispute in the parking lot.

Which was relatable, because I was currently in the midst of a more muted version.

Despite the mass quantities of caffeine I'd ingested, when we got back to the room earlier, my body had declared a time-out. I stumbled to the bed, slept for five hours, and awoke to find Kat staring at me. I haven't been in a lot of long-term relationships, but I'm a quick study, and what I've learned is that when your girlfriend glares at you like that, it's never good.

So bearing in mind what my mom had threatened, I decided it

was time to tell Kat everything. Warts and all, right? And if she decided that she didn't want to be dating a former con artist who *might* also be a person of interest in a cartel murder in Miami six years ago, well, that was her choice.

It was oddly liberating. Terrifying, too, obviously—but liberating.

Except Kat wasn't having the reaction I'd expected; instead, she just sat there looking puzzled. "So your parents are not real estate developers?"

"What?" I asked, perplexed.

"Your mother told me they were here to scout a new location for a retirement community. She said that's what they do, that they have a nationwide contract."

"Let me stop you right there," I said, holding up a hand. "Did my mom ask you for money?"

Kat shifted uncomfortably. "She invited me to participate in a unique investment opportunity."

"Of course she did," I groaned. "But you didn't say yes, did you? Or . . . oh God, please tell me you didn't give her any personal information."

"Like what?" Kat asked, eyes wide.

"Anything," I said, ticking them off. "Driver's license, credit cards, bank account numbers . . ."

"No, just my phone number. And you are frightening me, Amber," Kat said.

"Sorry." I ran a hand through my hair and exhaled hard. "Okay. There's not much they can do with a phone number, especially if you don't pick up, which you shouldn't. Like, ever. I'd feel terrible if they took advantage of you."

Kat shrugged. "How much damage could they do?"

"You'd be surprised," I muttered. Man, I was thirsty. Although a shot of tequila was starting to sound more appealing than water. "My parents are professional liars—as in, they literally lie for a living so that people give them money. And they've been doing it for so long, I doubt they could tell the truth now if they tried."

Kat eyed me dubiously. "And you were also a liar?"

My knee-jerk reaction was to get defensive, but instead, I drew a deep breath and owned it. "Yeah, I was. That's the thing about being raised by liars. I grew up thinking that was normal, that everyone lied and pretended to be all sorts of things they weren't: bankers, lawyers, . . . real estate developers," I added pointedly. "And when I was old enough to realize that most people weren't like that, it seemed like a game. Like anyone who actually worked for a living was an idiot and deserved to be taken advantage of."

"But then you stopped," Kat said slowly. "After your girlfriend was killed in Miami."

"Yeah," I said, bracing for the flood of memories from that day. Oddly, it wasn't as bad as usual. Maybe I was finally getting past that particular trauma. Forcing myself to meet Kat's eyes, I said, "After Stella was killed, I went straight. I took out loans, went to college, got my degree in psychology . . . all of that was true."

"Loans?" Kat cocked her head to the side.

Shit. Is this a good time to tell her the rest of it, too? That seemed like a lot of explaining for one day. And in addition to feeling like there was sand in my throat, I was hungry. Besides, my parents didn't know about the serial killers, so it wasn't a weapon in my mother's arsenal.

Save it, I decided, telling myself that I didn't want to overwhelm Kat. "That's kind of an even longer story," I hedged. "Can I explain that part tomorrow?"

"Amber . . . are you lying to me right now?"

"What?" I frowned at her. "No, of course not. I swear, everything I just told you is true."

"No, I mean . . ." Kat bit her lip. "I just wonder . . . am I a mark? I mean, even if it just started that way, I would understand—"

"No, baby." I took her hands in mine and scooted closer to her. "I swear, I never saw you like that. I'd already put all this behind me when we met."

"Really?"

"Really," I said firmly, deciding not to tell her that I'd had a bit of a relapse last spring. Because that hadn't been by choice. And I was not even tempted anymore.

Right?

A knock at the door and then Dot called out, "It's stakeout time! Are you girls ready to catch an asshole?"

"Be right there!" I called back. I leaned in and kissed my girlfriend, then rested my forehead against hers and looked into her eyes. "I'm crazy about you. You know that, right?"

"I am crazy about you, too," she whispered.

"Great. Then let's go handle some toxic masculinity."

— — —

Everyone had assembled back in the Mayhem dining room to get corner assignments and final instructions from Dot. Kat was walking ahead of me; when she hit the doorway, she stopped dead and I nearly crashed into her.

"Oh my," she said, sounding awed.

Peering around her, I had to agree. There were fewer folks than had been crammed in that morning, but those in attendance were a sight to behold. A third of the room was composed of a wide variety of women in miniskirts, six-inch heels, tube tops, and blond wigs. I recognized Portia; she was in full dominatrix leathers and a blond wig that cascaded down to the small of her back. A significant number of the rest looked like they'd just stumbled off the set of a noir flick: trench coats, fedoras, wide shoulder pads, and kitten heels—clearly an assortment of Dot's Fatal Femmes. The few people left were dressed in black, like Kat, and like Grace, who leaned against the far wall with her arms crossed over her chest, looking bemused.

"Amber," Kat said breathily. "This might be the best vacation I have ever taken."

"It's a trip, all right," I agreed. "C'mon." I couldn't see Dot, but Marcella was standing by the TV mounted in the corner, dressed in her former uniform: a minidress, towering heels, and a blond pageboy wig. She was talking on a cell phone with her finger blocking her opposite ear. Behind her, a chyron was ticking off the usual litany of bad news: the wildfire still raging in Colorado, a hurricane in Louisiana, a brutal murder in Arizona. We made our way over to Marcella, wending carefully through the crowd. The prevailing mood was anticipatory, chatter bouncing off the walls. A table in the center of the room was piled with snack bags and bottles of water. Beside it, a second table held canisters of pepper spray. The rest of the tables had been cleared to the room's perimeter.

"Yeah, me too. Love you," I overheard Marcella say as we got within hearing distance.

"Hey," I said awkwardly after she hung up.

"Nice outfit," Marcella said.

I couldn't tell if she was being sardonic, but Kat brightly chirped, "Why thank you! Amber bought this for me today."

Marcella quirked an eyebrow. "Did she now?"

"We didn't pack a ton of black since we were coming for a wedding," I said defensively.

Marcella smirked. "You should know better by now."

"Yeah, tell me about it."

"I am going to explore the food options." Kat leaned in and pecked me on the cheek. "Any requests?"

"Grab some of those Takis," I said.

I watched as she practically skipped to the table, immediately striking up a conversation with a cocktail waitress who had sat near us the night before. After a beat, Marcella said, "She seems to be enjoying herself."

"Yeah. This trip isn't turning out exactly how I promised, so I'm glad she's making the best of it."

"Please. Look at her. Like a pig in shit." Marcella took a drag off a vape pen. "Not too late to throw a blond wig on her."

Did she just call my girlfriend a pig? I frowned and said, "Thanks, we're good." Maybe coming over here wasn't such a great idea. Marcella seemed to be in a mood. "Who were you talking to just now?"

"Why? You jealous?"

"Just curious."

"Okay, everyone, listen up!" Dot called out as she bustled into the room. She wore a trench coat and fedora and was carrying a sheaf of papers. "Skeeter has come up with corner assignments and a few basic rules to follow to keep you all safe. That goes double for you blondies, hear?"

A general murmur of agreement. Skeeter stood behind her, wearing a muumuu and turban; their beard was dyed lavender to match. "Send up someone from your group to collect instructions. If you don't have a group, no worries. We'll get you sorted in two shakes."

A person peeled off from each cluster. It was only then that I realized most of the crowd was grouped in trios, and we didn't have anyone in a blond wig. Nervously, I scanned the room. Kat came back over, her purse bulging with snacks. "I grabbed ours!" she said, waving a piece of paper. "And three pepper sprays, so we are all set.

We are to go to a motel called the Prickly Pear. Isn't that a fantastic name? Marcella, are you coming with us?"

Marcella and I both looked at Kat, then at each other. She smirked at me. "That okay with you, Amber?"

"Why wouldn't it be okay?" I said, matching her tone.

"It is settled then," Kat said decisively, linking an arm through each of ours. "I feel like we might be the lucky ones!"

"We better be," I said. "I got money riding on this."

CHAPTER FOURTEEN

LURED

Gina was sitting in the Getaway motel's back office, three episodes into the new season of her favorite show, when the outer bell jingled, signaling that someone had just entered the reception area. She sighed and put down the pint of ice cream she'd been digging caramel bits out of, then hastily pulled the itchy brunette wig back on, calling, "Coming!"

A guy in a baseball cap stood with his back to her, hands tucked in his pockets, watching the film playing on the TV mounted in the corner. Gina stood behind the desk and said, "You want a room?"

Belatedly, she saw the slip of paper Marcella had taped to the back of the desk that read **WELCOME TO THE GETAWAY MOTEL. CAN I HELP YOU?**

The guy didn't seem to care, though. He turned, stepped up to the desk, and smiled at her. "You poor thing," he said, gesturing to her hair. "What happened?"

Self-consciously, Gina straightened the wig and said, "Chemo."

"Well, isn't that a shame. Hope you beat it."

"Thanks," she said warily, sizing him up: old, white, dressed like he was going camping. Should she ask if he was looking for a date? Marcella had threatened to kick her out if she treated the guests as johns, but Marcella wasn't here, and maybe just this once . . .

Gina's eyes drifted up to the security camera mounted in the corner, and she sighed. Not worth it. "So do you want a room or not?"

"Actually, I had a question for you." Seeing her expression, he laughed and said, "Oh, nothing bad, I assure you."

Gina didn't laugh along with him; she wasn't in the mood. She felt like shit thanks to whatever that asshole had drugged her with last night, and she really wanted to get back to her show. This guy was standing in the way of all that, and even more annoyingly, it didn't seem like he was getting a room anyway. "What do you want?"

He adjusted his ball cap. "This is the place where those murders happened last May, is it not?"

He had kind of a funny way of talking, more formal than his clothes.

Last May, Gina had still been living with Jordan in his van—before he took off and ruined her whole fucking life. She'd heard rumors about what had happened at the Getaway, but the details were vague. And based on Marcella's attitude, she'd gathered the topic was off limits.

Gina shrugged. "I guess. I don't really know anything about it."

"So you weren't working here then?"

Gina shook her head. She wasn't even working here now, not really, but he didn't need to know that. "Nope."

"I see." He rubbed his chin.

"Why?" Gina asked.

"Well, I suppose I'm just curious."

Gina nodded, thinking, *Whatever, creepo.* "Well, if that's all—"

"Actually, is there any chance I could see the room where it happened?"

Gina was already shaking her head. She knew this scam; she and Jordan had pulled it themselves a few times. You asked to see a room, like you wanted to "inspect" it before committing to paying for it, and then as soon as the door was opened, you surreptitiously called the front desk. While the manager hurried back to answer the phone, you showered, brushed your teeth, shit, and left without paying. It was pretty much the only time Gina had felt clean on the road; she'd gotten really good at taking a thirty-second shower. "Marcella wouldn't like that."

"Marcella?" he asked, leaning in. "Is she the owner?"

"No." Gina hesitated. Maybe there *was* a way to make some money off this weirdo. And the canister of pepper spray Dot had given her was tucked in her pocket, so if he tried anything, she could spray him and run. "Um, if you want, I could show it to you? For a fee," she said pointedly.

"Oh my, that would be absolutely lovely." He beamed at her. "Thank you so much."

The guy dug a wad of cash out of his jacket pocket and peeled off a twenty-dollar bill, offering it across the counter.

Gina frowned. She should have asked for more, but it was too late now. What the guy didn't know was that she wasn't exactly sure which room the murders had happened in. Not that it really mattered, because he probably didn't know either. She eyed the rack of keys on the wall, debating. The closest empty room was number eleven, but Marcella always said that room was off limits. Which definitely fit with a room people had died in. Hell, maybe it even *had* happened there. Regardless, it suited her purposes. Gina grabbed the key and said, "C'mon then."

He stuck to her heels as she led the way across the parking lot and up the stairs and hovered a little too close as she unlocked the door. Some primal sense switched on, making her scalp prickle as it dawned on her that maybe bringing a stranger to a motel room wasn't a great idea, considering the fact that just last night she'd been drugged and shaved in a similar scenario. Gina tucked her right hand in her pocket, wrapping her fingers around the pepper spray trigger. With her left, she unlocked the door and stepped aside, waving him past. "Go ahead. But I only got a minute, so be quick about it."

She stepped back to put some distance between them as the guy walked inside and flipped on the light.

Almost immediately, he called out, "I believe there's been a mistake. Someone is clearly staying in this room."

"No they're not," Gina said with a frown. She'd been here for months, and this room had always sat vacant. No way Marcella would have rented it out. Besides, if she had, there wouldn't have been a key available. Out of curiosity, she stepped inside. He wasn't lying. The bed was unmade, and the garbage can overflowed with empty fast-food wrappers. *What the fuck?*

She heard the sound of a toilet flushing, and then another guy stepped out of the bathroom. Seeing them, he froze.

Gina's breath caught in her throat as the realization hit: *They're a team, working together.* The old guy had lured her up here, where they would finish the job they'd started last night.

She shrieked and yanked out the pepper spray, fumbling and nearly dropping it. She spun on the old guy, but he was too fast and bolted for the stairs. Growling deep in her throat, Gina charged his accomplice. All the accumulated rage of the past few months—hell, the past year—coursed through her. She held down the trigger and sprayed directly into his open mouth. The guy fumbled for her, and she shoved him back with a surge of what felt like superhuman strength, hurtling him into the far wall, where he fell to the ground, clawing at his face.

Then Gina turned and ran like hell.

CHAPTER FIFTEEN

MANHANDLED

This is not as fun as I thought it would be," Kat grumbled.

"Told you," I said, popping a Taki in my mouth. We were sitting in my car, parked across the street from the Prickly Pear Motel. The ubiquitous neon sign advertised **LO RATES** and **FREE SATELLITE!** below a cactus that added spikes with every subsequent illumination. Based on the steady stream of cars pulling into the parking lot and disgorging mismatched couples (usually an old, heavy white guy and a young woman in high heels and a miniskirt), most of the guests were paying by the hour. Maybe by the minute. Every single one of the sex workers was a brunette or redhead, which made me wonder if Dr. Aboud had any wigs left in his store.

I held out the bag to Kat, but she shook her head. "I am too nervous to eat."

"Are you?" I tilted my seat back and stifled a yawn. We'd been parked here for nearly two hours, and I could easily fall back asleep, despite the energy drinks we'd been mainlining. A bathroom was going to become a pressing necessity soon. I checked my watch:

nearly midnight. "I'm starving. With any luck, this asshole will show early enough for us to grab a decent meal after."

"As long as I get to use this first," she said, holding up the pepper spray canister.

"Easy." I shifted her hand so the canister wasn't aimed directly at me. "I like being able to see."

"Sorry." Kat sighed heavily, then picked up Dot's flyer and skimmed it for the hundredth time. "So it says if we suspect we have the right person, we are to contact Dot immediately and she will redirect everyone to our location. We are not to approach on our own." She looked at me. "But he is not supposed to be dangerous, is he?"

"Anyone can be dangerous if they're cornered."

"I suppose that is true." Kat frowned. "Once everyone comes, then what?"

"Great question, babe. Dot said she's got that part covered."

"What does that mean?"

"Not sure. Guess we'll find out." I stretched my arms above my head and arched my back. "Oof. I'm gonna be sore tomorrow."

"Your friend is waving to you."

"Yeah?" I straightened. Through the windshield, I could see Marcella. She'd pulled on a fuzzy bolero over the pink leopard minidress that accentuated every curve. Not that I was looking. I cleared my throat and said, "She's supposed to text if something's up."

Marcella made a gesture of exasperation and then crossed her arms over her chest.

"Perhaps you should go see what she wants," Kat said.

"Yeah, I better," I sighed. "Hang tight. And save me some gummy bears, all right?"

I got out and slumped over to Marcella. "What's wrong?"

"I'm bored," she said, taking a hit off her vape pen.

"You're bored?" I raised an eyebrow. "What do you want me to do about it?"

"Entertain me," she said.

I choked out a laugh. "I thought the whole point was not to blow your cover."

Her eyes trailed over me and she said, "You can pass. Those jeans are tight enough."

I shifted uncomfortably. While Kat had kitted herself out in all black and looked like she was on her way to an art heist, I'd stuck with my usual: dark jeans, T-shirt, boots, and a motorcycle jacket. "I don't know," I said. "You think a lot of johns go for lesbian chic?"

"The chicks do." Off my look, she said, "Sometimes we get those. Makes for a nice change of pace."

"I'll bet." A limo with two girls poking through the sunroof blew past. They whooped at us, and Marcella blew them a kiss. "I didn't think you were still working."

Marcella's lips quirked. "I'm not. Just managing the Getaway these days, and believe me, that shit is full-time. Thought I'd hung up these heels for good, but I owe Dot, so . . ." She shrugged.

"Yeah." I realized I was nodding excessively and forced myself to stop.

"So is it serious?"

"Is what serious?" I asked.

Marcella nodded toward the car. I could see Kat in the passenger seat, polishing off the gummy bears. She grinned and waved. "Oh, um . . . kind of, yeah."

"Huh." Marcella said. "She seems okay. For a rich bitch."

After all the psychology I'd studied during the past four years, you'd think I'd be better at navigating awkward conversations. You'd be wrong. But I'd had something on my mind for months, and this was as good a time as any to get it out there. "Listen, I should apologize."

It was her turn to look puzzled. "For what?"

"For the way things ended with us." I drew a deep breath. "It was shitty of me to just take off without saying goodbye."

"Super shitty," Marcella agreed.

"I know, and I'm really sorry. It's just, after what happened with Jessie—"

"After I got her killed, you mean," Marcella interrupted, her voice hard.

"It wasn't your fault."

"Yeah, it was." She met my eyes squarely. I realized that I hadn't appreciated until now how clear her gaze was; definitely not the same as before. "I gotta make amends, right? I mean, you put together a whole plan to catch that asshole, and I fucked it up and got Jessie killed. I have to live with that."

I started to interrupt, but Marcella put a hand on my arm. "I mean it, Amber. I'm sorry. I should've gotten in touch with you. But I knew you were coming for the wedding, and I figured better to tell you in person, right?" She bit at her thumbnail. "I didn't know you'd be bringing someone, though."

I was surprised and moved. The depth of emotion in her voice was clear, and it sparked a similar feeling in me. I drew a deep breath and said, "Wow, so we're doing step nine right here, huh?"

"Well, this *is* kind of my natural habitat," Marcella said with a grin, indicating the street corner with a sweep of her arm.

We were laughing when Kat approached. Smiling shyly, she asked, "Is everything all right?"

"Yeah, it's fine," I said, feeling a pang of guilt even though I hadn't been doing anything wrong. "What's up?"

"Dot has been texting you," she said, handing over my phone.

"Sorry, babe. Guess we aren't the lucky ones." I read the texts and said, "Oh shit. We gotta go."

"What's wrong?" Marcella asked.

"He's at the Getaway," I said over my shoulder, already hurrying back to the car. "Everyone's meeting there."

"What?" Marcella blanched. "But no one's even working that corner tonight! I left Gina to watch the desk!"

"All I know is Dot said to get there as fast as we can," I said, turning on the engine.

Kat slid into the passenger seat, looking pale. As she buckled her seat belt, I checked my mirrors before swinging the car around. "Is everyone okay?" she asked worriedly.

I chanced a glance back at Marcella. She was sitting in the back seat, chewing on a nail and glaring out the window. "I don't know," I said honestly. "Let's hope so."

— — —

The Prickly Pear was relatively close to the Getaway. Still, by the time we got there, a half dozen cars were already parked haphazardly in the lot. A bunch of folks were milling on the second story walkway; another group clustered outside the office on the ground floor.

I parked right beside Grace's sedan. Marcella had the door open and was out before my car had come to a full stop. I could hear wailing from inside the office. Kat and I exchanged a glance and then followed her inside.

The reception area was mostly how I remembered it, although the battered desk had been replaced by a sleeker mid-century one, and the carpeting was new. A rack of pamphlets for local attractions lined one corner, a set of chairs flanking it. Framed noir posters decorated the walls, and a small TV mounted in the corner showed noir movies on a loop.

The crying came from the tiny office behind the desk. Grace stood in the doorway, her back to us. She shifted and met my eyes, her expression inscrutable.

Excusing myself, I eased past the people crammed inside the lobby and came up beside Grace. Gina sat in the chair at Dot's desk, a brunette wig askew on her head and her face in her hands. Dot and Marcella had crouched down to console her.

"What happened?" I asked in a low voice.

"Apparently the attacker came after her again." Grace said. "He tried to lure her into a room on the top floor where his partner was waiting, but she pepper-sprayed him. One guy ran, and the other is being held upstairs."

"Shit, really?" I frowned. "There were two of them?"

"Which would explain why my algorithm failed," Grace said, with an unseemly amount of satisfaction. "The parameters did not account for multiple attackers."

"How did they find her?" I asked. "I mean, Marcella said no one was even stationed over here."

"We're not sure. She hasn't been very forthcoming," Grace said disapprovingly.

"Gina, honey, have some water," Dot said gently, offering her a glass. "It'll help, I promise."

Marcella looked up. "Does anyone have a Xanax?"

"I do!" Kat offered.

As she dug through her purse, I said, "You do?"

Kat threw me a look. "Yes, Amber. I have a fear of flying."

"Oh." I frowned. Had she told me that? Seemed like something I should know about my partner, right?

Kat hurried forward and offered a pill to Gina, who gulped water to wash it down. Her breathing gradually slowed, the sobs abating.

"Now then, that's better." Dot patted her knee. "Why don't you start at the beginning?"

"I just—I don't know what's wrong with me!" Gina wailed, throwing her head back. "Why does this keep happening?"

"Easy, hon," Dot cooed.

"What happened?" Marcella asked.

Gina dissolved in sobs again. "He . . . he . . . came to the desk. And asked to see the room."

"Wait, what?" Dot frowned. "He asked for a room?"

"No, he asked to see *the* room. Where the guy died?" Gina sniffled. "So I took him up there, and when I opened the door, there was another guy waiting!"

"So the guy inside the room attacked you?" Dot asked.

"Didn't give him the chance," Gina sniffed. "I screamed, and the first guy took off, and I sprayed the other one, then I ran down here and locked the door and called you, and Portia was closest so she showed up, like, right away."

Whooping and cheers from the group upstairs—it sounded like there was a real party going on up there. I was starting to get a bad feeling, though. Mainly because whoever had attacked Gina appeared to be interested in what had happened at the Getaway last spring. Was there a connection between him and Gunnar? Grace had stiffened, clearly thinking the same thing.

"Why did you take him to see the room?" Marcella asked.

Gina avoided her eyes and shrugged.

"I told you to just answer the phone," Marcella said in a harder voice, straightening and crossing her arms. "This guy try to pay for a date?"

"No!" Gina retorted. "He just offered twenty to look at the room. That was it!"

"Fucking lookie-loos," Dot said. "We get them all the time." Her phone beeped; she checked the screen and frowned. "Huh. Skeeter is saying that they had the guy, but he ran."

"What?" I frowned. "Where's Skeeter?"

"Over at the Super 8 near Henderson."

Another buzz on her phone. Dot winced as she read the text. "Oh my. Candy's group just pepper-sprayed someone, too. Maybe this wasn't the best idea."

"Um, Gina?" I asked. "Is it possible this wasn't the same guy who attacked you last night?"

Gina stopped sniffling and glared at me. "That room is supposed to be empty!"

"She's not wrong about that," Dot said, getting to her feet and straightening her trench coat. "Let's go see what this character has to say for himself."

I gestured for Kat to follow. Grace branched off as we strode through the parking lot. "Where are you going?"

"There were two motels connected to my brother," Grace said in a low voice. "I need to check on Mother."

"Oh shit." It hadn't even occurred to me. Grace's brother had died at the Getaway, in the room everyone was currently thronging. But he'd actually been staying next door at the Buggy Suites. And both motels had been mentioned in most of the news coverage. "Probably just a coincidence, right?"

"I'd prefer to check."

"Okay. Let me know if you need anything."

Grace was already trotting away, headed toward the vacant lot that separated the motels.

"What is going on with Grace?" Kat asked.

I shook my head. "Long story."

Another round of cheering erupted as we mounted the stairs to the second floor. The walkway was crowded, the atmosphere jubilant. People were drinking canned margaritas and peering in the motel room window. They cleared a path for Dot.

"We got him, Dottie!" someone called out.

"Yeah, happy wedding, girl!"

"Portia's making him pay all right!"

A muffled howl issued from inside the room.

I stayed close to Dot as she wove through the crowd, accepting everyone's glee with a thin smile. "Hell, toots," she murmured. "I got a bad feeling."

"You and me both," I said.

When we finally reached the doorway, I took a deep breath to steady myself. The last time I'd been inside this room, Gunnar had been lying dead on the floor and Jessie was in the bathtub, the cord that strangled her still wrapped around her throat.

I felt Kat's hand on my arm. "What's wrong?"

"Nothing." I exhaled slowly, thinking *It's just a motel room. Nothing in there can hurt you.* Then I stepped inside.

It was packed, wall-to-wall people. And I'm not the tallest person, so at first I couldn't make out what was going on. But then someone shifted, providing a clear view of what everyone was fixated on.

I clapped a hand to my mouth and said, "Oh shit."

A rickety desk chair had been moved into the space between the bed and the bureau. Portia stood behind it, still wearing her full dominatrix regalia, although she'd taken off the wig. In front of her, a guy was tied to the chair with elaborate ropework, a ball gag in his mouth. His eyes bulged as he attempted to scream around it. Portia was brandishing an electric razor; she grabbed hold of a clump of his hair, shaved it off, and then waved it around to the overwhelming approval of the crowd, who whooped and applauded. Thanks to the pepper spray, the guy's eyes were bright red and teary, and half of his head had already been shaved bald.

"Oh my," Kat said. "This is all very dramatic. That is the man we were trying to catch?"

"Holy crap," I said. "It's BJ."

"Who?"

"Dot's friend's nephew. He used to help run the motels."

"So then he is supposed to be here?" Kat sounded confused. I couldn't blame her; I was feeling pretty damn confused myself. My understanding was that BJ had left in a huff after his aunt Jessie willed the place to Dot instead of him. But apparently, he was back in town.

"Bernard Jones Veasey," Dot thundered, hands on her hips. "What on *earth* are you doing here?"

Bernard Jones, aka BJ, tried to speak around the ball gag. Dot nodded at Portia, who flicked it off with one hand.

BJ coughed a few times and then whined, "What the hell, Dot? These crazy bitches tied me to a chair!"

That statement did not go over well with the crowd. Portia stepped forward and smacked him across the face open-handed. "Shut up, maggot," she said imperiously.

BJ shrank back from her as much as possible, considering how well he was bound.

"I asked what you're doing here," Dot repeated. "Come clean, or I let Portia get on with it."

"And I'm just getting started," Portia purred, turning on the razor beside his ear. "You have no idea how creative I can get with this thing."

"What? No! I didn't do anything!"

"Try again," Dot said. "Because far as I knew, you were still in Stockton."

BJ lowered his eyes, glaring at the floor. "My mom kicked me out. And I remembered that this room is usually empty."

"Mm-hmm. And how did you get in?" Dot asked sternly.

"Still got a master key," he said, so low I could barely hear him.

"And the other guy?"

"What other guy?"

"Your partner," Dot said.

"The asshole who's been helping you drug and shave girls," Portia chimed in.

BJ looked mystified. "What asshole?"

"Uh-oh," I said.

Kat murmured in my ear, "What is it?"

"Not who we're looking for, apparently," I murmured back.

"Wrong guy," Marcella called from the door. "Clear a path!"

People shifted to let her through. Marcella stalked in, a disgusted expression on her face. "Gina thinks maybe she made a mistake."

"Damn straight she did!" BJ said, his chin wobbling. "I didn't do nothing to no one! I should sue!"

"Oh, I dare you to," Portia said, bending down to tickle his cheek with her nail. "That would make my week."

"You broke into my motel!" Dot said.

"Yeah, well . . . I had no choice," he muttered.

"You're lucky that's all she shaved," Marcella said. "If I'd caught you, it would've been a hell of a lot worse, you little shit."

"I—I had nowhere else to go!" BJ started crying. In spite of everything, I couldn't help but feel sorry for him.

Portia waved the razor around. "So am I finishing the job, or what?"

"Don't touch me!" BJ shrieked. "Aunt Dot, make her stop!"

I felt my phone buzz in my pocket. As the conversation devolved into a four-way argument, I stepped outside to answer it.

It was Grace. And she sounded uncharacteristically rattled.

"Amber, come quickly. I need help."

CHAPTER SIXTEEN

THE WOMAN IN QUESTION

"What is it?" Kat asked after seeing my expression.

"Grace needs help with something," I said. "Um, would you mind waiting here?"

"You're leaving me?" Kat said, an edge to her voice. "Again?"

"Just for a sec, promise," I said. "It's just, I'm not sure Grace would be comfortable having you there. And it might not be safe."

"Fine." Kat jutted her chin up. "I want to see what happens to this BJ anyway."

"I promise I'll be quick," I said, leaning in to give her a peck on the cheek. Kat turned her head so it just grazed her. She was clearly pissed off, but I couldn't worry about it now. For Grace to ask for help, something must be seriously wrong.

"Can I borrow that?" I asked, gesturing to the pepper spray.

Kat held it out for me to take. "Can I have the car keys?"

"Yeah, sure," I said, digging them out of my jacket pocket.

"Thank you."

"Listen, baby—"

"You better go," Kat snapped. Then she turned to the crowd and called out, "Excuse me please, I would like a margarita if there are any left?"

Someone handed her a can, and she took a big swig. I hesitated but then turned away. I'd make it up to her when I got back.

I took the stairs two at a time and then raced across the vacant lot that connected to the Buggy Suites next door. I eased through the gap in the fence bordering the parking lot and stopped dead.

Floodlights had been lit, making it glaringly bright. The parking lot was completely empty, no cars. And the door that led to Grace's mom's room was wide open.

I went to the open door and knocked tentatively. "Um, hello?" The room was empty, the covers on the bed in a tangle. I swallowed hard. *Is her mom okay?*

"Through here!" Grace called. I followed her voice back to the main apartment.

Grace was sitting in front of her monitors, tapping at the keyboard. Security camera footage flashed past at several times the normal speed.

"What's up?"

"The new idiot attendant who was supposed to be watching Mother didn't lock the door," Grace said in a hard voice. "Apparently someone knocked on the office door and she went to see who it was. When she got back, Mother was gone."

"Oh shit." I ran a hand over my face. "What can I do?"

"You can help me look," Grace said grimly. "I'm reviewing the surveillance footage now. Once I get a sense of which direction she went, I'll go after her. You remain here in case she returns."

"Yeah, sure," I said. "Whatever you need. Um, where's the attendant?"

"I fired her," Grace said.

"Oh, okay." Seemed harsh, but understandable. Although it would have been helpful to have someone else looking. I watched as Grace slowed down the video and then rewound it. A guy entered the parking lot from the street, on foot. He was wearing bulky, dark clothing and a ball cap. He walked up to the door marked **Office** at the very front of the building, the one currently farthest from us, and knocked. I watched him rock back and forth on his heels, waiting. Then he knocked again.

"You think that's the same guy who went to the Getaway?"

"Possibly. He came here first, however." Grace pointed at the time stamp.

"Huh." While I watched, he knocked one final time, then shrugged and sauntered back the way he'd come.

A moment later, the door popped open and a small figure in scrubs poked their head out. The attendant stepped outside and scanned in both directions; then she went back inside. We watched another few minutes of video at lightning speed; nothing moved until Grace hurried into the frame, coming through the vacant lot the same way I had. She went straight into her mother's room, leaving the door open behind her.

"Are there any other ways out?" I asked. "Or maybe an area the cameras don't cover?"

Grace sat back, frowning. "No. There are no blind spots. I made sure of it."

"Weird." I turned back toward the door. "You checked everywhere?"

"Of course I checked everywhere!" she snapped, rewinding the video.

I held up both hands defensively. "Just asking, sheesh. Could she have gone out a back window, maybe?"

"All of those are sealed shut for safety."

"Well, then she has to be here somewhere."

Grace threw up her hands. "Where?"

I tried not to react; I'd never seen Grace this flustered, and I'd watched her stare down serial killers. Twice. "I'm just gonna take a look around, okay? You keep checking the footage."

Without waiting for a response, I made my way back to her mom's room. Standing and facing the empty bed, I tried to imagine her mom's mindset. She lived in fear of her husband showing up. She'd been rattled by a stranger knocking at the office door. In her mind, the threat was outside, so it was unlikely she would've gone there.

But where then? I tried the door to the connecting room on the other side; still locked.

Then I heard a small noise. I cocked my head to the side and strained to listen.

It was coming from the closet.

"Hello?" I called out, noticing that the door was slightly ajar. "Grace's mom?"

Silence. I went over to the closet door and rapped lightly with my knuckles. Then I carefully eased it open.

It had been converted to a deep walk-in closet. At first glance, it was empty: plastic bins filled with clothing, a long line of hanging dresses and coats, built-in shelves and drawers.

And a pile of clothes heaped in the back, which could've been mistaken for laundry if it wasn't trembling slightly.

"Um, hi," I said, settling down on my haunches. "Just wanted to make sure you were doing okay."

The top of the pile shifted slightly, revealing white hair and an eye gazing suspiciously out at me. I smiled encouragingly. After a beat, a hand reached out and slowly peeled back more clothing, revealing her entire head. I was careful not to react.

I hadn't gotten a close look earlier, but now I could see that Grace's mom was an older version of her—the same icy blue eyes and delicate features. She eyed me uncertainly, as if trying to place me. She was shivering, which was no surprise; thanks to the open door, it was frigid inside the room.

"Hey," I said softly as I texted Found her to Grace. "It's okay. I'm a friend."

She eyed me suspiciously and then croaked, "Close the door, it's not safe! He's out there!"

"Yeah?" I said. "Who's out there?"

"Father," she rasped, leaning forward. The way she said it made the hair on my arms stand up.

"Gotcha," I said. "Okay, I'll go close the door."

I got up slowly and went to close it. Coming back, I eased down into a seated position and wrapped my arms around my knees. "We haven't met," I said. "I'm Amber."

She was still regarding me uncertainly, which I couldn't blame her for. "Amber."

"Yup. I'm a . . . well, I know Grace."

That seemed to register. She shifted forward, sending clothes cascading, as she said urgently, "We need to protect Grace."

"Okay," I said agreeably. "Happy to help."

"Mother," Grace said firmly from the doorway. "You have to go back to bed."

"Grace?" Her voice was reedy.

"Yes, Mother. Let me help you." Grace stepped forward and extended a hand, but her mom shrank back into the closet.

"He was here!" she hissed. "Father came for me!"

"That wasn't Father," Grace said firmly.

This agitated the elderly woman further. She waved an arm, pointing toward the door. "I heard him! Plain as day!"

Looking impatient, Grace started toward her. Her mom shrieked and cowered back. Grace swore under her breath. "Mother, if you don't get back into bed, I'm going to have to sedate you again."

"No! It's not safe! He's come for us, Grace, he knows what I did. He's going to punish us. Punish us, Grace!" She was becoming overwrought, shaking with emotion.

"Hey, um . . . want me to try?" I said hesitantly.

"Be my guest," Grace said, throwing up her hands. "I have to get the medication ready anyway. Please make sure she doesn't hurt herself."

"Yeah, sure." After she left the room, Grace's mom regarded me warily. I hesitated, then sat on the floor facing her. "How about we just sit for a moment?"

She eyed me and then said, "Father."

"Right, I heard," I said, nodding. "Sounds like that was pretty scary."

Tentatively, she straightened slightly. Looking at me intently, she said, "He wants to take the other one. Don't let him!"

"That's awful," I said sympathetically. "So sorry to hear that."

"Yes." She edged a bit closer, almost to the closet door; it was like trying to coax an animal. "He knows, you see."

"Knows what?"

"Knows that I called the FBI. I had to. He was going to break Grace, the same way he broke Gunnar." Her eyes filled with tears. "He was going to take her, too."

Grace reappeared in my peripheral vision. I made a small motion for her to stay where she was, then said, "You did the right thing."

"Yes," she nodded, a look of satisfaction on her face. "Too late for Gunnar. But I saved Grace."

I made a show of yawning and then checked my watch. "Wow, would you look at the time. Pretty late. I'm tired. Are you tired?"

A long beat, during which she regarded me suspiciously, as if this was a trap. Then she slowly shook her head. "Not safe. He's out there."

"I think he left, actually." Turning to Grace, I said. "You checked, right? And he's gone?"

Grace stood there frowning, holding a hypodermic needle. Seeing my look, she nodded and said, "Yes, Mother. I checked everywhere. He's gone."

"Well, that's good news, right?" I slowly got to my feet and stretched my arms above my head. "What do you think? Ready to go back to bed?"

Grace's mom seemed to be engaged in a silent debate. Finally, she stood all the way up and crossed her arms against the chill. "It's cold in here," she complained.

"Right? It's freezing." Mirroring her, I crossed my arms and shivered theatrically. "Let's get you under the covers, okay?"

Still eyeing me skeptically, she acquiesced, letting me take her elbow. Gently, I guided her back to the bed. She let me tuck her in, then motioned for me to come close. I leaned in, and she said in a low, urgent voice, "You need to kill him. Before he kills us."

The way she said it sent chills up my spine, especially because her voice was uncannily like Grace's. But I carefully kept my face blank and nodded, saying, "I hear you."

Seeming satisfied, she leaned her head back against the pillow and closed her eyes. Within a minute, her chest was rising and falling regularly.

When I turned around, Grace was tucking the hypodermic needle back into a medical kit. She motioned for me to follow as she headed back toward her living quarters. Avoiding my eyes, she said, "Thank you. I hate having to sedate her."

"Yeah, of course. No problem."

Grace set the medical kit down on the kitchen counter and braced both hands on it. Lowering her head, she breathed out hard and then laughed abruptly.

"You okay?" I asked awkwardly.

"I'm fine." She shook her head without meeting my eyes. "I need to call the service and see if they'll send someone else."

"Sorry this happened," I said. "The guy must've rattled her."

"She thinks she sees Father every day," Grace said wearily. "Sometimes multiple times a day. Anything sets her off."

"That sucks," I said.

"She liked you," Grace said after a beat. "That's unusual for Mother."

"Oh, that's nice." I hesitated. "Anything else I can do, or should I head back?"

She didn't appear to have heard me. "I don't know. Maybe Chuy is right, and I should put her back in a home."

I stood there, not knowing what to say. Grace had always seemed so self-assured, so certain of everything; seeing this side of her was deeply unnerving.

"I need a drink." She turned to face me. "Do you want a drink?"

I hesitated. Kat was still waiting at the Getaway; I should get back to her. But that would leave Grace to drink alone. And frankly, I could use one. Grace's mom's voice still echoed in my ears. "Yeah, sure."

Grace was already pulling a bottle of vodka out of the freezer. She poured a few fingers' worth in two tumblers and brought them over. Personally, I would've preferred a mixer, but she didn't offer and I didn't ask. I raised my glass in a toast and then took a sip.

She downed hers in a single gulp.

"Yowza. Okay, then," I said. "Did you want to call the service? Or, I mean, I can call them . . ."

"No point. I doubt they'll find anyone willing to come at this hour. And at the rate we're going through them, they're probably going to stop sending people altogether. Mother can be a handful, as you've seen." While I watched, she refilled her glass. Picking it up, she swirled the liquid inside and gazed at it ruminatively. "I wish she still possessed enough faculties to understand the news about Father."

"Uh, what news?" I asked, wondering if I'd missed something.

"He's gone."

"Gone? As in . . . dead?"

She nodded. "Apparently the supermax was threatened by the wildfire, so they were relocating inmates to a different facility. There was an accident on the highway, and his bus was overtaken by flames. There were no survivors."

"Oh shit." Awkwardly, I added, "Sorry."

"Sorry?" Grace frowned at me.

"Well, yeah. I mean, I know he was awful, but he's still your dad, right?" My parents were con artists who basically abandoned me when I was fifteen, but if they died, I'd still feel something. I wasn't sure what, but something.

"Yes." Still avoiding my eyes, she said, "But Gregory hadn't been a father to me in a long time."

"Believe me, I get that. Um, how do you feel?"

Grace shook her head slightly. "Honestly? I don't know."

"That's normal." At least, I assumed it was; I hadn't studied the psychology of grief yet, so all I had to rely on was my lived experience. And I remembered not feeling anything for a long time after Stella died. "All this seems like a lot."

"You have no idea." She sighed and rubbed her eyes. "I thought that with Gunnar gone, everything would be easier. But instead, it's just a mess. I'm a mess."

I stared at her. I didn't know how to deal with this version of

Grace. Hesitantly, I offered, "You're a good daughter. Even if it doesn't work out, you tried. That counts for something."

Grace barked a sharp laugh. "Mother would never agree, not if she was able to think clearly. The irony is that Father was always my favorite. Growing up, Mother was basically a ghost." Moodily, she downed another gulp.

I was definitely not touching that one. "Anything I can do to help? Seriously, whatever you need."

"No thank you, Amber." Grace sighed and rubbed her eyes. "I apologize for dragging you into this."

"No problem, really. Hopefully we'll catch this guy, and things'll settle down."

As if on cue, my phone rang. I picked up. On the other end, Dot sounded breathy. "Hey, kiddo. Any chance you're still with Grace?"

"Yeah." I frowned. "How'd you know?"

"Kat told us before she took off."

"Oh. How'd she seem?"

"Upset, I'm afraid."

"Fabulous," I sighed.

"She'll be fine, doll. But listen, we think Bambi's group might actually have run into the guy."

"Really?"

"Yes. He managed to get away but left behind a bag with a razor and a bottle of chloroform." Voices in the background. Dot said something I couldn't quite make out and then her voice came through clearly. "We were thinking maybe Grace could trace his license plate for us?"

"Um, this might not be the best time," I hedged.

"What is it?" Grace asked, refilling her glass. She was hitting the booze like it was water, which was also extremely out of character.

But then, she'd just found out her dad was dead, so she wouldn't be getting any judgment from me. I covered the receiver and said, "Dot wants you to trace a license plate. But I can tell her you're busy."

"I would be happy to do it," Grace said, setting down her glass. "Tell her to text it to me."

"You sure?"

"Positive, Amber." She looked and sounded more like herself as she added, "Now if you'll excuse me, it's been a long night. Please see yourself out."

– – –

I scrolled through news alerts during my Uber ride back to the Mayhem. Gregory Grimes wasn't the only famous psychopath who had perished in the prison bus fire; the flames had also taken a cartel boss and a domestic terrorist. *Good riddance,* I thought, enlarging the main photo. It was an overhead shot, probably taken by a drone. The bus had been knocked on its side and shorn in two. It was wrapped around the semi, as if the truck was the meat in a prison-bus sandwich. The bus's side windows were charred black, and wisps of smoke still cloaked the edges of the scene. I let out a low whistle; no one walked away from something like that. I felt bad for the truck driver and prison guards, but based on the list of dead prisoners, the world was now a slightly better place.

It was nearly two a.m. when my Uber pulled into the Mayhem parking lot, and most of the room lights were extinguished. Someone was sitting at the firepit on the balcony, however. As I got closer, I recognized Dot. She was staring into the flames, sipping from a champagne flute. She'd removed her headscarf and kicked off her shoes. I hesitated, then climbed the stairs.

"Hey," I said. "Want some company?"

Dot started, putting a hand to her chest. "Oh my, you gave me a fright."

"Sorry."

"S'okay. I was just a million miles away."

"How's Gina?"

"Sleeping, thanks to your gal's pills and a couple strong shots."

"That's good. Do you think the other guy had anything to do with it?"

"The lookie-loo?" Dot shook her head. "Doubt it, hon. 'Fraid this got away from us a bit. I'm guessing there are a lot of pepper-sprayed johns regretting their life choices tonight."

"Well, that's not necessarily a bad thing."

"True. Like I said, Bambi seems pretty sure they had him, but we'll see. Hopefully Grace can track down that plate number."

"I think she appreciated the distraction," I said.

"Hm." Dot examined me. "Everything okay with her?"

"More or less."

"She seems tired."

"Yeah." I hesitated; it didn't feel right to tell Dot about Grace's father. It would probably be all over the news tomorrow, anyway. "Family stuff."

Dot sipped her drink. "Sometimes, getting exactly what you want throws you for a loop."

"Pretty sure she didn't get exactly what she wanted," I said, picturing her mom. "She's definitely struggling."

"Well, she's a smart cookie. She'll figure it out. Anyway, I didn't want to lose out on beauty sleep right before the wedding. But when I got back here, *boom*!" She snapped her fingers. "Wide awake."

"Me too," I said.

"Pour you a tipple?" she asked, wagging her glass at me.

"Sure." Mixing champagne with vodka was probably going to produce a serious hangover, but at the moment, I didn't care. Anything to avoid the confrontation waiting back in my room. Dot went over to a cabinet built into the wall, opened a panel, and withdrew another flute. "That's pretty cool."

"Jessie's idea," Dot said with a smile as she came back. She poured champagne into the flute and handed it to me. "We spent a lot of nights spilling the tea out here. Whenever I'm feeling a little blue, I come out and raise a glass."

I frowned. "Why are you feeling blue? You're not having second thoughts, are you?"

"About getting hitched?" Dot smiled and shook her head. "It's not that, toots. It's just . . . I'm sad that Jess won't be here to see it." Staring down into her glass, she twirled the champagne and then added, "Sometimes I just feel kinda lonely, y'know?"

It was funny; I never would've thought that of Dot. Everyone I'd ever met in Vegas seemed not just to know her, but to genuinely care about her. But then, you could be surrounded by people and still feel alone. "I get that," I said finally. "I'm really sorry. I wish Jessie was here, too."

"I'm not much of a believer," Dot said, leaning forward. "But let me tell you something. This morning, I woke up and saw a hummingbird, right outside my window. A hummingbird, here in Vegas! And I knew it was her."

"Yeah?"

"Oh, definitely. She always had a soft spot for those. Think I'll put up a feeder when we get back from the honeymoon." Topping off her glass, she motioned to mine. I nodded, and she refilled it. "Anyway, toots, you seem pretty happy with that gorgeous new girlfriend of yours. Are you?"

"Sure," I said. "I should get to the room, actually. Kat's probably wondering what happened to me."

"Oh, she's not back yet."

"Wait, what?" I frowned. "Where is she?"

"Got a call back at the Getaway and said she had to go help someone. And away she went." Dot made a waving motion with her free hand.

That was perplexing; who in Las Vegas would call Kat for help? Aside from me, she didn't know anyone. I pulled out my phone and texted, but she didn't respond.

Dot settled back in her chair, the flickering flames reflecting her red hair as she watched me. After a long beat, she said, "Word of advice, hon? Be careful with that one."

"With Kat?" I frowned, a little hurt. "Why? Don't you like her?"

"Oh, sure," she shrugged. "But rich folks aren't always what they seem, in my experience."

"Well, I think she's great," I said gruffly, getting to my feet. "Thanks for the drink, Dot. I'll see you tomorrow—"

"Now, don't get your knickers in a twist." Dot reached out and patted my arm. "Ignore me, I'm just tired. And speak of the devil, here she comes."

My Audi pulled into the lot. We both watched as Kat parked in one of the few empty spaces and climbed out. She turned to talk to someone in the passenger seat. When I saw who it was, I muttered, "You have *got* to be kidding me."

Dot leaned forward to peer over the rail. "Who's that with her?"

"My parents," I said grimly, watching as my father lumbered out of the back seat.

"Your *parents*?" Dot set down her glass, an expression of shock on her face. "Hell, kiddo. You didn't tell me they were in town."

"Trust me, it wasn't a pleasant surprise."

"I see. Well, you know I'm no stranger to tricky families. You think they want a room?"

"Probably. Along with a kidney and whatever else you're willing to give."

"Number four is open if you want," Dot offered.

"Give me a sec to find out what they're doing here."

"You want me to come with?"

"Nah, I got this."

"Suit yourself." Dot drained her glass and stood. "I'm gonna hit the hay. Here." She dug a key out of her pocket. "Opens any room in the joint. Family rate is thirty a night."

"What do you charge assholes?"

She grinned, showing her dimples. "Sixty."

"Sixty it is." I offered her the bottle, saying, "Don't forget this."

Dot snorted. "You keep it, dollface. From the look of things, you'll be needing it. Just tell them to keep it down, okay? Number three likes to whine about noise. See you at the fitting tomorrow. One o'clock—don't be late!"

As she headed toward the room at the far end, I descended the stairs. Kat and my parents were talking in low voices. As I approached, they fell silent.

"So," I said. "What the fuck is this?"

"Language," my mother tutted.

"I am sorry, Amber. I did not know where else to take them," Kat said apologetically. She looked as spent as I felt. "They called and said they needed help."

"I'm not blaming you," I said reassuringly, taking her hand. "I know whose fault this is. The two of you should be ashamed of yourselves." I stepped forward and jabbed a finger at my mother. "I told you to stay away from us."

"Well," my mother said stiffly. "I didn't have much choice. *Someone* had to bail your father out of jail."

"Jail?" I turned to my father. He looked ashen and had an institutional smell that I immediately recognized. "What did you do?"

"It was a misunderstanding," my father said hoarsely.

"You know what?" I said, holding up a hand. "I don't actually care. Why didn't you go back to your hotel?"

My parents exchanged a look, then my dad cleared his throat and said, "Because we don't technically have one, honey."

"We were sleeping in the car." My mom's hair was a mess, her makeup smeared. A few tears rolled down her cheeks as she said, "But then it got towed, and your father was just trying to get it out of the impound lot, and there were dogs! I mean really, we could sue the pants off them, he's lucky he wasn't ripped to absolute *shreds*—"

Kat squeezed my hand and shot me a look. I sighed. "You can stay here for *one* night," I said, holding up a finger. "One. I'll cover it, but I have terms."

"I really don't appreciate your tone, dear," my mother said.

I motioned for her to shush and continued, "I will get your car out of impound tomorrow, and you will get in it and drive away. You're going to lose her number," I said, pointing at Kat. "And you're going to leave us alone. Deal?"

My mother's eyes narrowed; I could practically see her calculating. Before she could open her mouth, I said, "This is not up for discussion. Either you agree, or you sleep on the street."

"We're your parents," my mother said plaintively. "Would you really abandon us?"

"In a fucking heartbeat," I said. "It runs in the family. So what'll it be?"

My parents exchanged a glance and then my father nodded

wearily. I handed him the key. "Room four. Be quiet, and don't make a mess."

Pulling Kat behind me, I headed for the stairs.

"Sweet dreams, girls!" my mom called out.

"Unbelievable." As we passed the firepit on the way to our room, I grabbed the champagne bottle by the neck. Once inside, I closed the door and collapsed on the bed.

"Amber—"

"Listen," I said. "I get why you helped them—you're a nice person, and they're really, really good at taking advantage of nice people. But we've gotta talk about boundaries, okay?"

"Yes, of course." Kat crossed the room and perched on the edge of the desk, holding out a hand for the bottle. I passed it to her, and she took a long swig. "I just thought, even though they might not be the best people, they're your family. And I have the money to help them, so I might as well. Besides, I wasn't even sure you were coming back tonight."

"What's that supposed to mean?"

She shrugged, avoiding my eyes. "You just seem awfully busy with other women."

"Oh, please," I scoffed. In the small corner of my mind that was still sober, a voice was yelling at me to shut up and play nice. Unfortunately, the rest of it was verging on sloppy drunk, and that part was not in the mood for drama. "You're overreacting."

"Am I?" Kat crossed her arms and glared at me. "You have barely looked at me since we got here! Or touched me. And every time I turn around, you are either staring at another woman or going off with her!"

"These are my friends," I said defensively.

"They seem like a lot more than that," she sniffed.

"That's ridiculous," I mumbled.

Not quietly enough, as it turns out, because Kat immediately snarled, “Did you just call me ridiculous?”

Looking back, this is the moment when I should have apologized. But I was tired, and grumpy, and as I already mentioned, drunk. So instead I snapped, “If the shoe fits.”

Kat glared at me, spun on her heel, and left the room. And I, like the grown-ass adult that I was, fell back onto the bed fully dressed and passed out cold.

CHAPTER SEVENTEEN

SATAN MET A LADY

Gina knocked again; no answer. *Where the hell is Marcella?* Even though it was super late, everyone knew she barely slept. Gina stamped her feet to warm up; she probably should've put on real clothes instead of just grabbing a beanie and throwing a jacket over her PJs. But she'd expected Marcella to come through for her.

No such luck. Frustrated, she tried again to take a hit off her vape pen but got nothing. The cartridge was completely empty, and it was her last one. Gina groaned. She'd crashed out after everyone took off, thanks to a couple shots of tequila and a Xanax. But a few hours later she snapped awake, convinced she'd heard a noise. She'd spent a half hour trying to get back to sleep before finally giving up. Figured she'd stay up smoking and scrolling but then realized she'd drained her nic pen.

And now she was fully awake and itching for it, and Marcella wasn't answering. Which meant she had to go all the way to the corner store for a new cartridge.

Gina sighed and shuffled through the parking lot in her platform UGGs. None of the lights were on in the rooms around her, and the street ahead was empty. The wind had picked up, and it cut straight through the thin material of her pajama bottoms. She swore under her breath. The past couple days had been truly fucking awful. First that creep knocked her out and shaved her head. Then all the drama tonight, and the way Marcella had treated her, as if it was her fault that some idiot was squatting there. *Of course* she'd assumed they were a team and this was all part of their plan. And yeah, maybe she shouldn't have taken the guy's money in exchange for showing him the room. But it wasn't like she was getting paid to watch the front desk; she'd basically been forced into doing it "as a favor."

Whatever. At least she'd gotten twenty bucks out of it.

From here on out, Marcella could answer her own damn phone. As it was, Gina was probably going to have to get a job, something temporary just to cover basic expenses. She sure as hell wouldn't be earning much until her hair grew back; the convention crowd wasn't going to pony up cash for a bald chick. Gina scratched at the hat; even the cotton irritated her scalp. All in all, her life totally sucked right now, and no one seemed to care.

Gina yanked open the door of the all-night bodega and went straight to the counter. "You got watermelon cartridges?"

The old guy behind the counter nodded and reached up to grab one. "This'll give you popcorn lungs, you know." He made an exploding motion with one hand. "Like that. Little holes all through 'em."

"So fucking what," Gina snarled.

The guy shrugged, taking the twenty. "Just sayin'."

"Yeah, well, mind your own fuckin' business," Gina grumbled, snatching the cartridge off the counter. As she stomped back toward the motel, she ripped open the wrapping and tossed it on the ground.

Screw that guy, screw Marcella, and screw everyone else in this shitty fucking town. Maybe it was time to move back to Tempe. She could crash with Belinda for a while. Work the fancy hotel bars in Scottsdale. Less competition there anyway; she could probably make a killing.

Distracted by trying to slot the new cartridge into the vape pen, Gina didn't notice the car tailing her. Not until she stopped to take a hit and caught movement in her peripheral vision. Turning, she startled; the guy who had asked to see the room was right behind her. He smiled wolfishly, showing all his teeth.

"Fuck!" Gina gasped. "You scared me!"

He tutted. "You really shouldn't employ such coarse language. It's not ladylike."

"Sorry," she mumbled, taking him in. He was average height, pretty old, and dressed in a bulky parka and corduroys. Just like earlier, he looked harmless enough. But harmless guys didn't follow you around in the middle of the night, did they? Gina dug around in her coat pocket for the pepper spray; with a sinking feeling, she realized she'd left it in the office.

Gina stepped back to put some distance between them, and his eyes narrowed. "I imagine you're surprised to see me. But then, we have some unfinished business, don't we?"

"Nah, I showed you the room," she said, edging back farther. "You want to see it again, it's another twenty."

He cocked his head to the side. "That glimpse was hardly worth what I paid, don't you think? And I must say, your behavior was very rude. Someone should teach you some manners."

His voice went hard on that last bit in a way Gina definitely didn't like.

"Fuck you," she spat, turning to bolt. But she barely got two feet before tripping on her pajamas. She went sprawling, scraping her palms and sending the vape pen skittering away. Suddenly panicked, she scrambled, trying to regain her footing.

She was yanked back up by her jacket. She yelped and then felt something sharp at the base of her spine. "That is an extremely sharp knife you're feeling, and if I press harder, you will never walk again," he said softly. "Now then. You and I are going to have a little chat. Then we'll get down to business."

CHAPTER EIGHTEEN

THE RACKET

I'm the last person who would ever claim to be a relationship expert; prior to this, my longest had lasted two months and ended spectacularly badly. But I have picked up a few things that I'd love to share:

1. When you wake up in a motel room and your partner refuses to speak to you or make eye contact, it generally means that they're upset. And if they're just muttering to themselves in German while throwing you the occasional dirty look? Also not a great sign!

2. When you check your watch and realize you've got ten minutes to shower, change, and get to a bridesmaid dress fitting, so you don't have time to dive into a long apology? Well, if that's the case, you might as well embrace the fact that your relationship could end right now!

But it's not as if I didn't try. I rolled over and immediately said, "I am so, so sorry, Kat."

Kat was already awake and fuming. She sat against the headboard, laptop propped on her knees, probably searching for flights back to San Francisco. She threw me a withering look, then turned her attention back to her computer.

"Um, dog or cat? Or hey, what if we throw a third option into the mix, like an iguana?"

"I do not want to play," she said curtly.

The clock to her right read 12:45, which meant that even if I left immediately, I was going to be late.

"Are you looking at the clock?" she asked accusingly.

"No! I mean . . ." I sighed and ran a hand through my hair. "It's just . . . I'm supposed to meet Dot and Marcella for the fitting, and so while I really, really want to explain—"

She glared at me and shouted, "Really?!" Then she slammed her laptop shut and stormed off to the bathroom, muttering under her breath.

Tentatively, I went over and rapped on the door with my knuckles. "Um, Kat?"

No answer. Which was problematic, because I really needed to pee. And brush my teeth and shower. Or at the very least, slather on some deodorant. And everything I needed to accomplish those things was locked in the bathroom with her.

But it seemed like explaining that would not go over well in the current climate. I leaned my forehead against the door and swore softly to myself. Then I called out, "Listen, I get that you're pissed, and you have every right to be. I'll be back soon, and I swear I'll make it up to you then. Okay?"

No response. I found a wet nap in my backpack and quickly

smeared it under my arms, hoping it made a dent in my burgeoning ripeness. Then I left, making a quick pit stop at the lobby bathroom on my way out.

So yeah, not winning any girlfriend-of-the-year awards.

- - -

"Oh, honey, you *didn't*," Dot gasped, hand to her mouth.

"Well, that explains the stank," Marcella said with a smirk.

"Sorry," I muttered, sinking down even farther in the tatty armchair. We were ensconced in a costume design shop near the Strip. Giant headdresses lined the walls, overlooking four battered worktables, a dozen dress forms clad in little more than strands of pearls and feathers, and racks filled with beads, chains, and zippers. If I hadn't been feeling so despondent over the state of my personal life, I would've been enjoying how cool this all was.

True to form, Dot wasn't getting mass-produced bridal attire from a chain shop, but custom dresses made to her specifications. "So who is this person?" I asked, my attention drawn to a male mannequin in a tiny thong.

Dot and Marcella exchanged a glance and then Dot said, "Toni? She's the best. Arrived a few years back and is already the go-to costumer for all the hot shows."

"Yeah, and she's pretty hot herself," Marcella said with a grin.

"Anyway," Dot added quickly, "Toni simply insisted on kitting out the entire bridal party as her gift."

"Wow," I said. "That's really generous."

"Isn't it?" Dot said. "She's a great gal."

I checked my watch again; we'd been sitting there for twenty minutes. "And when will hot Toni be arriving?"

"There's some sort of sequins emergency," Dot said apologetically. "Shouldn't be too much longer, though."

It was hard not to think that I could've used that extra time to patch things up with my girlfriend—if she even was still my girlfriend. I hadn't intended to share my relationship drama, but when I showed up looking much worse for wear, Dot understandably had some questions.

"Kat will cool off," Dot said reassuringly. "Don't you worry."

"Maybe," I sighed. "I don't know. We haven't had a real fight before this."

"Well then, you got some making up to look forward to!" Dot shot me a wink and then leaned forward to check her reflection in the mirror and smoothed an eyebrow. "If you want, I can have my friend get you a table at Delmonico tonight. Best steaks in town, and very romantic."

"Yeah, I'm not sure if steak's going to cut it," I grumbled, picking at a hole in my jeans. "She's pretty pissed. Wouldn't even talk to me."

"Shouldn't have fallen asleep." Pointing a finger at me, Marcella added, "Never go to bed angry. That's a rookie mistake."

"Seriously?" I asked. "You, too?"

"Well, Marcella's not wrong, hon," Dot said. "I mean, if Jim spent our whole vacation running off with a couple hot gals, I'd be pretty steamed."

"Nothing happened," I said, exasperated.

"No one's gonna believe that," Marcella said smugly. "I mean, hell, look at me."

Dot laughed. I shook my head and said, "Don't encourage her."

"Aw, I'm just so tickled to have both of you here with me," Dot said. "I've missed you, dollface."

"Yeah," I said. "I missed you both, too." Sitting here with them, it felt like we'd picked up right where we left off. If I'd learned anything, it was how rare and precious that was.

"Oof," Marcella said. "Both of you give it a rest." But she was grinning, too.

"Besides, aren't we doing another stakeout tonight?"

"I can't decide," Dot said. "People got a smidge too enthusiastic yesterday."

"What was the total again?" Marcella asked. "Four johns sprayed?"

"Five, actually." Dot shook her head. "So going forward we'll keep it simple. Just the core group."

"What about the license plate you asked Grace to check out?" I asked.

"No word yet."

I wondered if Grace was okay; she was an expert hacker, so tracking a license plate shouldn't have taken this long. Maybe she was dealing with her mom again? Should I text her, or was that weird? And when had this all gotten so complicated? I sighed and said, "She'll probably have it soon."

"Sure hope so. Maybe this time, we get lucky."

"As long as we're done with stakeouts," Marcella grumbled. "I need a break from those heels, my feet are killing me."

"My everything is killing me," I mumbled, rubbing my neck.

And then the door flew open and an actual goddess swept in.

Toni turned out to be a stunning Black woman, nearly six feet tall, with close-cropped hair and green eyes. And calling her "hot" was a stark understatement. She wore high-top sneakers and a bright blue jumpsuit that I couldn't have pulled off on my best day. I goggled as she gushed, "I am so sorry, beautiful people! Someone who shall remain nameless split her hot pants, and I don't have to tell you what it's like working with those divas. You'd think it was a national emergency. Hey, lover."

I tried not to react as Toni bent down and gave Marcella a long, deep kiss. I clocked Dot looking at me with concern and tried to settle my features into something that hopefully passed for normal.

Toni straightened and turned to the rest of us. She clapped her hands together and exclaimed, "You must be Amber!"

"Yeah, um, hi," I said, pushing up to my feet and extending a hand. "Really great to meet you."

She grabbed it and pulled me in for a hug. "I was so sorry to miss the bachelorette party, I heard it was a blast! Unfortunately, I had to deal with a *Magic Mike* emergency."

"What kind of emergency?"

"Girl, you don't even want to know," she scoffed. "Anyway, I've heard so much about you from Marcie."

"Really?" I said, wondering exactly what Marcella had shared.

"Don't worry." She held me at arm's length and grinned. "It was mostly good. Now let's get you ladies done up. Baby, you want to go first?"

"You're just trying to get me naked," Marcella purred.

"Always," Toni said with a wink. "Now come on into my office."

As Toni led Marcella to a small fitting room at the far end of the workshop, I turned to Dot and said in a low voice, "So they're dating?"

Dot gave me a sympathetic look. "For a month or so now. They hit it off at an NA meeting."

"Really?" I frowned. "I thought part of recovery was waiting a year to start a new relationship." Hearing the plaintiveness in my voice was embarrassing.

Dot came over and perched on the arm of my chair, patting my hand. "Have you ever known Marcella to follow the rules? But Toni's been real good for her. She's been sober for years." She paused, then added, "And I figured maybe it's for the best, what with you having a serious girlfriend and all. Probably good that you've both moved on."

"Yeah, sure," I mumbled. "I'm happy for her."

Dot chuckled. "You don't have to pretend with me, hon. But I promise, someday you'll say that and actually mean it."

Marcella stepped out and my heart gave an extra thump: She looked unbelievable in a black velvet dress with cutouts and a plunging neckline.

Dot clapped her hands together and said, "Oh, it's perfect!"

"Good to hear," Toni said. "It was a little hard to see the seams in the pictures you gave me, so I had to do some guesswork. What do you think, babe?"

Marcella stepped onto the platform and did a full turn, inspecting herself in the mirror. "I think my ass looks amazing."

Silently, I agreed. Dot looked absolutely giddy. "You're a dead ringer for Linda Darnell in *Fallen Angel*."

"*Fallen Angel*, huh? Guess that tracks," Marcella cracked.

"Oh, stop. Seriously, though, you'd love it. Definitely her best film," Dot said. "She was such a talent. Did a lot of westerns, too."

"Shame you didn't pick one of those, I love working with fringe." Toni dropped to her knees to pin the hem.

Marcella frowned and said, "Can't you make it shorter?"

"There's a big slit up the back," Toni said, running a hand up her calf. "Don't worry. People'll see plenty of these gorgeous legs of yours."

Marcella bent and kissed her again while I tried not to squirm. *You're happy for them*, I reminded myself. *You love Kat. Even though she currently isn't speaking to you, overall it's a great relationship. Right?*

"All done!" Toni got to her feet and playfully batted at Marcella as she went in for another kiss. "Stop distracting me and go take this off—carefully, watch the pins. Amber, you ready?"

"Sure," I said. "Who am I supposed to be?"

"I always got a real Cathy O'Donnell in *They Live by Night* vibe from you," Dot said, drawing a circle in the air with her finger. "Girl next door, natural beauty. She wears these fabulous coveralls in the film, but that seemed a little casual, so we're going with her premiere look."

"You saying I'm not a natural beauty?" Marcella called from behind the curtain.

"I'm saying you don't leave the house without putting on your face," Dot retorted.

"She's got you there, babe," Toni laughed.

Every time she said "babe," I had to fight an inward cringe. I smiled weakly. "Someday you're going to have to give me a crash course on the best noir flicks."

"Anytime, toots. Now shake a leg." Dot shooed me toward the changing room. "Toni has to get to a fitting for the new Cirque show."

I passed Marcella as she came back out in her regular clothing. She threw me a lazy grin and said, "Better hope your dress is killer. Wouldn't want to overshadow you up there."

"We both know that's happening no matter what," I scoffed.

She laughed and squeezed my arm. I tried not to flush, noticing Toni watching us. Turning to Dot, she said mildly, "Do these two ever stop flirting?"

"Not that I've seen," Dot snorted.

"Well, lucky I'm not the jealous type," Toni said, holding back the curtain for me. "Now be careful with the zipper; it's a bit tricky."

"Got it. So you're doing a Cirque show, too?" I said, stooping under her arm. "That's cool." A dark green dress was draped over a hanger. I shrugged off my clothes and carefully stepped into it, easing the fabric over my hips.

"I'm doing three of them! It's been a busy year," Toni said from the other side of the curtain. "Definitely can't complain."

"As if," Marcella chimed in. "Toni's never complained about anything in her life."

"Now that's not true. But nobody ever died of a positive attitude and gratitude," Toni said. "Spend too much time focused on the bad, that's all you'll see."

"Ain't that the truth!" Dot said.

"Hell, you two should be a couple," Marcella snorted.

"Taking that as a compliment, babe," Toni said. "We could all benefit from being more like Dot. Amber, you need a hand?"

"All good. Should've brought heels to try with it, though." I tugged the bottom of the dress to straighten it and then stepped out.

Dot shook her head and said, "Damn. I really should've gotten less-sexy bridesmaids."

"I got some leftover fabric from *Blue Man Group* if you want to stick them in black turtlenecks instead," Toni joked.

I stepped in front of the mirror. Even without heels, I looked amazing. The dress fit like a glove and hugged my curves perfectly. It even made my legs look longer, thanks to the asymmetrical hemline. I turned and grinned. "Dang. *My* ass looks great, too. Thanks, Toni."

"That's my motto," Toni said through a mouthful of pins as she checked the fit on the sides. "Making women's asses pop since twenty-fifteen."

"I know you make mine pop," Marcella said.

"Enough already," Dot said. "You're making me blush, and you know I eat that sort of thing up."

"All right, you're set." Toni eyed me approvingly, "Not many adjustments for either of you. I'll have them done by tomorrow morning. Now I'm gonna have to kick you out. Dot's right, I got another meeting to get to." Toni glanced at her watch and sighed. "Happy to be working, but this week has been brutal."

"Don't we get to see the bridal gown?" I asked.

"Sorry, hon. Saving that for a big reveal," Dot said. "Y'all get to see it when you help me get ready Saturday."

"Okay." I sighed. "Any suggestions on how to get my girlfriend to speak to me again?"

"Flowers, chocolate, bath bomb, face mask," Toni said, ticking them off on her fingers. "You can rehearse what you're going to say while I help you out of this, 'kay?"

"Okay," I grumbled. I watched her blow Marcella a kiss before leading me back to the fitting room, and for a minute, I actually did feel happy for them. Marcella had had a tough life, and she'd worked hard to pull herself together. She deserved someone as cool as Toni. Hell, they basically defined #relationshipgoals for me now.

"You two are super cute," I said.

"Aw, thanks," Toni said. "Can't wait to meet your girl. This wedding is going to be one for the ages."

"Definitely," I agreed, not knowing then exactly how prophetic those words would prove to be.

— — —

It was late afternoon when I got back to the Mayhem. This time, I was prepared. I'd stopped at a store along the way and bought everything Toni had suggested, including a souvenir sweatshirt to satisfy Kat's soft spot for American kitsch. I struggled to bring it all to our room without dropping anything, which was especially challenging when I tried to dig out my key. Plus, largely courtesy of Toni, I had a whole speech prepared. A pretty darn good one, too, if I do say so myself: heartfelt and moving and definitely enough to convince any reasonable person that I should be forgiven.

I was so prepared, in fact, that I launched into it before the door had closed behind me. "Sweetheart, I'm a total idiot and I'm so sorry that I've ruined—"

I peered around the precariously balanced two dozen roses and frowned. The sheets were rumpled, but there was no sign of my erstwhile girlfriend. "Um, Kat?" I called out. "You in the bathroom?"

I checked: no Kat.

"Well, shit," I said, dumping my peace offerings on the bed and plunking down heavily beside them. Had she gone back to San Francisco? And if so, did that mean we were over?

Also, was it a bad sign that I felt just the slightest twinge of relief at the prospect? *Stop it, Amber,* I chided myself. *You're a grown-up now, in a grown-up relationship. And grown-ups don't bail when things get a little rough.*

Of course, it might not even be up to me anymore. Just in case, I should make sure the roses didn't die. Disgruntled, I went to find an ice bucket to stick them in.

Which was when I spotted a note on the bureau, because Kat's finishing school had emphasized the importance of handwritten communication. It read:

> *Amber—*
>
> *Your father was badly hurt. We took him to Acute Urgent Care on Sahara Avenue. Please meet us there.*
>
> *Kat*

— — —

I don't even remember the drive. It turns out that you can have terrible parents who abandon you, who you don't see for years, and still the thought of losing one of them is a gut punch. I went into a kind of fugue state. Somehow, I must have parked and made my way to reception because I found myself standing in front of a desk staring down at a frowning woman in scrubs.

"Miss? Are you okay? Can I help you?"

I stared at the woman in front of me, momentarily drawing a blank. Then I said, "I think my dad is here?"

"What's his name, hon?"

"Perry Austin."

Her fingers flew over the keyboard and then she nodded. "He's down the hall, that way," she said, pointing past me.

I pushed through the double doors she'd indicated and scanned inside each room as I passed. Most were empty. The whole time, I was saying a silent prayer that he was okay. "Badly hurt" could mean a lot of things, right? After all, this was urgent care, not a hospital.

When I finally found his room, I paused on the threshold. My dad was lying on an examination table, eyes closed, a cast on his arm and a collar around his neck. He looked small and pale. My mother sat beside him, holding his good hand. Kat was leaning against the wall by the windows. They all turned their attention to me as I demanded, "What the fuck happened? Dad, are you okay?"

"He is most definitely not okay!" my mom said angrily, as if this was somehow my fault. "He nearly broke his neck!"

"Now, Sarah, just calm down," my dad said wearily. "I'm fine."

"And his arm!" Mom exclaimed, gesturing to the air cast. "Broken in two places!"

"Yeah, I can see that," I said, annoyance overtaking my concern. "So what happened?"

"He was in a car crash," Kat explained. Avoiding my eyes, she added, "The details are a bit . . . confusing."

"I thought your car was impounded," I said suspiciously.

"It was! I mean, it is!" Mom said.

"So he was walking, and a car hit him?"

My parents exchanged a glance. I shook my head. I should've known. "What did you do?"

"Your father tried to solve our little problem," my mother said frostily. She cast a quick glance at Kat, then said, "I told you we owed some people money. Well, they offered a way to pay them back."

"Oh, for fuck's sake." I threw up my hands. "Please tell me you weren't dumb enough to do a swoop and squat."

"We didn't have a choice," Mom said stiffly.

"What is a swoop and squat?" Kat asked, eyes wide.

"It's a scam where you basically cause a car crash," I said, folding my arms. "One car blocks in the target, then the other swoops in front of them and slams on the brakes, forcing a rear-ender."

"But . . . the crash is real?"

"Very real," I said. "And super dangerous for whoever is in the swoop car. Which I'm guessing was you, Dad?"

"They were going faster than they were supposed to," my dad said apologetically. "It was only meant to be a little fender bender."

"I can't believe you!" I shook my head. "You know better than that." Most self-respecting grifters considered swoop and squats beneath them. They were high risk and low reward—or worse. The con hinged on having a bunch of willing victims piled into the car that got hit; usually, those victims were desperate people risking their lives. The mark would hit the swoop car, then be persuaded to fork over cash to cover the vehicle damage and injuries, rather than involving insurance companies.

It was a coin toss, though. Some owners would refuse to pay and insist on waiting for the cops, or demand an exchange of insurance information.

And sometimes, the victims' injuries were severe. People had even died.

If my parents were stooping to those tactics, they must be in worse trouble than I thought. *Not your problem*, I reminded myself, although seeing my father all banged up was definitely challenging my resolve. "Well, I told you to leave us out of it," I said resolutely. "Kat, let's go."

She threw me a withering look. "No."

I sighed. "C'mon, baby, let's go somewhere we can talk. I promise to make it up to you."

"You were right," Kat said, exchanging a look with my mother.

My eyes narrowed, and a swell of rage filled my chest. Turning on my mom, I growled, "What have you been telling her?"

"Nothing!" my mother protested, holding up her hands. "Kat is just such a lovely person, I thought she deserved to know a little more about you."

"*You* don't even know me," I said. "We haven't spoken in nearly a decade!"

"I'm your mother, dear," she said placidly. "Of course I know you."

"You can't listen to her," I said to Kat. Gesturing to my mother, I added, "She'll say anything. This is the person who forgot to buy Christmas presents one year, then told me Santa didn't come because I did a bad job of pretending to have leukemia."

"Which was better than telling you he didn't exist!" my mother said.

"No, it *really* wasn't!" I snarled.

A nurse poked her head in. "Mr. Austin, I'm afraid we're going to have to ask your visitors to leave. Some of the other patients are complaining about the noise."

"Oh, I'm going, all right." I whirled on my girlfriend and demanded, "Are you coming?"

Kat hesitated. Her eyes shifted between my mother and me. Finally, she nodded. "Yes, I am coming."

I held out my hand, and she took it. As we walked down the hall my mother called after us, "Her real name is Emily!"

CHAPTER NINETEEN

DESPERATE

When Gina woke up, it took a second to get her bearings. She was cold and uncomfortable. Her eyes were covered and her whole body ached, especially her head, which felt like it had been stuffed with wool. She was lying on something hard and slick.

Gina opened her mouth to say, "What the fuck?" and discovered that she couldn't. Her eyes and lips were taped shut, and her hands and feet were bound together with what also felt like tape. She couldn't move at all. Couldn't stand. Couldn't scream.

That's when she started to panic. She thrashed, her body knocking against something hard and cold. Wherever she was felt narrow, slightly wider than her shoulders. Was it a box? Or worse—a coffin? She tried to scream through the tape, but the sound came out so muffled it was barely audible.

A wave of dizziness nearly overcame her. Her lungs hurt; she wasn't getting enough air. Feeling herself start to slip back into unconsciousness, Gina forced herself to relax. Carefully, she drew deep breaths in through her nose until her pulse settled. And as she did that, memories flooded back in.

The old guy with the knife. *Shit.* He'd forced her to his car and made her take some pills that knocked her out. But why? What else did this sick fuck want from her? He'd already taken her hair.

"Oh, good, you're awake!" a hearty voice boomed from somewhere to her right.

Gina jerked away from it, banging her shoulder painfully.

A low chuckle and then the voice said, "Easy, now. No need to be dramatic. If you behave yourself, this will all be fine."

Gina dared allow herself the tiniest bit of hope. Maybe he'd covered her eyes so she couldn't identify him. He wore disguises, right? That's why she hadn't recognized him last night. Maybe he was going to let her go as soon as she gave him whatever he was after.

"All righty then. If I remove the tape, are you going to be a good girl?"

She nodded.

A pause and then he said, "I should tell you, there's no point in screaming. We're somewhere no one will hear you." His voice hardened as he added, "And if you do scream, I'll cut out your tongue. Do you understand, young lady?"

Gina hesitated, then nodded again. She couldn't help yelping in pain as he ripped the tape off her mouth. The sudden ability to take in big gulps of air practically made her cry from relief. She filled her lungs greedily as he said, "Let's get started. I have some questions for you."

"Okay." Gina's voice came out raspy, like it hadn't been used for a while. How long had she been here? She'd assumed just a few hours, but could it have been longer? Another wave of panic swelled inside her; she fought it back. Panicking wasn't going to accomplish anything. She had to be smart about this. "I'll give you a blow job if you let me go," she croaked.

A long silence. She cocked her head, listening; was he going to take her up on it?

When he finally spoke, his voice was low, so quiet she could barely hear him. "So you really are just a filthy little whore."

Gina shrank back again, shaking her head and stammering, "No, I just—I thought—"

"Silence!" he hissed.

Gina clamped her mouth shut.

"Now, then," he said in a completely normal voice. "Please explain what happened last night. I'm particularly curious about the women who visited the motel after my departure. Any information you provide would be greatly appreciated."

"Um, I'm not sure," Gina said. "I don't know a lot of them. Most are Dot's friends."

"And who is Dot, exactly?"

"She owns the motel. But Marcella manages it." Should she be telling him all this? Would he go after them next?

Well, if so, too bad. Gina could only afford to worry about herself right now. And if that meant telling this asshole everything she knew about Dot and Marcella down to their bra sizes, that's what she was going to do.

"And the motel next door? The Buggy Suites?"

"That dump? No, that's not Dot's," she said, puzzled by the question. "I got crabs from the sheets once, it's nasty."

"I see." Another pause, as if he was debating what else to ask. "And why was everyone congregating last night?"

"Um . . ." Should she lie? Or would that just piss him off more? Probably safer to stick with the truth; after all, it hadn't been her plan. "To try to catch you."

He laughed sharply. "To catch me? Goodness."

"Yeah." Emboldened, she said, "I had nothing to do with it; it was all Dot and Marcella's idea. And their other friend, she does something with computers." She searched for the name. "Georgia, I think? Something like that. Anyway, they got pretty mad about you shaving people's heads. But like I said, I had nothing to do with it."

"Shaving heads?"

Gina frowned. He sounded mystified. "Yeah. Like the other day, when you drugged me and shaved my head."

A long pause, then he chuckled again. "Oh my. Is that what happened to your hair?"

Gina's heart sank as the realization hit: *This isn't the same guy.*

It was someone much, much worse.

"Well, thank you for being so forthcoming," he said smoothly.

"Sure." She swallowed, then said hopefully, "You gonna let me go now?"

The strip of tape was pulled back across her mouth. Gina screamed against it, bucking wildly. There was a note of regret in his voice as he said, "I'm afraid not. Bad girls like you need to be punished."

Something wrapped around her throat. Gina struggled, but it was no use. He pulled it taut, and the darkness behind her eyes became absolute.

CHAPTER TWENTY

THEY LIVE BY NIGHT

We drove back to the motel in silence. Between the fatigue and the rage still churning in my gut, it was hard to compose a coherent thought or figure out exactly where to begin. Because it turned out I was furious with Kat. The fact that she'd taken my mother's side, even for a moment, well . . . that stung more than anything.

For her part, Kat stared out the window, avoiding my eyes. When I glanced at her, for a moment it felt like I was looking at a stranger. In spite of myself, I flashed back on the night we met.

When my college diploma finally arrived in the mail, I'd immediately headed to the local lesbian bar that had become my second home (in fact, I'd chosen my San Francisco apartment largely because it was stumbling distance away).

The bartender and I were already on a first-name basis, probably because I tipped generously and flirted shamelessly. That night, I'd harbored hope that maybe our flirtation would evolve into something more. But mainly, I was in the mood to celebrate: I'd survived two serial killers and had an actual, legitimately earned college degree. I wasn't taking any of those things for granted. So I'd swept in and announced that the next round was on me, which elicited cheers from the women nestled at tables around the room. One round had turned into two, and as the night progressed, things got a bit hazy.

But one moment stands out crystal clear in my memory. I was in the bathroom, staring blearily at myself in the mirror. I had definitely been overserved, and the evening was threatening to take a turn. I tried to check the time on my phone but was having a hard time reading the numbers—a sure sign that I'd best be on my way.

Then I heard snuffling coming from one of the stalls. I hesitated, aware that in my current state of inebriation, I wasn't really capable of offering assistance. But I was planning to become a therapist, right? Which (I assumed) meant it was ostensibly my job to intervene if someone was shedding tears in a public space.

So I lurched over to the stall and tentatively rapped on the door with my knuckles. "Um, hello?"

The sniffling paused and a voice quavered, "Do you need something?"

"Funny, I was gonna ask you that," I said, bracing myself against the door to keep from falling over. "Everything okay?"

Another sniffle and then the voice said, "I am fine, thank you so much for asking."

Her tone was oddly formal, in a way that clashed starkly with our environment. It made me smile. "All right, well. I'm not actually a shrink yet, but I'm going to be, if you want to talk about it."

The door popped open. I'd been leaning against it and almost fell in, catching myself at the last moment. Which is when I found myself face-to-face with one of the most gorgeous women I'd ever seen. She was a few inches taller than me, with long blond hair. Not even the puffiness from crying could diminish those green eyes. My throat went dry, and I fumbled for something to say that wouldn't make me sound like an idiot. "Um, do you need a tissue?"

She held up a wad of toilet paper. "No, thank you. I am all set."

"Okay. If you need anything else, I'll be at the bar."

"You bought me a drink," she said, tilting her head to the side. "Thank you for that."

"Oh, um, you're welcome." I wasn't great at chatting up beautiful women sober, and drunk it was an impossibility. Plus, I could feel my stomach churning. *Don't you dare puke!* I told myself sternly. Out loud I said, "I like your accent. Where are you from?"

"Germany."

"Yeah? That's cool. Your English is great, though."

She quirked a smile. "Do you think so? I am self-conscious about it, because it is my weakest language. May I ask, why did you buy everyone a drink?"

"I'm celebrating," I explained. "I got something today that I've waited a long time for."

"I see. And why are you not celebrating with friends?" I couldn't detect any snark in the question despite its bluntness; she seemed genuinely curious.

"Um, I don't really have any here yet," I said, painfully aware this made me sound like a loser. "I'm pretty new in town."

She brightened. "Really? I am also new!" Jutting out a hand, she added, "Katarina von Rotberg. But you can call me Kat."

"Hi, Kat." Bemused, I took the hand she was offering and shook it. "Amber."

"Nice to meet you, Amber," she said. "Now, if we are going to be friends, you will need to buy me another drink."

And that's how it started. I switched to club soda and gradually sobered up while we ensconced ourselves at a corner table. One thing led to another, and we ended up closing down the joint. Kat told me all about her life and how she'd spent the past few years bouncing around the globe, trying to find a place to stay for a while.

"So how do you decide?" I'd asked. "Gut feeling?"

"Yes, I keep waiting for that," Kat said, a tiny frown furrowing the spot between her eyebrows. I had to resist the urge to smooth it out with my thumb. "Nowhere has felt quite right. I did love Haarlem in the Netherlands, but it was a bit too rainy."

"Not a huge fan of rain myself," I said. "So how do you like San Francisco so far?"

"It is a lovely city," she said decisively. "Very European."

I grinned, charmed by her careful enunciation of vowels and her clipped endings. "So if you don't mind my asking, what was up earlier?"

"You mean, why was I crying?" she asked.

"Yeah. But you don't have to talk about it unless you want to," I amended.

"It is fine." Kat flushed red. "A bit embarrassing, however. You see, I came here with a date."

"Oh," I said, deflating. Of course someone this stunning had a girlfriend. Feeling like an idiot, I said, "So the two of you had a fight?"

"Yes." She looked up at me from beneath her lashes and added, "I said that the girl buying drinks was very attractive, and she took offense."

"Really?" I said, perking up. "So was this a serious relationship, or . . ."

Kat was already shaking her head. "Hardly. We only met last week."

"Well, I'm sorry for causing drama," I said. "Not my intent."

"I am actually grateful," Kat said, shifting closer so that our knees were brushing. "Because this is turning out to be a much better date."

The rest, as they say, is history (or herstory). Kat came home with me that night and basically never left. And up until now, we hadn't argued about anything more serious than where to go for brunch.

Which proved that my parents were still masters at ruining absolutely everything they touched. Perry and Sarah Austin: living embodiments of Murphy's Law.

I pulled into the Mayhem parking lot, squeezed into one of the few remaining spots, and turned off the car. We sat for a minute in silence. Kat put a hand on the door to get out, but I reached over to stop her. "Listen," I said firmly. "One of the things I love about you is that you're such a good person. You really want to help, and that's a great trait. But there are some people who will see that and take advantage of it. Like my parents."

"Your father was terribly injured," Kat said stiffly, without meeting my eyes. "They called and asked for my help. Should I have turned them away?"

"Honestly, yes," I said with a sigh. "I'm sorry, but that's just how it is."

"Well, it is no longer a problem," she said, shaking off my hand and getting out of the car.

"Wait, what does that mean?" I asked suspiciously, hurrying to catch up. Because if my parents were deep enough in the hole that they were willing to risk their lives (well, my dad's life) in a swoop and squat, it was highly unlikely that a single collision would cover their debt. No bookie or loan shark was that generous.

"I have taken care of it," Kat said breezily over her shoulder as she marched up the stairs to our room.

I groaned. *Shit.* This was exactly what I'd been afraid of. I hustled after her, catching the door before it closed. "Kat, what did you do?"

She grabbed her suitcase from the closet and tossed it on the bed.

"It was not so much money for me. I took it out of my trust and gave it to your mother."

I winced. "Fuck. How much?"

"It does not matter," she said stiffly, pushing past me to get to the bureau.

"It matters to me," I said, grabbing her arm to stop her. "So how much did my mom get from you?"

Kat shook off my hand and said haughtily, "I gave them ninety thousand dollars."

I swore out loud. "Wow. They really got you, didn't they?"

"They did not 'get me,' Amber. Your mother admitted to everything you said," she said defensively, jutting up her chin. "But she was not lying about them being in trouble with bad people. She said without the money, they would be hurt even more. Unlike you, I could not just stand by."

I felt another flare of rage. Before I could stop myself, I spat, "How could you be so stupid?"

Kat froze. "What?"

I should have taken a deep breath and counted to ten. Better yet, I should've left the room entirely and come back when I'd cooled off.

But I didn't do either of those things. I was absolutely livid, and in the moment it was impossible to separate how much of that anger belonged to her and how much to my parents. So I doubled down. "I said, how could you be so stupid? I warned you about how they operate. Even if they *do* owe someone, there's no way they're in that deep. But you forked over ninety K like it was nothing—like an easy fucking mark. So you know what? This is your own damn fault."

Kat stared at me. I'd never spoken to her like that before. I knew I'd gone too far, but it was too late to take back my words. And I wasn't a hundred percent sure I wanted to; deep down, I believed in what I'd said. Still, the expression on her face gave me pause.

Slowly, she said, "You think it is my fault your parents robbed me?"

I actually didn't think that—in fact, I was ready to go back and confront my parents. But the part of me that wanted to fix it for her was being seriously overpowered by a different voice in my head that said, *Screw her. She sided with your mom. She can go to hell.* I shrugged. "Hey, it's not so much money for you, right?"

There was a long pause as we faced off against each other, engaged in some sort of silent duel. Kat was breathing hard, her shoulders heaving. We stood a few feet apart but miles away. Then something occurred to me. "How did you pay them?"

"What do you mean, how did I pay them?" she asked sharply.

"It's the middle of the night in Germany, right? Is your money guy just on call twenty-four/seven?"

"Of course," she said, tossing her hair. "That is what he gets paid for."

My eyes narrowed; that felt off. Kat definitely wasn't telling me something, I could sense it. "I thought international transfers didn't go through right away."

"I wouldn't know anything about that," she retorted. "They don't bother me with the details."

"Must be nice. How about we call him right now and get some of those details."

Kat stared at me. "Are you calling me a liar?"

"You just made the transfer, right? A professional money manager should be able to do something. Maybe get in touch with the bank and have the payment stopped. That's what you pay him for, isn't it?" I shot back.

Kat glared at me, jaw set. Crossing the room in three quick strides, she jabbed a finger into my chest. "Do you really think you can talk to me like that? *You?*"

I fell back a step, startled. Kat sounded like a different person. Her face was flushed, and she was breathing hard as she continued. "You're nobody, you hear me? Nobody! You're *just* like your parents. Trash."

I fell still. There was silence for a long moment. Then I said, "Trash, huh? That's what you think?"

Kat's face shifted and she held up both hands. In a rush, she said, "Amber, I am so sorry. I did not mean that. Please—"

"No, you did," I said, cutting her off. Stepping back, I drew a deep breath. I knew that later I'd feel everything: anger, sadness, regret. But right now, the rage had cooled to a block of ice in my gut. I nodded toward her suitcase. "Finish packing."

"No, Amber, please!" She grabbed my arm. "Let's talk about this."

I shook my head. "We're done talking."

"Do you . . . are we . . ." Her eyes glistened with tears. "Are we breaking up?"

"I try not to date people who think I'm trash," I said in a flat voice. My insides were roiling, but I wasn't about to let her see that. My phone buzzed with a text. I pulled it out: It was Dot, asking me to call her.

"Please, Amber. Don't leave like this," Kat pleaded, coming toward me.

I held up a hand to stave her off. "Just don't, okay? I need some space."

Kat stood by the bed looking distraught, hands dangling by her sides. I waited to feel the usual rush of love sparked by the sight of her, but there was nothing. It was as if she'd wiped all the emotions out of me with a single word.

And maybe that wasn't such a bad thing. Opening the door, I said, "Call your money guy. Maybe there's something he can do."

I stormed toward my car, a dull roar filling my ears. I should've called Dot back to see what she wanted, but I was so angry I wasn't a hundred percent sure I could form a complete sentence. I just needed to get in my car and drive somewhere I could calm down and think. Part of me was tempted to keep going until I reached San Francisco. I visualized throwing all of Kat's stuff out the window of my apartment, watching it drift down to Dolores Street. Or better yet, dumping it in the trash.

I stopped next to my Audi and placed both hands on the hood, leaning over to collect myself. *It's over.* My first real adult relationship had just completely imploded. New emotions started to penetrate the anger: grief and sorrow and, to be honest, more than a little relief.

You know what made the whole thing even worse? Digging through my pockets and discovering I'd left the car keys back in the room.

"Shit," I groaned. I couldn't go back there. I'd rather buy a whole new car than deal with Kat staring at me with that stricken expression on her face, the word *trash* ringing in my ears.

"What's wrong, kiddo? You look like someone just sneezed in your soup."

I turned at the familiar voice; Dot and Marcella were sitting in her convertible, eyeing me like I was losing my shit. Which wasn't far off base.

"Damn," Marcella said. "You look pissed."

"It's kind of been a rough day," I said through gritted teeth.

They exchanged a look, then Dot said, "Well, we were just coming to find you. Grace finally got a hit on that license plate, and we're headed to meet up with her. Why don't you hop in?"

I shook my head. "I'm not going to be good company right now."

"What else is new?" Marcella muttered. Off my look, she shrugged. "What? You've been kind of a drag since you got here."

"Hush, Marcella," Dot reprimanded her. Lowering her sunglasses, she said, "Gotta be honest, toots, you don't look in any shape to be driving. And it's no good being alone when you're in a snit. If nothing else, this will be a distraction. And you can tell us all about it on the way there. 'Kay?"

I hesitated. I desperately wanted to go somewhere—anywhere, really—but without car keys, my options were limited. Deciding, I hopped in the back.

"Buckle up, buttercup," Dot said, pulling out of the parking lot. "I got a good feeling about this! Grace said the plates were stolen. That's suspicious, right?"

"Sure," I mumbled, chin on my hand as I glared out the window.

"Anyway, she's trying to get a bead on where the car is right now. Said something about checking security cameras all over town."

"Took her long enough," Marcella grumbled.

"Now, Marcie," Dot chided. "It was plenty fast, considering the circumstances. I feel awful about bothering her with this when her dad just died."

"Good riddance," Marcella muttered.

"Amen to that, but he's still her father. And remember, we're not a hundred percent sure it's even the right person. This time, we're not gonna rush into anything. BJ is still pretty riled up about getting his head shaved."

Marcella snorted, and I grinned in spite of myself. "Go ahead and laugh," Dot added. "He's trying to get a bonus, calling it 'combat pay.'"

"Tell him if he keeps pushing, his bonus will be ten more minutes with Portia," Marcella said. "She can finish the job."

"Truth be told, I do feel a little bad. Poor kid looks like a plucked chicken." Dot pulled into the left turn lane and put on the blinker. "Here's the odd thing, though. Grace asked to meet up at the Buggy Suites."

"Aren't they still closed?" Marcella said, frowning.

"Last I checked." Dot caught my eye in the rearview mirror. "You know anything about that, toots?"

"Um—I'm sure she has her reasons," I hedged.

"Guess we'll find out soon enough," Dot said. "So back to the business at hand. You and your gal are still tussling?"

"You could say that," I muttered. "She said I was trash."

"She *what*?" Dot exclaimed. "The nerve!"

"That bitch," Marcella agreed.

"Well, I did call her stupid," I said, shifting uncomfortably. My anger was ebbing, and all sorts of other feelings were swooping in to fill the void. Maybe *I* was actually the asshole in this scenario.

Or maybe something else entirely was going on. But every time I tried to catch hold of it, my mind forced it away. I twisted the Rolex she'd given me around my wrist.

"Is she stupid?" Marcella asked.

I shrugged. "She definitely did something dumb."

Dot caught my eye in the rearview mirror and frowned. "Still doesn't justify name-calling, Amber."

I shrugged, embarrassed. "Maybe I overreacted."

"I meant by her," Dot said.

"Can't trust someone like that anyway," Marcella said knowingly.

"Someone like what?" I bridled.

"Rich," Marcella said.

"Technically, I'm rich, too."

"Not like her. That's generational wealth. It's different."

I opened my mouth to argue, but she was right. The past few

months had made that painfully clear. But that wasn't what was bothering me. "You don't even know her," I said defensively. "Besides, she was just trying to help my parents."

"Hold up. Your *parents*?" Marcella asked, turning in her seat to face me. "The fuck is going on?"

I sighed. "It's a really long story that I'm not up for telling."

"Suit yourself," Marcella said, turning back around.

"I didn't mean—"

"It's fine," Marcella snapped. "You said you didn't want to talk about it. So maybe we should just stop talking about it."

"It'll work out if it's meant to be, kiddo," Dot said, shooting Marcella a look. "Probably good for you both to take a beat and cool off."

"Yeah, probably," I agreed, sinking back in my seat.

"Anyway, I'm glad to have you with us. I just hope it doesn't turn out to be another wild goose chase." Dot sighed. "I swear, if I'd known it would be this hard, I wouldn't have gotten you all involved."

"I actually think this has been good for Grace," I said. "She needed a distraction."

"Poor lamb," Dot said. "She handling it okay?"

I shrugged, remembering her downing shots the night before. "I guess she's doing about as well as could be expected. Stuff with her dad was . . . complicated."

"I bet," Dot said. "Well, here's hoping she's got the right creep. If this isn't wrapped up by the time Jim gets home tomorrow, I'll have to put a pin in it."

"I told you I could handle this alone, Dottie," Marcella said. "You didn't have to come."

"Yeah," I chimed in. "Shouldn't you be having a spa day or something?"

"Me and Jim are getting mani-pedis and massages at the Wynn

tomorrow afternoon," Dot said. "And hell, I wouldn't miss this for the world. I bet we get lucky."

"Sure," I agreed, opting not to share what I was really thinking: Based on how my week was going, luck wasn't in the cards.

– – –

Dusk was falling as we arrived at the Buggy Suites. Dot steered into the lot and parked between Grace's sedan and a little Honda that probably belonged to the nurse. The remodeling banner snapped in the wind, and a plastic bag skittered across the back fence. I turned up my coat collar against the chill and climbed out, regretting the fact that I still hadn't bought a parka; Vegas in November was much chillier than San Francisco.

"I simply don't understand why we couldn't meet at the Getaway," Dot said, hands on her hips.

Marcella leaned against the hood, arms crossed over her chest. "When Slimy Stanley sold this place, I was kind of hoping it would get torn down."

"I just hope they don't make it too nice," Dot said with concern. "The last thing the Getaway needs is competition right next door."

"Oh, you don't have to worry about that," I said. "It's not a motel anymore."

Dot frowned at me. "How do you know?"

"Because I'm the new owner," a voice said from behind us.

I turned. Grace was framed in the doorway of her new living quarters. As usual, she was dressed all in black and carried a cattle prod.

"Hang on a sec," Dot said. "What do you mean, you're the new owner?"

"I purchased the property a few months ago," Grace said. "As an investment."

Marcella made a strangled noise. I met her eyes and said, "Yeah, I know."

"You bought the Buggy Suites? But—why?" Dot asked with what seemed like professional indignation.

"We can discuss it on the way," Grace said, checking her watch. "I need to be back by six to interview a new attendant for Mother."

Marcella raised an eyebrow. "Wait, *your* mom is here, too? What the fuck is going on?"

"Like I said, long story," I sighed.

"If he changes locations, I might not be able to track the car," Grace said, striding toward us. "So we should take full advantage."

Dot was still gaping at her. "But—"

"Time is pressing," Grace insisted, climbing in the back seat. "I texted the address to you, Dot. Shall we?"

The three of us looked at each other, and I shrugged. What the hell—at least it would offer a distraction from my relationship drama. As Dot started the car, she shook her head. "I just can't get over it. Stanley told me he sold out to some group that was going to turn it into condos or something."

"Well, it's definitely 'or something,'" I muttered.

"You should torch it and start over," Marcella said. "I got crabs once from the sheets."

"As I told Amber, the exterminators were extremely thorough," Grace said. "I also discarded all of the original furniture."

Dot said, "I guess what's bugging me, hon, is that you were right next door this whole time and never reached out! I could've helped with whatever you needed."

Grace was looking out the window blankly. When she finally responded, she said, "In all honesty, I'm not accustomed to asking for help."

"I get that," Dot said, her voice softening. "And I'm not saying you have to either. But if that ever changes, I'm here. Oh, and my condolences for your loss."

"Thank you," Grace said. "Although I haven't spoken to Father since I was ten years old, and given the circumstances, grief seems inappropriate."

"Still. Even when parents are real pieces of work, it's hard not to feel something when they go."

Grace looked uncomfortable. "I suppose. But at the moment I would prefer to focus on coming up with a plan."

"We got the cattle prod, right?" Marcella said. "How much more of a plan do we need?"

My phone buzzed with a text: Kat. I tucked it back in my coat pocket without reading it. It started ringing. I checked the screen: Kat again. Well, she was persistent, I'd grant her that.

"Maybe you should pick up, hon?" Dot suggested from the front seat.

"Not ready to talk to her yet," I muttered, turning on do not disturb mode.

"Are you referring to your girlfriend?" Grace asked.

"Yeah. We're kind of in a fight right now."

"Are you?" Grace asked. "Then perhaps this is a good time to tell you—"

I held up a hand to cut her off. "I get it, no one else likes her. But I'm really not in the mood for 'I told you so' right now, okay?"

Grace eyed me for a beat, then said, "As you wish."

"Thanks." I settled back against the seat and crossed my arms over my chest. "Let's just focus on catching this asshole."

"Here we are!" Dot announced. "Dino's Lounge."

"I hate this dive," Marcella said.

"It's not a dive," Dot protested. "Krissie runs a clean place."

"There's no such thing as a clean karaoke place," Marcella scoffed.

"Wait, the guy who has been drugging and attacking girls is hanging out at a karaoke bar?" I frowned. "You think he's looking for another victim?"

"No way. No one works this joint, they wouldn't make a dime," Marcella said.

"Maybe *he* works here?" I offered. "As a bartender or something?"

"Or he's a big fan of shitty singing."

"I just hope it's really him this time." Dot looked nervous as she turned off the car.

"I believe it is," Grace said. "In addition to running the license plate, I performed a meta-analysis of every car that passed the victims' locations for weeks prior to the attacks. Then I cross-referenced those license plates against local residents and performed a demographic analysis—"

I held up a hand to stop her. "Listen, Grace. I'm sure whatever you did was super nerdy and way beyond our ability to understand and also boring. Does that sound about right?"

"I would dispute your framing, especially the boring part," she sniffed.

"Jumping ahead," I sighed, rubbing my eyes. "You're saying you're pretty sure we got the right guy this time?"

"Yes. A car bearing that license plate was in this parking lot a half hour ago."

"So now what?" Marcella asked. "We just go in and zap him?"

"Damn straight," Dot said with determination, digging the cattle prod out from underneath the driver's seat. Brandishing it, she added, "We're bringing down this asshole tonight."

CHAPTER TWENTY-ONE

CORNERED

Dino's was lit up like a pinball machine. The sign in front stated in all caps: **GETTING VEGAS DRUNK SINCE 1962**. Which would be appropriate for pretty much any establishment in town, but whatever.

"We're looking for a black 2018 Kia Forte, Nevada plates, 8KGC52," Grace said, hopping out. We all clambered after her.

"Okay," I said, suppressing a yawn. "How about I take this end of the parking lot, and you—"

"Found it!" Dot called out giddily. She was standing behind a small black sedan a few cars down from the front entrance. We hurried over. Dot gestured to the license plate and said, "Kia Forte, 8KGC52."

"Okay," I said. "We still need to make sure it's the right guy and not just some weird coincidence."

Grace frowned. "Of course it's right. According to my algorithm, there's a ninety-six—"

"Yeah, well, that's not a hundred percent," I interrupted. "And as someone who's been on the receiving end of your cattle prod, I'd like to make sure. So let's try to come up with a plan before we start zapping random strangers."

"Fine." Grace sighed, checking her watch. "But as I mentioned, we are on a schedule."

"How about a couple of us stay out here in case he tries to leave," Dot said. "And the other two go inside, see if they can spot him?"

"That'll work," I said.

"C'mon, then." Marcella grabbed my elbow. "You can be my wingman."

My arm buzzed where she touched it. Swallowing, I said to Dot and Grace, "That work for you two?"

"Sounds good, kiddo." Dot nodded. "Grace and I'll keep an eye out here."

"Please hurry," Grace said.

"Yeah, yeah," I said, waving her off. "You got plans. I heard you."

I turned to find Marcella stripping off her flannel shirt to reveal a strapless corset that barely contained her breasts. "Um, what're you doing?"

"Baiting the hook," she said, leaning into the side mirror to tousle her hair. Aside from the corset, Marcella was wearing tight jeans and sneakers, which didn't exactly scream "sex worker," but she looked hot enough that it probably wouldn't matter. My throat certainly went dry as she walked in front of me. Maybe it wasn't the worst thing in the world that I'd basically just broken up with my girlfriend.

But Marcella is with Toni, I reminded myself. *And you've decided to stop being such a dirtbag.* Easier said than done, but hopefully the effort counted for something.

I followed Marcella through the parking lot. At the entrance, she turned and cocked an eyebrow at me. "You ready?"

"Yup," I said, holding the door for her.

Marcella sashayed through. Inside, the lighting was dim and hazy with a distinctive red tint. A long bar ran down one side of the room, and the rest of the space was crowded with high-top tables. Despite the fact that it was pretty early in the evening, the place was packed. Bartenders hustled back and forth to fill orders for the folks stacked two deep at the bar. Every table was taken; a hubbub of voices pierced by an occasional shriek of laughter. Like every other dive bar I'd frequented (definitely not a short list), the air stank of stale beer and vomit.

I winced as our ears were assailed by a sudden loud wailing noise. "Fuck," I said. "What *is* that?"

Marcella gestured toward a small stage in the corner where a large man on his knees belted into a microphone. "'I Will Always Love You,'" she said. "That high E is a killer. I can hit it, though."

"You sing?" I asked.

Marcella tilted her head. "Yeah, of course. You didn't know that?"

"Nope," I said, scanning the room. There were at least a dozen guys who fit Grace's composite. "I didn't think there'd be so many people here this early."

"Dino's is always packed," Marcella snorted. "This actually looks like a slow night for them."

"Great," I sighed. Eyeing the karaoke stage, I said, "I guess we could say something happened to the Kia to get them out to the parking lot? Just need to put our names on the list."

"Good idea. Leave it to me." Marcella sauntered up to the stage and said something to the singer in a low voice. He nodded and handed the microphone to her as the song wound down.

"Hey, I'm next!" a guy at the bar protested.

Marcella ignored him, leaning over to talk to the DJ. A moment later, the first strains of ". . . Baby One More Time" belted from the speakers. Marcella threw her head back and launched into the opening verse. Cooing the lyrics, she proceeded to act out the full Britney video, moving her hips, running her hands up her body . . . by the time she hit the chorus, I desperately needed a drink.

I ordered a beer and sipped it while I scanned the crowd. Hopefully this wouldn't turn out to be a bust. At least it was a distraction from my relationship drama. I heard Kat's voice hissing *trash* again and winced. It was the worst thing she could have said because deep down, it was exactly what I'd always feared she thought of me. *Focus, Amber,* I chastised myself. *That's a problem for later. Get this done and then you can deal with it.*

Marcella finished and bowed with a flourish, clearly relishing the enthusiastic applause. Ignoring the agitated guy reaching insistently for the mic, she shouted, "Thank you, Las Vegas! Also, if your black Kia Forte is parked in the lot, someone sideswiped your car. I got their plate number, if you want it, meet me outside."

Then she tossed the mic and hopped off the stage. When she reached me, she grabbed my beer and took a long swig, leaving a lipstick mark on the rim. "Nicely done," I said approvingly.

"Thanks," she said. "Now let's go deal with this asshole."

– – –

Grace and Dot were waiting in the car when we walked out. Dot rolled down her window and said, "Did you find him?"

Before we could answer, a middle-aged woman in skintight jeans, cowboy boots, and a denim jacket came barreling out the door and charged past us. She went straight to the Kia and started to examine it.

"Well, shit," Marcella muttered.

"You sure you got the right car, toots?" Dot asked worriedly.

"Positive," Grace said, but even she looked perplexed.

"And it was definitely a guy who attacked Gina and the others?" I asked dubiously.

"Even with the disguises, I'd imagine the girls could tell the difference," Dot noted. "Oh dear, she's coming over."

Dot was right; the woman was charging our way, and she looked pissed. Planting herself in front of Marcella with her hands on her hips, she barked, "You think it's funny to mess with people?"

"Yeah, kinda," Marcella retorted, stepping forward with her chin up.

"I think there's been a misunderstanding," I said in a conciliatory tone. Pointing to the Kia, I asked, "Is that your car?"

"Why?" The woman was in her late forties, petite, with big hair and a thick layer of makeup that poorly concealed acne scars.

"What's your name, hon?" Dot asked.

"Sandra," she said warily.

"Are you the sole driver of that Kia, Sandra?" Grace asked, coming to stand beside us.

The woman's eyes narrowed as she took us all in. "The fuck is going on?"

"Listen, I know this is kind of weird," I said. "But we think someone has been using your car to commit crimes."

"You don't look like cops," she said suspiciously.

"FBI," Grace said smoothly, producing a badge seemingly out of nowhere. I gawked as she added, "We have evidence that backs up these claims."

I waited for Sandra to call bullshit on us. But instead, she asked, "What claims?"

"Assault," Grace said. "The victims are all sex workers."

Sandra sucked in air through her teeth, her brow darkening as she spat, "Son of a *bitch*!" Then she wheeled around and tromped back toward her car, calling over her shoulder, "You want to arrest that bastard? Follow me."

– – –

We barely had time to pile into Dot's car before Sandra tore out of the parking lot. She gunned the engine, cutting in and out of the few other cars on the road as we struggled to keep up.

"Holy cow, this is like a real car chase!" Dot exclaimed, bending low over the steering wheel. "Where do you think she's taking us?"

"More importantly," I said, throwing a pointed look at Grace, "what do we do when she expects the *FBI* to arrest him?"

"I brought zip ties," Grace said blithely.

"Of course you did," I muttered.

"I think maybe she'll kill him before we have to do anything," Marcella said. "She seems pretty pissed."

"Do I even want to know why you have a fake FBI badge?" I asked Grace.

"Who says it's fake?"

Before I could answer, the Kia screeched to a halt in front of a dilapidated-looking casino. Sandra charged out, arms swinging, clearly on a mission. We hurried to follow as she threw open the front door and huffed inside. You could practically see steam coming out of her ears as she checked to make sure we were still in tow. Nodding curtly, she led us through the labyrinthine casino floor.

It was a far cry from the other establishments I'd seen in Vegas: The ceiling was low, the carpet threadbare, and several of the slot machines bore handwritten **OUT OF ORDER** signs. The few people gambling looked like they might not technically be alive.

Sandra blew through, not sparing a glance for anything until she reached the far end of the casino. We had to practically break into a jog to keep up. She finally stopped in front of a ragged black curtain. A faded sign on an easel beside it featured a top hat and read **THE AMAZING PRESTIGO! SHOWS EVERY HOUR ALL DAY LONG!**

Yanking back the curtain, Sandra bellowed, "Dwayne, you no-good motherfucker!"

I peered past her. The room on the other side was tiny, just a handful of chairs facing a small platform with black velvet stapled to it. The only person in the audience was a guy who, from the look of things, had been rudely awakened by the yelling. Without meeting our eyes, he got to his feet and shuffled back to the main casino floor.

"The Amazing Prestigo" turned out to be a doughy-looking guy in his forties who was every bit as nondescript as Grace's computer-generated composite picture. His tuxedo was as worn as the carpet, and ragged sneakers poked out from the frayed cuffs. He stood on the platform behind a rickety-looking table with a splayed deck of cards and—yep, you guessed it—a top hat. Dwayne blinked at us, startled, while Sandra stomped to the "stage." She jabbed her index finger into his chest to punctuate every word as she hissed one long stream of invective, "You useless piece of *shit* I hope they lock you up *forever* I knew you weren't really working all those nights how *dare* you I want your shit out of my place *tonight* hear me? To-night—"

She drew a deep breath, clearly preparing to continue the tirade. Before she could, Grace stepped forward and said, "Excuse me, sir? We have some questions for you."

If Dwayne was surprised at being confronted, he gave no indication of it. "Yeah, sure. Just let me get my things," he said, scraping the cards into the top hat.

"Your friend can get those for you," Grace said smoothly. "Let's go outside to talk."

"You're in for it now, Dwayne," Sandra said with satisfaction. "These are feds. And there's no way in hell I'm bailing you out this time."

"Like I said," Marcella murmured in my ear. "We should just hand him over to her."

"Aw, c'mon, Sandra," he whined. "I got a problem, I know that. But I love you."

Which was apparently the wrong thing to say because Sandra turned a few shades redder and started pummeling him with her fists, screeching.

"Does this place have security?" I asked, checking over my shoulder. The last thing we needed was some burly rent-a-cop who might not be as easily swayed by a fake FBI badge.

"Even if they do, he's not a paying customer," Marcella reasoned.

"Yeah, but still. This isn't exactly low-key."

Dwayne had put his arms up to protect his face and was making yipping noises as he tried to fend off Sandra's assault. Luckily for him, she tired quickly. Her arms fell by her sides, and she heaved soft, hiccupping pants as tears streamed down her face, leaving mascara trails in their wake. I felt awful for her. If there was one thing I could relate to, it was how gutting it was to be let down by your partner.

Dot stepped forward and wrapped an arm around Sandra's shoulders, saying, "C'mon, hon. Let's get you a drink."

"You're going to miss the fun," Marcella warned.

"This was enough fun for me," Dot said. "You gals make sure he gets what's coming to him, though, 'kay?"

"Mother*fucker*!" Sandra snarled again, turning and spitting at

Dwayne's feet. Then she allowed herself to be led meekly from the room.

Dwayne had red marks on his face from where Sandra had slapped him, and what little hair he had was mussed. Mutely, he held out his hands for cuffs; clearly this wasn't his first rodeo. When a few beats passed, his look of resignation turned to puzzlement. "So am I under arrest, or what?"

"That largely depends on you, Dwayne," Grace said.

I stared at her, wondering how far she was willing to take impersonating an FBI officer. It would be the height of irony if, after all the crimes I'd committed, this was the one I went down for.

"Yeah?" His eyes turned calculating. "What, you want cash? 'Cuz I don't have much on me, but I can get some—"

"Are you trying to bribe a federal officer?" Grace asked, sounding genuinely perplexed.

"No?" he said. "I mean, maybe?"

Marcella made a disgusted noise. "Wow. We got ourselves a real criminal mastermind here."

He blinked. "What's this about, anyway?"

"Serious crimes, Dwayne," Grace said. I had to hand it to her; she made a very convincing fed. "You're in quite a bit of trouble. Felony assault of at least four victims that we know of."

"I didn't assault anyone!"

"Shaving someone's hair against their will counts."

"Oh, that." Dwayne shuffled his feet. "I want a lawyer."

"I have a question," I said. "Why hair?"

Dwayne shrugged. "Dunno. But it's not like I hurt anyone."

"You drugged them," Marcella said menacingly. "And made them bald. How is that not hurting them?"

Dwayne looked embarrassed. "You gotta understand, ladies. I have a condition. Besides, is there even a law against it?"

"Are you kidding?" Marcella growled. "Fuck arresting you. We should take you out to the desert and bury you where no one will find the body."

"Whoa, whoa, whoa," Dwayne said, holding up both hands. "I didn't mean to hurt anyone. Please, just give me a chance. I swear I'll stop . . ."

I frowned. Dwayne's eyes were darting all over the place in a way that was strikingly familiar; that's exactly what my mom did whenever she was about to bail. My focus shifted to his hands, which had slipped into his pants pockets. "Hey," I said warningly. "Keep your hands where—"

Before I could finish, Dwayne flicked his wrist and yelled, "See ya, suckers!"

There was a loud *bang!* and we were suddenly enveloped in a huge cloud of smoke.

CHAPTER TWENTY-TWO

THE UNSEEN

Whatever Dwayne had set off quickly filled the small room, contaminating the air. The smoke was thick and cloying. My eyes stung, and my lungs burned. I bent over double, hacking. Turned in a circle but couldn't see anything and immediately lost track of which way was out. A wave of panic swelled in my chest, and I started hyperventilating, which only made the coughing worse.

Someone hit me from behind. "Ow!" I exclaimed, lashing out.

"It's . . . me . . ." Marcella choked. "Can't . . . see."

I felt her hand bat at me, grabbed it, and tried to suss out the exit. The smoke seemed thinner off to my right. I groped forward slowly, patting the air until I encountered something solid: one of the chairs. Pulling Marcella behind me, the pair of us coughing and wheezing, I fumbled us from chair to chair. It was as if the room had expanded along with the smoke; an eternity seemed to pass before my hands brushed against the velvet curtain blocking the door. I swatted at it, trying to find an opening, then gave up and dropped to my knees, lifting it from the bottom. A blast of fresh air slipped beneath, and I gulped it greedily; it stank of stale smoke, but compared to what we were coming from, it was the sweetest air I'd ever tasted. Holding up the curtain, I waddled forward on my knees until I was all the way out.

Somewhere nearby, an alarm was blaring. I could feel Marcella right behind me and edged forward to give her room. We both stayed on all fours, hacking and gasping for air. My eyes wouldn't stop tearing, so I wiped them with the back of my hand to clear my vision. After a full minute, Marcella choked out, "Mother. Fucking. Magicians."

I managed to gasp, "At least he didn't shave us." She made a strangled noise; it took me a second to realize she was laughing, too. I started cough-laughing along with her, straining my already aching lungs. The smoke must have triggered the fire alarm because there was no one in sight, and red emergency lights flashed along with the shrieking siren. No sprinklers, thankfully, but that probably meant this place wasn't up to code. Not that I cared. The last thing I needed was to end the night by getting soaked.

Marcella had mascara streaks running down her face and a cocktail straw in her hair.

"Hang on," I said, reaching over to pluck it out. "You've got something—"

I moved to grab the straw, not realizing that my foot was still entwined in the velvet curtain. Thrown off balance, I lurched forward and fell directly into Marcella, knocking her down and landing on top of her. She made a small "Oof" sound as I basically crushed the air out of her lungs.

"Sorry," I gasped. "I didn't mean to—"

But apparently I did, because suddenly we were kissing. And not just a little peck either. We were all over each other, rolling around on the floor, her tongue flirting with mine, her tears wet against my cheeks. My brain had completely checked out, and my body had apparently decided that the floor of this godforsaken casino was the perfect place to devour Marcella.

In the periphery of my awareness, someone cleared their throat. I opened one eye and saw Grace standing above us, gazing down with a familiar expression of disapproval. "If you're not too busy," she said archly, "I believe we can still catch him."

"Oh, yeah. Sure," I said, disentangling myself from Marcella while avoiding her eyes. We both clambered awkwardly to our feet. I swiped the tears off my cheeks and meekly followed Grace toward the casino entrance. I didn't check to see if Marcella followed; I could feel her at my heels and frankly was too mortified to face her. I'd basically come on to her like some sort of horny teenager. I was lucky she hadn't smacked me.

Grace led the way back to the casino entrance. A few people still sat at slot machines in defiance of the bleating alarm. They didn't spare us a glance as we passed. "Why didn't you grab him?" I asked, hurrying to catch up to her long strides.

"There must have been another exit from the room," she said. "I waited, but Dwayne didn't emerge. So I did a quick circuit of the casino."

"Thanks for all the help," I grunted.

A smile quirked the corners of her mouth. "You seemed to be managing just fine."

She pushed open the outer door, and I was hit by a wave of sweet, actual fresh air. I gulped it in greedily, folding my arms against the chill. A small cluster of people were chain-smoking as they waited to be let back into the casino. No one seemed particularly perturbed, so maybe the smoke bomb was a regular part of Dwayne's act. Dot's convertible was still parked behind the Kia, but there was no sign of her or Sandra.

"Shit," Marcella sighed. "We lost him."

I finally let myself look at her. She'd managed to remove the straw from her hair, but her cheeks were flushed. And she was definitely avoiding my eyes.

My phone buzzed in my pocket. Checking it, I found a text from Dot: AROUND THE CORNER IN THE ALLEY.

I held it up to show the others and then the three of us made our way around the building. The alley was long, narrow, and filled with overflowing dumpsters.

I spotted Dot about halfway down, hands on her hips. Sandra was with her, brandishing a cattle prod over a prone Dwayne. When we were a few feet away, she jabbed him in the leg with it, and he shrieked and writhed on the ground.

Dot waved cheerily at us. "Oh, good, you got my text!"

"How the hell did you find him?" I asked. Sandra barely seemed to notice us. Dwayne was gibbering at her, spittle surrounding his mouth. He waved his hands wildly, pleading for her to stop, but she jabbed him again with the cattle prod.

"Soon as that alarm sounded, my girl Sandra here knew exactly what was up," Dot said, nodding toward her. "Figured Dwayne'd be trying his ol' escape routine, so we hustled out here and intercepted him." Leaning in, she added sotto voce, "I turned down the zapper, but someone should probably step in. She's been going like this for a while now."

"Hopefully he doesn't have a heart condition," I said.

"I'm hoping he does," Marcella said, crossing her arms over her chest as she looked on approvingly. Tilting her chin up, she said, "Hey, Sandra, you zap him in the balls yet?"

Sandra seized on this inspiration. I winced as Dwayne made noises that would probably haunt me for years to come.

"Damn. Well, we got him," I said. "Now what?"

Dot made a face. "Good question, kiddo. Truth be told, I didn't really think this far ahead."

"For starters, we're definitely shaving his head," Marcella said.

"Not much to shave, though, is there?" I said dubiously.

"The rest of him, then."

Eyeing him distastefully, Grace said, "I would prefer not to participate in that."

"Me either," I muttered, making a face.

Sandra shoved the cattle prod into Dwayne's belly and pressed the button as he yelped, "No, no, no, no!"

Both of them suddenly froze. Sandra held up the cattle prod, examined it, and then frowned. "Dead battery," she noted with disappointment. "You got another one of these?"

"Maybe we jam some of those smoke bombs down his throat?" Marcella offered.

"Help yourself," Sandra said, nodding toward a small pile of brightly colored balls a few feet away. "I dug those out of his pocket."

"Actually," I said, stepping forward, "Maybe we should give Dwayne a bit of a break, yeah? I think he's fully charged."

He threw me a grateful look. I hunkered down so that we were eye-to-eye. Lowering my voice, I said pleasantly, "So Dwayne. How can we make sure this doesn't happen again?"

"It won't, I swear," he said, trying to smooth out his hair. "I'm not a bad guy."

"Good guys don't drug women," Dot said.

"She has a point, Dwayne," I said.

"Listen," he said earnestly, leaning forward. "These girls aren't like you and me. They almost expect it, all right? They know it's dangerous out there. But they're choosing to do it anyway, see? So it's like . . ." He snapped his fingers and concluded, "Cost of doing business."

Marcella's foot was connecting with his chin before I even registered it. Dwayne went sprawling, coming to rest with his head nestled against the side of a garbage bag.

"Out cold," Dot noted.

"Lucky for him," Marcella said. "'Cuz if he kept talking, I was probably gonna kill him."

"You okay?" I asked, reaching for her.

She shrugged off my hand and snapped, "I'm fine."

"So," Dot said. "What the hell do we do with him now?"

I cut a look at Sandra, who waved me off. "Don't worry about me, honey. Dot told me you're not FBI. Shame, though. I'd love to see him behind bars."

"She's coming to the wedding," Dot added, patting Sandra's shoulder. "Hell of a gal."

"That's great, but it doesn't really help with the problem at hand." I gestured to Dwayne. "Ideas?"

We all stared at him. His shirt had pulled up, revealing a small, pale potbelly.

"I still vote that we drive him out to the desert and bury him alive," Marcella suggested.

I shook my head. "He's an asshole, but murder seems a little extreme."

"I could destroy his credit history," Grace offered.

"Hell, he's already done that himself," Sandra snorted.

"Can't we have him arrested? He basically confessed," I said.

"Jessie's cousin said if we want anything to stick, we'll need at least one eyewitness," Dot said doubtfully. "Maybe Gina?"

"Unlikely," Marcella said.

Dwayne groaned; he was coming around.

"Well, we gotta do something to make sure he doesn't bother the girls anymore," Dot said. "You think you can convince one of the others to testify against him?"

"It won't be easy," Marcella said doubtfully. "None of them have a great track record with the cops."

"There is the other thing," Sandra said slowly.

"What other thing, hon?" Dot asked.

Sandra seemed to be engaged in an inner debate. Finally, she shook her head and said, "Fuck it. If I'd known what he was up to, I would've turned him in myself."

"Turned him in for what?" I asked.

"Car theft," Sandra said. "He and his idiot buddy found a way to steal Kias. But they haven't figured out how to sell them yet, so I got, like, five of them sitting in my yard."

"Six if we count the one parked out front, I'm guessing?"

Sandra gave me a cagey look. "Maybe I already owned that one."

"He used different cars!" Grace said, sounding delighted. "That's why the algorithm was ineffective."

"And once again, you're focusing on the wrong thing," I said. "Can we figure out how to nail him for car theft without implicating Sandra?"

"We can sure try. I'll make a call," Dot said, already pulling out her phone.

"And I'm taking these," Marcella said, bending to scoop up the smoke bombs. "They look fun."

– – –

Dwayne ended up in Dot's trunk after all. About halfway to Henderson, he started pounding on the inside of it.

"He dents my car, I might let you bury him in the desert," Dot muttered.

"I can kick him again if you want," Marcella offered.

"How much farther?" I asked, repressing a yawn. Since arriving in Vegas, I'd barely slept. Between dealing with my parents, fighting with Kat, and catching a head-shaving magician, the emotional turmoil of the past few days had been a lot. It felt like if I closed my eyes, I'd sleep for a full day.

"Think we're almost there," Dot said, following Sandra's Kia off the next exit.

Thankfully, she was right. Sandra made a few turns before pulling into the driveway of a split-level ranch that had seen better days. It sat in a predominantly unfinished development; the cul-de-sac sported four other houses at various stages of construction. Based on the state they were in, the work seemed to have been abandoned years earlier.

"Well, this is grim," I said under my breath.

"Great setting for a murder," Marcella said. "If we change our minds."

I dragged myself out of the car as Sandra gestured to all the Kias crammed in her dusty front yard and said, "See? Fucking idiot."

"So what's the plan?" I asked Dot.

She nodded toward the street, where a dark sedan had just pulled up. "Remember how Jessie had a cousin in law enforcement?" She nodded toward the car. "That's them."

The person striding toward us bore a striking resemblance to Jessie, without the elaborate makeup. They were tall and imposing, with short-cropped salt-and-pepper hair. They strode into the yard and took in the scene. "Hey there, folks, I'm Deputy Riggs. Thanks for the call, Dot. Looks like a solid tip. Where's my guy?"

The thumping from my trunk ratcheted up a few notches. Deputy Riggs raised an eyebrow. "It was kind of a citizen's arrest," I said lamely.

They marched over and popped the trunk. Dwayne blinked up

at them, wide-eyed, and then gasped, "Officer, thank God! These crazy bitches beat me up, and kidnapped me, and—"

Riggs hauled him out of the trunk by one arm as if he weighed nothing. As they smoothly flipped him around and slipped cuffs on his wrists, they said, "Dwayne Baird, you're under arrest for grand theft auto, and I'm guessing a hell of a lotta other things. We can chat all about it on the way to Clark."

"But—" he sputtered, "these aren't mine!" He pointed at Sandra and said, "They're hers! This is her place! I don't even live here!"

"You're my witness?" Riggs asked.

"Hell yeah, I am," Sandra said, crossing her arms over her chest. "Came home and found all these cars here. Asshole was trying to turn my place into a chop shop. Lock him up and throw away the key."

Dwayne was led away sputtering and protesting. Riggs called back, "Now that we got him, if any of the victims are willing to come forward, just let me know and we'll tack on the charges."

"Thanks, Lon!" Dot said with a wave.

"Sure thing. See you at the wedding."

I watched as they drove away. Dot was hugging Sandra and exchanging information with her. Grace was examining her phone as if it held the key to the universe.

And Marcella was watching me. I met her eyes, then quickly looked away. I wasn't sure whether I felt guilty for cheating on Kat because, based on our fight earlier, that was probably over. But I really liked Toni, and I felt shitty for maybe messing up their relationship, too. I repressed a yawn, jammed my hands in my pockets, and slumped back to Dot's car. The adrenaline in my system was dissipating, exhaustion taking its place.

"Best wedding present ever!" Dot declared, coming back over to us. "Wasn't that just a hoot and a half?"

"I'm glad it met expectations," Grace said.

"Oh, it was all that and a slice of cake! The look on Dwayne's face when he came out that door and Sandra tased him! Wish I'd been recording, because I could watch that on a loop. Now, who's up for toasting our success?"

I caught Marcella's eye, and we both immediately shifted our gazes. Grace was still frowning at her phone.

"I don't know, Dot," I hedged. "I'm pretty tired."

Dot waggled a finger at me. "Don't you dare. It's early yet, and you are way behind on bridesmaid duties. 'Fraid I'm calling in that chit."

"I could use a drink," Grace said, out of nowhere.

I gaped at her. "Really? I thought you had places to be."

"The person I was going to interview just canceled, and Chuy agreed to stay late. And as Dot said, a celebration would appear to be in order."

Marcella shrugged. "I mean, I have to go back to the Getaway anyway."

"Aces!" Dot clapped her hands together. "I've got a bottle stashed there that I've been saving for the perfect occasion. Shall we, ladies?"

— — —

"Here's to the best damn bridesmaids a gal could hope for," Dot said, raising a glass. She'd produced a bottle of champagne from the laundry room; a little warm, but still delicious. We were all ensconced in the rickety patio chairs outside the Getaway office.

"I'm not a bridesmaid," Grace said.

"I still got a day left to change your mind!" Dot said with a wink. "Anyway, I just want to say how much I appreciate you all."

"Thanks, Dot," I said as she clinked her glass against mine, then Marcella's and Grace's.

Grace had already knocked back her first glass and was well on her way to finishing a second, I noted. But I figured she was still entitled to a little overindulgence. Besides, she could walk back to the Buggy from here.

Marcella, meanwhile, was still avoiding my eyes. Despite Dot's exuberance, the atmosphere among the rest of us was notably muted.

A chirp from Dot's phone. She made a face. "Ah, hell. Probably Jim checking in. He should've hit San Diego by now."

"That's sweet," I said, sinking farther down in the patio chair and swallowing another yawn. All I wanted was to head back to the Mayhem, get a different motel room, and crash out for at least twelve hours. Tomorrow, I could attempt to sift through the ashes of the life I'd built during the past six months. Tonight, I didn't have the energy to think about it.

Grace was brooding into her champagne coupe. Marcella sucked on her vape pen, a thoughtful expression on her face. Dot's phone chirped again. She checked it, then gasped and covered her mouth with one hand. "Oh no!"

"What now?" I asked wearily, already certain that whatever it was, I'd probably rather not know.

"It's Farina from the Motel 6 over on Tropicana. Her housekeeper found a dead girl in the tub. Strangled." Dot looked up, an expression of dread on her face. "She was bald."

"Oh shit," I said. "Could it have been Dwayne?"

"I hope not. He's a real creep, but he didn't strike me as a killer," Dot said dubiously. "I'll give Lon a heads-up about it, though. Maybe they're linked?"

"Who is it?" Marcella said in a thick voice.

"I don't know, hon," Dot said. "Farina offered to send a pic she took, but—"

"Yeah, I don't want to see that," Marcella snapped.

"Me either. She said the girl is young, though."

"I'm texting Gina," Marcella muttered. "She better be okay."

"Oh, gosh, I hope so. Let's check in with the other girls, too. I'll try Jade and Mystique."

As they tapped at their phones, I noticed that Grace wore a strange expression. "What's up with you?"

"It's an odd coincidence," she said in a low voice.

"What is?" I asked.

"That's the motel where my brother stabbed me."

"Huh. Yeah, that is weird." My mind was spinning. "Could it be a copycat?"

Grace abruptly pushed back her chair and got to her feet. "I need to check on Mother."

"Right now?"

"Yes." She was already trotting off into the night.

"Well, bye," I said, feeling disgruntled. I swirled my drink and finished it.

"Jade is fine," Dot announced. "Mystique, too."

"Nothing from Gina," Marcella muttered.

"Does she usually get back to you right away?"

"No," Marcella said. "And she's kind of pissed at me."

"So maybe she's just dodging you. I'll try her, too," Dot said. "Cover our bases. And let's not get into a lather before we know for sure."

"No matter what," Marcella said darkly, "it's probably someone we know."

At that, we fell silent. Finally, Dot sighed and rubbed her eyes. "Well gals, I'm beat to hell, and there's nothing more to be done tonight. If I hear anything from Gina, I'll let you know. C'mon, Amber, let's head back to the Mayhem."

"Okay," Marcella said, still staring into her drink. As I got to my feet and started to gather up the glasses, she snapped, "I'll clean up. Just go."

I held up both hands. "Sheesh, sorry. Just trying to help."

Marcella looked ready to spit fire. "All I know is, every time you show up, people start dying."

"Hey!" I protested.

"That's hardly fair, Marcie," Dot said wearily.

Marcella shrugged. "Just calling it like I see it."

I bristled and snapped, "Really? *I'm* the one who gets people killed?"

Marcella shot to her feet. "That asshole wouldn't even have known we existed if it weren't for you! And Jessie might still—"

"That's enough, both of you!" Dot said sharply, clapping her hands together. Startled by her tone, we both fell silent. Sternly, Dot wagged a finger at us. "We *do not* turn on each other. Not ever. It's been a long day, and we're all worn out. We probably won't hear anything tonight anyway, so let's get some shut-eye."

Dot straightened her coat and turned toward the car. Chastened, I followed at her heels.

We didn't say a word the whole drive back to the Mayhem, each lost in our own thoughts. The Vegas streets were busier tonight, nightlife revving up as the weekend approached. Just the thought of it exhausted me. I closed my eyes and dozed briefly, only waking when Dot eased into the Mayhem parking lot.

She turned off the car. Rubbing my eyes, I said, "Thanks, Dot. Sorry about everything."

"Not your fault, kiddo." She reached out and patted my knee. "Just ignore what Marcie said. She still feels guilty about Jess, and now that another girl was killed, well . . . I think it's hitting home."

"Yeah, I get that." My head hurt, and it was becoming increasingly difficult to keep my eyes open. But the thought of going back to the room I shared with Kat, answering her questions, having—God forbid—yet another relationship talk . . . I didn't have it in me. "Any chance there's another room available?"

"Place is pretty full with wedding guests, kiddo. We could see if your folks checked out of four?"

"Probably not, unless a bookie caught up with them." I wanted to deal with my parents even less than Kat.

Dot hesitated, then said, "The only open room is number five. And I kinda figured you wouldn't want that one."

My whole body tensed; room five was where Gunnar had dumped one of his victims last spring. But even as I started shaking my head, I hesitated. It was just a motel room, after all. And considering the Mayhem's checkered past, it probably wasn't the only room a body had ever been found in. Based on the law of probability, people could've died in every room in the joint.

"I'll take it," I finally said.

"You sure, kiddo?" Dot said dubiously. "I can always give you my place."

"No." I shook my head. "It'll be fine."

"All right, then. Let's get you sorted."

I followed her into the lobby. BJ sat with his feet propped on the reception desk, head tilted back and mouth wide open, dead asleep. Dot snorted and shook her head, then cuffed his feet off.

BJ startled awake with a jolt as his feet hit the floor. He nearly fell off his chair, flailing wildly to catch himself. Then he paled and muttered, "Oh shit."

"Watch your mouth, Bernard," Dot snapped. "I've had a helluva day, and coming back to find you sleeping on the job gives me half a mind to send you packing again." She leaned in and sniffed, then narrowed her eyes. "You better not have stunk up my office with weed either."

BJ shrank into the collar of his T-shirt. "It's medical," he mumbled.

"Oh, really?" Dot braced both hands on the counter. "You want to try again?"

"Sorry, Aunt Dot."

"I swear, one more strike and I kick you to the curb. Now get the key to number five. Amber's staying there tonight."

His eyes flicked toward me, and he frowned. "I thought she was in twenty."

"Did that sound like a question?" Dot said. "Mind your p's and q's, and get her the damn key."

He ran a hand through his hair, making it stand up in tufts. "Um, see, I might've rented that room, though."

Dot's eyes narrowed. "Rented it to who?"

"Old guy came in." BJ looked sheepish. "Said he was interested in true crime and wanted to stay in the murder room."

"And I bet you tacked on a surcharge?" Dot demanded.

"No," BJ grumbled, but the way he avoided her eyes was a dead giveaway.

Dot sighed and turned to me. "Sorry, kiddo. Looks like you're stuck with my place after all."

My mind was spinning, kicked back into gear by something BJ had said. "So this guy asked for that room specifically? By number?"

BJ shook his head. "Nah, he just wanted the one where the girl was found dead in a tub. Said it was his hobby. Maybe you should ask him to join your club, Aunt Dot."

Dot and I exchanged a look. I pointed to the camera in the corner. "Does that thing work?"

Dot was already circling the desk. Pushing past BJ, she said, "You're working a double."

"What? But I got plans—"

"You want to keep this job and whatever you charged him on top of the room fee? Then you're working tonight." Dot waved for me to follow. "C'mon, kiddo. I can bring up the footage in here."

I came around the desk, giving BJ a wide berth as he grumbled to himself.

Dot settled behind her desk in the manager's office. She tapped away at a laptop and then motioned for me to come closer. Obediently, I hunched down and peered at the footage playing onscreen; compared to Grace's giant panoramic displays, this was puny and not nearly as clear. Dot rewound at eight times normal speed. We watched what was basically a time-lapse of BJ sleeping, scratching himself, spilling soda . . . as it progressed, Dot shook her head and murmured, "How he managed to reach adulthood is frankly beyond me."

"Is that the guy?" I asked, leaning in. Another figure had appeared. He moved in reverse, walking backward toward the desk. Dot went back farther, all the way until he entered the office three minutes earlier. Then she hit play.

We both watched as a guy in a bulky down jacket with a hat pulled low over his eyes entered. He moved slowly, like a big cat. Glanced toward the camera, then shifted his shoulders slightly. "Doesn't want us to see him," Dot noted.

"Yeah," I said. "Definitely seems suspicious."

We watched as BJ and the guy talked. Then the old guy handed over a wad of bills, and BJ passed him the key.

"That little bastard," Dot snorted. "I should dock his pay."

As he was about to leave the office, the guy suddenly turned fully to the camera and tilted his face up.

Dot hit the pause button. A shiver made its way up my spine. He was staring right at us, as if he could see us through the lens. "Fuck," I said. "That was no accident."

Dot didn't reply. I tilted my head to look at her; she was gaping at the screen and had gone unusually pale. "Dot? You okay?"

"That's Gregory fucking Grimes," she finally choked out. "The Cannibal of Shaker Heights. Here, in my motel."

CHAPTER TWENTY-THREE

FOLLOW ME QUIETLY

Oh shit," I breathed. "He's supposed to be dead. Are you sure?"

"Positive. Do I call the police?" Dot's voice was thin and strained, her eyes still locked on the screen.

"They probably won't believe us," I said, my mind racing. "We should call Grace first anyway."

"Yes, that's a good idea. I'll call her right now. She'll know what to do. Won't she?" As Dot picked up her phone and dialed with shaking hands, I wondered if Grace already knew. She'd left so abruptly, rushing back to check on her mom . . . I suddenly remembered the fear in the woman's eyes as she hissed, "He was here!" Could she have been right after all?

"Yeah, she'll know how to handle it. When was this?" I asked, trying to read the tiny numbers at the bottom of the footage.

"Forty-five minutes ago," Dot said, a tremor in her voice. "Why would he come here? I don't understand."

"He seems to be going everywhere that has a connection to Gunnar," I said. "Especially the places where he left victims."

"But what does he want?"

"What's wrong?" BJ asked from the doorway.

"Nothing," we said in unison.

"Stay on the desk," Dot ordered. "And don't fall asleep!"

"You guys suck," BJ grumbled as he left the room.

"Gotta be honest, toots," Dot said, her voice still quavery. "I think we better call the cops, too."

"Let's just see what Grace says." While I was no fan of the cops, Dot was right. I had a pretty good idea how Grace would respond to that, though.

"She isn't picking up."

BJ poked his head back inside.

"What now?" Dot snapped.

"Thought you'd want to know the guy in number five is leaving."

"What?" Dot gasped. We exchanged a look and then rushed to the door. Through the window overlooking the parking lot, I saw a guy in a parka climbing into a battered sedan.

"Oh no!" Dot wailed. "What do we do?"

"We follow him." The words left my mouth before I even knew what I was saying.

Dot gaped at me. "Really?"

"We have to. We can't let him get away," I said decisively. There really was no other option. For all we knew, he was on his way to kill another girl. And I wasn't about to let that happen. "Try Grace again."

Dot hesitated. "I think I'm too shook up to drive right now."

"I can drive," I said. "C'mon, let's hurry."

— — —

"Where on earth is he going?" Dot asked.

"I don't know." We'd been following the sedan for a few minutes. Gregory Grimes was a surprisingly sedate driver, going well below the speed limit, to the point that cars passed him, honking angrily. Granted, he'd been in prison for a couple decades, so maybe his driving skills were rusty. The downside for us was that this did not make him easy to follow. "What's up this way?"

"Not much," Dot said. "Maybe he wants to check out the Neon Museum. Or he's leaving town."

A small part of me actually hoped for that. Maybe Gregory "Gruesome" Grimes had decided he'd had enough of Sin City. Would it be so bad if he became someone else's problem? That someone being Grace, obviously. I suspected that she'd actually be thrilled to have a family member to chase again. Repressing a twinge of guilt at the thought, I said, "Is she still not picking up?"

Dot shook her head. "Nothing yet."

"Text her," I said.

"I already did," Dot said, throwing up her hand. "I've texted '911' three times now!"

"It's Grace, so it helps to be more specific," I said. "Text 'We're following your dad, answer the damn phone.'"

"Worth a try, I s'pose," Dot said.

Three cars ahead of us, Gregory Grimes put on his turn signal.

"Oh no," Dot said.

"What?"

"That's the parking garage for the Fremont Street Experience," Dot said. "It'll be packed at this hour!"

"So lots of potential victims."

Dot nodded. "Plenty. And tons of ways in and out. It'll be hard to keep track of him."

Dot's phone rang. As she picked up and put it on speaker, I called out, "About time!"

"You're certain it's Father?" Grace asked, sounding surprisingly calm.

"Yeah. Dot recognized him right away."

"I must have watched his *Dateline* special five times," Dot said. "He looks exactly the same, just a bit more gray in his hair."

A pause, then Grace said flatly, "I suspected he'd survived once I read about the murders in Colorado and Arizona."

I couldn't read her tone; did she want condolences or congratulations? "Listen, we're right behind him," I said, edging toward the barrier gate. Grimes was a car ahead of us. I shivered as he reached out the driver's side window for the parking ticket. He grabbed it, the arm raised, and he pulled ahead. "We're in the Fremont Street Experience parking garage."

"You should not have followed him," Grace said disapprovingly.

"Too late," I said. "We already did. So grab a cattle prod, and get your ass over here."

"I'm just getting Mother settled."

"She okay?"

"I moved her somewhere safe as a precaution, so yes, she's fine for the moment. Frankly, I'm more concerned about you. Father is extraordinarily dangerous. Do not approach him under any circumstances."

"Wasn't planning on it," I said. "Just trying to keep him from grabbing another victim."

"Grace, should we call the police?" Dot's voice was bordering on hysteria.

"Every news outlet has announced that my father is dead, so I doubt they'd believe you. It would probably be treated as a crank call. It's best if I handle this." I heard a door close in the background and then she continued, "I will be there in ten minutes. Please be careful."

"You know me," I said, "*Careful* is my middle name."

Grace scoffed audibly. Ahead of us, Grimes turned into a parking spot. I exchanged a glance with Dot. Her color was high, her eyes wider than normal. Still, she nodded at me. I eased into a spot on the opposite side of the aisle and turned off the car. I watched in the rearview mirror as Grimes headed toward the stairwell.

"You should stay in the car," I said. "I got this."

"That's okay, kiddo," Dot said. "It's gonna be packed in there, so it'll be hard to keep an eye on him. And he might just be dumping the car. Best if both of us go."

"You sure?" I asked doubtfully.

Dot nodded. "A hundred percent. And I'll reach out to see if there's anyone nearby who can help."

"Great." The stairwell door closed behind Grimes. If we didn't hurry, we might lose him. Still, I was finding it hard to get out of the car. It was like I was suddenly planted in the leather seat, unable to move.

Dot reached over and squeezed my arm reassuringly. "We got this," she said. "Right?"

"Right," I agreed. Taking a deep breath, I opened the door and forced myself to climb out.

– – –

Dot wasn't kidding; the place was absolutely packed with drunk tourists. As we exited the stairwell, I gaped at our surroundings. The Fremont Street Experience was a long corridor that extended in both directions. The storefronts lining it were a blur of blazing neon lights and towering screens that rivaled Times Square. Although we were technically outside, an arched roof overhead functioned as a giant digital screen. "Good thing I'm not a seizure risk," I said, blinking as my eyes adjusted to the glare.

"Yeah, it's something else," Dot agreed. "Goes on for blocks and is attached to a bunch of casinos, so keeping tabs on him is gonna be tricky."

"There he is," I said in a low voice, gesturing with my head.

I felt a little frisson of fear as Grimes turned sideways and bent to examine something in a shop window. He was still wearing the parka and ball cap, brim pulled low. He didn't look all that threatening. Passing him on the street, I wouldn't have given him a second glance.

"How do you want to do this?" Dot asked anxiously.

I shifted to see his reflection in the window we were facing. "Stick together. Try not to look at him, okay? Like, not at all. I'll keep an eye on him."

"And if we lose him?"

"We split up. But Grace will be here soon to take over." I was already texting an update on our location to Grace, although I was sure that she'd find us regardless; I swear she'd implanted a tracker or something on me.

"Okay." Dot was wringing her hands and looked every bit as stressed as I felt. To reassure her I said, "Listen, it's going to be fine. I doubt he'll do anything here, it's too public. We just need to keep him in sight, yeah?"

"Yes. Okay." Dot's phone pinged, and she checked it. "Oh good, a few of the Femmes are coming to help."

"Great," I said, secretly wondering if a bunch of overeager amateur sleuths might do more harm than good. But too late. And maybe the more eyeballs we had on this asshole, the better.

Dot suddenly squeaked and clutched my arm, staring past my shoulder.

"What?" I asked, swiveling to see what had her so spooked.

Gregory Grimes stood mere inches away, grinning widely as he said, "Well, hello."

CHAPTER TWENTY-FOUR

THE DARK CORNER

I gulped, forcibly repressing an overwhelming urge to run away screaming. I could hear Dot breathing hard, probably doing enough panicking for the pair of us.

So I dug deep into my wealth of experience at putting up a front and regarded him with what hopefully came across as mild curiosity. "Can I help you with something?"

"Yes, I believe you can." His smile was creepy, the forced rictus of a game show host. "I realize this might sound terribly forward, but do we know each other?"

"What?" I asked, thinking, *What the fuck?* Was he toying with us? Could he possibly know that we were connected to Grace? "Um, no, I don't think so."

He nodded, pursing his lips. "Yes, I did not think so either. But I couldn't help but notice you looking at me, and so of course, I wondered. Wouldn't want to be rude."

"Nope, never seen you before in my life. Sorry for the confusion." I took a small step back. "Anyway, we've gotta get going. Right?"

A long beat. I shifted to see Dot's face: She looked absolutely petrified and was wringing her hands like Lady Macbeth in Act V. I put a hand on her elbow and said loudly, "Let's go see if we can find that snow globe you were looking for. Have a good night."

"You as well, young lady," he said.

I steered Dot away, risking a glance back after we'd gone ten feet. Grimes was still planted in place. Hands in his pockets, he rocked on his heels, watching us.

"Be cool," I said in a low voice.

"Is—is he gone?" Dot asked, voice quaking. "Ohmigod, he knows who we are. He knows what we look like! Oh my God, Amber!"

"It's okay," I said, rubbing her arm. I never should have brought her; this was way too much. Too much for me, too, really. *Where the fuck is Grace?* "We'll just stay out here where it's nice and public and keep our distance."

Dot was shaking. I felt awful. Less than forty-eight hours to her wedding, and I was dragging her through an outdoor pedestrian mall in pursuit of a serial killer? If they handed out awards for worst bridesmaid, I was a shoo-in. "Maybe you should just head back to the car."

"No," Dot said, shaking her head vigorously. "I'm not leaving you alone. It's okay, I'll be fine."

I checked back over my shoulder again, only to discover that Grimes had vanished. "Shit!" I muttered, turning around fully to scan the crowd. "He's gone."

"What?" Dot whipped around as well, going up on her toes to try to see.

"So this is where the party's at!" someone exclaimed from behind us. Turning, I recognized Skeeter and Portia. Portia must have come straight from work; she was wearing another immaculate suit. Skeeter, conversely, was dressed in full camouflage attire, which—thanks to the fact that they were six-foot-three—only served to make them more noticeable.

"Oh, thank God!" Dot said. "Reinforcements."

"Where is he?" Portia asked, peering around us as if we were hiding Grimes somewhere. Gesturing to the leather handle jutting out of her purse, she said, "I brought my best whip. It'll come in handy if he gets frisky."

"I still have my pepper spray, too," Skeeter said, holding up the canister. "This time I promise to wait until we're sure."

"Smart thinking," I said, relieved. There was safety in numbers, and they could stay with Dot and keep her calm. "Listen, why don't you all find a safe spot to keep watch in case he comes back this way."

"What are you going to do?" Dot asked, grabbing my arm as if to physically restrain me.

"I'm gonna make sure he doesn't get past us," I said, nodding in the direction I thought he'd disappeared. "Tell Grace to head in from the other side, and we can surround him."

"I'll come with you," Portia offered, looking a bit too zealous for my taste.

"Better if I go alone," I said firmly. "Just stick together and stay in touch by text."

"You sure about this, hon?" Dot asked nervously. "I think maybe we should stay paired up."

She wasn't wrong, but I also didn't want to paint a target on Portia's or Skeeter's backs. Plus, they weren't exactly subtle. And I was the one with a ridiculous amount of experience dealing with serial killers. "Don't worry about me. I'll be fine." Struck by inspiration, I opened my phone and said, "I'll turn on location sharing, okay?"

"Okay," Dot said, looking mollified.

"Herd him this way, and I'll show him what happens to scumbags in my town," Portia said, fondling the whip handle.

"Hopefully that won't be necessary," I said. "Just hang tight and watch out for each other."

With a final nod, I turned and dove into the crowd.

I moved forward as quickly as seemed wise, considering the fact that I was chasing a ruthless killer who was probably on the lookout for me. I couldn't spot the parka or the hat anywhere up ahead, though.

Because he tossed them, I realized, seeing them perched precariously atop an overflowing trash can. I swore aloud, turning in a slow circle. The problem was, there was no shortage of older white guys in the Fremont Street Experience. And the fact that I was too short to see over anyone's head wasn't helping. I crossed the corridor from right to left, dodging packs of drunk revelers toting giant drink glasses with straws. They all looked like crazed dolls to me, mouths agape as they tried to take it all in. Someone screamed overhead as they tore past on a zip line. I passed a small stage where scantily clad women were performing a cabaret show to the crowd. Then I dodged a couple of showgirls who fanned themselves with giant feathers, taking turns posing with passersby.

But there was no sign of Grimes. Had he ducked into one of the stores? Maybe gone through one and out a back exit? My stomach plummeted. I'd failed. I'd lost him.

As if on cue, Grace called. I groaned, then slipped in my earbuds, figuring I should keep my hands free. Pressing the button to connect the call, I said preemptively, "He's gone."

A long pause and then Grace said, "Explain."

"Not much to explain. We lost him." I ran a hand through my hair, irritated. "He must've recognized us somehow because he came right up to us. Freaked out Dot pretty badly. Then he was watching us, so we had to give him some space, and he slipped away."

"Amber," Grace said, her voice suddenly urgent. "Where are you right now?"

"I'm—" I looked up. "I'm in front of a White Castle, believe it or not."

"I'll be right there," she said. "Do not move. And Amber—"

"Yeah?"

"Stay alert."

"No shit," I snorted. "But I'm telling you, he's gone."

A long pause. I heard street noise in the background, a car horn. "Perhaps. But there's another possibility."

"Yeah?" I asked guardedly. "What?"

"He's hunting you."

As I opened my mouth to answer, the glaring screen overhead abruptly went dark and then loudspeakers boomed, "Enjoy Viva Vision, the largest video screen in the world! Tonight, Sha-kir-a, every hour on the hour! Please look up and enjoy the show!"

I wouldn't be enjoying it, though. Because something suddenly jabbed into my back from behind, and a low voice said, "Hello again, young lady."

— — —

"Amber? What's happening?" Grace said in my ear.

I swallowed hard. My throat had gone so dry it was hard to form words, but I managed to choke out, "Dude, what the fuck?"

"That's a knife at the base of your spine," he said conversationally. "If I increase the pressure, you will be paralyzed. So please, do not try anything foolish."

Overhead, the giant screen had flared to life again. Some sort of music video was playing across it, loud and distracting enough to entirely captivate everyone around us. Even if I screamed or tried to run, it would take precious moments for someone to react. The one time I would've actually loved to see a cop, of course there were none in sight.

"What do you want?" I asked, hyperaware of both the sharp object digging into my lower back and the fact that I still had Grace on the line. "Money? My wallet's in my back pocket, you can have it. Not much cash, but you can use my cards. I won't even cancel them."

"I'm not a common criminal." He actually had the audacity to sound indignant. "I would simply prefer to have a conversation somewhere a bit more private."

I was already shaking my head. "No thanks. I'm good right here."

"I'm afraid you don't have a choice." The tip of the knife pierced the skin of my lower back and I yelped, but the music was blasting too loudly for anyone to hear. "Come along, now."

"It'll be okay," Grace murmured in my ear. "I'm close. I can see you."

I surreptitiously ran my eyes over the crowd. "Where are we going?" I asked, probably too loudly.

"To satisfy my curiosity. I would very much like to find out why you and your friend were following me. Where is that captivating redhead, by the way?"

"She took off," I said, nauseated by his description of Dot. I never should've let her come; thank God she was safe with Portia and Skeeter. "You freaked her out."

A low chuckle. "Ah, well. I suppose you'll have to do."

The way he said that made my stomach turn. Unlike Dot, I didn't know much about Gregory Grimes. I'd seen a documentary about him a while back but had been pretty stoned at the time, and it hadn't seemed like information that I'd need to access at any point. Just goes to show you, right? But I seemed to remember he had a bit of a Dahmer kink, eating parts of his victims. I swallowed hard.

Grace better be pretty fucking close because I had no intention of joining the menu.

"That way, please," he said, nudging me toward the main exit on my left.

"It's okay," Grace said in a hushed voice. "Just do what he says."

I hesitated but then started walking. He kept one hand on my shoulder, the other held the knife against my spine. Consequently, we edged forward in an odd stutter step. It only took a couple minutes for us to emerge on the main street in front of the Fremont Street Experience. He motioned left and said, "This way, if you please."

At least now I knew where Grace's stiff formality came from. I shuffled forward, heart pounding, drawing short, shallow breaths. Every instinct was screaming at me to run. I'd been practicing, after all, and Grimes was much older, probably not in peak condition after decades of incarceration. *Should I just bolt?*

As if he sensed what I was thinking, the pressure of the knife increased and he whispered, "I would strongly advise against testing me."

"Wouldn't dream of it," I choked out. A bachelorette party passed by, shrieking and squealing, the bride-to-be flaunting a giant tiara made out of vibrators. Which was the sort of thing Dot should be doing tonight. Well, not exactly that—it wouldn't be her style. But she should be relaxing and enjoying herself, getting ready for her wedding. Instead, she was stricken with terror in a pedestrian mall, and one of her bridesmaids was on the verge of being skewered.

Well, fuck that. I raised my chin. Grimes was just another murderous bully, and I was definitely an expert on those. Conversationally, I said, "That prison bus crash looked pretty gnarly. How'd you get away?"

A long pause. He was guiding me along a nearly empty side street that flanked the White Castle. That was the weird thing about Vegas:

It was amazing how fast you could go from fighting through a crowd of people to being utterly alone. "So you know who I am."

"Oh, yeah," I said. "You're pretty famous."

"Am I?"

Was I mistaken, or was that a note of pride in his voice? *Keep him distracted.* "Definitely," I said. "I mean, I wasn't even born when they locked you up, and I've heard of you. That's pretty impressive."

A low chuckle, close to my hair. I could feel his breath along the nape of my neck as he said, "Well, that is gratifying."

We came up to a service alley that ran behind the Fremont Street businesses. It was filled with dumpsters and not much else.

"Turn in here, please," he said.

"What, down this alley?" I asked, pausing at the mouth of what pretty much screamed "Murder Alley." At a glance, I could see a half dozen spots where he could gut me like a fish and leave my corpse to be found later—probably much later. *Where the fuck is Grace? Is she still listening, or did she hang up?* "Uh, really?"

"Yes. Proceed." He jabbed me again.

"Ow! Jesus, stop poking me with that thing." If I survived this, my lower back was going to be a mess. Reluctantly, I shuffled into the alley. It felt like it was swallowing me every time we slipped into the shadows between floodlights. I swallowed hard against the dryness in my throat. *Keep him talking.* "So how did you escape?"

"I have always been uniquely able to recognize and seize opportunities," he said.

That's one way of putting it. "So you saw an opportunity to escape and took it. Then decided to come here? Why? If I were you, I would've headed to the border. Over to Mexico and gone."

"Of course you would have," he said disdainfully. "The act of a coward. But I had other business to attend to."

"Business?" I said casually. "Like what?"

"You're aware that my son, Gunnar, was killed here last spring? At the very motel where I saw you the other night, in fact."

Shit. So he'd stuck around to witness the mayhem that ensued after Gina freaked out. "Oh, right," I said casually. *I watched the life leave his eyes*, I wanted to say, but given the circumstances, that was probably a bad idea. "I guess I did hear something about that."

"The information I was able to obtain regarding his demise was terribly limited," Grimes said, as if we were discussing the weather. "So I thought I would come see for myself."

"Makes sense," I said, nodding. "So now that you've seen it, are you planning to head out?"

He issued a low chuckle that made the hair on the back of my neck spring up. "I'm afraid my business here has not yet concluded. I have reason to suspect that my daughter is currently in the area. Perhaps you know her?"

I shook my head vigorously. "Nope, definitely not." I wondered how much of this Grace was picking up through the earbuds—hopefully all of it. *Where is she?*

"Ah, well. Shame. You see, I've been looking forward to our reunion for quite some time now."

We were about halfway down the alley, and there was still no sign of Grace. Glass crunched as I stepped on the remains of a broken bottle. I was starting to feel desperate; I very much doubted he intended to let me walk out the other side. No, whatever he had planned would happen right here. I never should've let Grace talk me into playing along, never mind letting him bring me somewhere so isolated. At least back in the mall, I could have started screaming and people would have reacted. Here, I was on my own.

So. Fight or flight?

As if it was even a question. Grimes had at least fifty pounds on me, and I'd never been much of a scrapper; my usual MO was to talk myself out of sticky situations, not start throwing punches. And I doubted I'd be able to con a serial killer. It certainly hadn't worked with the other two.

Run it was. I sucked in a giant breath and shifted my weight slightly forward on the balls of my feet, the same way I started every morning.

And then I heard it—the sound of someone walking on broken glass.

I spun around.

Grace was standing right behind her father, arm raised, holding a hypodermic syringe. She looked frozen and wore an expression I'd never seen on her before.

Absolute, abject terror.

"Grace, do it!" I yelled.

Grimes drew himself up to full height and glared down at her, thundering, "Grace Anne, how *dare* you raise a hand to Father!"

Before I could react, he grabbed me and yanked me close to his chest, pressing the knife to my throat. My heart sank—*shit, I should have run.* He growled, "You choose *this* over me?"

"Grace, seriously, what the fuck?" I shouted. "Do something!" I could feel the blade against my neck, a trickle of blood sliding down as he increased the pressure. He was going to slit my throat, and Grace was just going to stand there and watch him do it. Her eyes were weirdly glassy, and she looked . . . smaller, somehow. Reduced.

Then she blinked, and her eyes cleared. Her jaw hardened as she stepped toward us. Grimes dragged me back, saying, "Stay right where you are, young lady. Any closer, and I will gut her."

"She's my kill," Grace said in a hard voice I didn't recognize at all; it was like another person had stepped in and taken over her body. *Christ*, I thought. *This again.*

I felt his grip loosen. *Okay*, I amended. *Not bad. String him along, distract him, give me a chance to run . . . not ideal, certainly, but I can work with this.*

"So this is not your friend?" Grimes asked.

Grace snorted. "As if I ever required friends. It's good to see you, Father. Now give her to me."

I couldn't see his face, but the knife pressed more insistently against my throat. I blinked back tears. I really did not want to die in an alley behind a White Castle. "I think not," he said, his voice so close to my ear I could practically taste his breath. "Why don't we take her with us? My car is close by."

"That's not how I work." Grace stepped forward and looked directly into my eyes. "I've been hunting this one for a while now. Months, in fact."

"Have you?" He chuckled. "That sounds unnecessarily complicated."

Grace shrugged. "You work your way; I work mine."

I couldn't get a read on what she wanted from me, so I tried to play along as best I could. "You're both fucking crazy."

Grace rolled her eyes—that, at least, was a gesture I was familiar with. "I'd hardly take advice from someone so naive."

"Naive?" I scoffed, eyes narrowing. "You know what? You can go to—"

Before I could finish the sentence, Grace stepped right up to me, practically nose to nose. I felt a prick in my stomach and thought, *What the fuck?*

She stepped back and tossed aside the hypodermic needle.

"Sloppy," her father said, a note of disappointment in his voice. "They'll find that."

"She's a former junkie," Grace said. "They'll assume it's an overdose. Besides, I always wear gloves." She held up a hand and waggled her fingers.

"Impressive," Grimes said.

"Yes, well. Gunnar was too flamboyant. That's how he got caught."

"Your brother did always tend toward the dramatic," he agreed, wrinkling his nose. "Perhaps this is better."

"Of course it is. I've doubled his body count, and no one's the wiser. Put her over there, against the dumpster," she ordered. "Then we should leave."

My vision was already starting to blur. I tried to protest that I wasn't a junkie, never had been, but my tongue was thick and my eyelids were starting to droop.

"No—" I gasped weakly, but my limbs had gone floppy and I couldn't do anything anymore.

Grimes lowered me against the nearest dumpster with surprising gentleness. He positioned me like a doll, arms dangling and legs sprawled out in front of me. "Please," I slurred again.

Grace hunkered down in front of me. I expected her to apologize, or to suddenly spin on him; this had to be part of some convoluted plan, right? She wasn't really killing me. She wouldn't.

Would she?

She lifted my chin so I was forced to meet her eyes. "I called you naive because your girlfriend is not who she appears to be."

"I know," I choked out. "Conning me?"

Grace cocked her head to the side. "Yes."

Even through the molasses seeping throughout my brain, things clicked into place. I think I'd known for a while; I just hadn't wanted to acknowledge it.

But it turns out Grace wasn't done kicking me while I was down. Leaning in again, she added, "Were you also aware that she's working with your parents?"

I stared at her. That couldn't possibly be true, could it? I pictured my mom and Kat, their heads together as I came into the room . . . *Shit.*

She patted my leg and said, "I'm truly sorry, Amber. But it had to end this way."

I could only watch as Grace got to her feet and turned. She and her father walked together toward the mouth of the alley, then disappeared. My mouth opened and closed like a fish. I tried to say something, but my brain was floating away, taking my body with it.

Suddenly, the effort required to keep my eyes open became unmanageable. As they drifted shut, I thought, *That bitch.*

CHAPTER TWENTY-FIVE

SO DARK THE NIGHT

I opened my eyes to find Dot inches away.

"Easy, doll," she said, stroking my hair. "You're okay."

"What happened?" I asked. My head felt like a bunch of monkeys had been pounding the inside of it with mallets. It was like the world's worst hangover.

"You tell me. I started to worry about how long it was taking, and then I got a weird text that said I should go find you, so we came looking. Luckily, Port carries Narcan in her purse."

"Always," Portia said. "Can't be too careful these days. They're putting goddamn fentanyl in everything."

"I'm just so glad it worked, I wasn't sure what was wrong with you! What the heck happened?"

I rubbed my forehead with my fingers. "Grimes got me."

"What?" Dot whipped her head around. "Where is he?"

"Gone. And Grace went with him," I said slowly as it gradually came back to me: Grace freezing up. The knife at my throat. And then—"She dosed me," I said indignantly. "She could've killed me!"

"Nah. Syringe is almost full," Portia said, holding it up. "She just gave you a little beauty sleep."

She and Skeeter hovered behind Dot, appearing to enjoy this a little too much for my taste. "Help me up?" I asked, holding out a hand.

The three of them hauled me to my feet. I stood there for a few seconds, trying to regain my balance. It felt like I was standing on the deck of a ship, the alley lurching beneath me in a way I really didn't care for.

"Focus, kiddo," Portia said, snapping her fingers in front of my face.

"Ease up, Portia," Dot said. "She's had a rough go of it."

I felt something on my back and reached around; when I drew my hand back, it came away wet. I held my bloody fingers up and stared at them, puzzled, as Dot shrieked, "Oh my God, Amber, are you hurt? Honey, let me check you!"

They all examined my lower back. "Just some scratches," Portia announced. "Not too deep. Shouldn't even need stitches."

"So we're not seeing a serial killer today?" Skeeter asked, sounding disappointed.

"Trust me, it's a lot less fun than you'd think," I mumbled thickly.

"Any chance you saw which way they went?" Dot asked anxiously. "Now we really should call the cops, right?"

I frowned, suddenly remembering the last thing Grace had said. *Kat is lying to me. She's working with my parents.*

Could that possibly be true?

I bent over and heaved; they all jumped back.

"Goddammit!" Portia snapped. "These are Louboutins! Don't you dare puke on them."

"Sorry," I gasped, hands on my knees.

Dot tentatively reached over and rubbed small circles on my back. "Poor thing. Do either of you have any water?"

Portia produced a small bottle from her purse and handed it over, an expression of distaste on her face. I gratefully rinsed out my mouth and spit. Took another few sips and tried to hand back the bottle. Portia wrinkled her nose and said, "All yours. Knock yourself out."

"Thanks." I slowly drank some more. I hated feeling logy like this; it was why I never did drugs. "So Grace texted you?"

"Well, I think it was her. It came from an unknown number."

"Yup, that's her." My mind was slowly revving back into gear. So even though Grace had dosed me, she'd sent the others to help. Which meant maybe she'd just been trying to protect me, in her own twisted way. And now she was going to try to deal with her father on her own.

The problem was, remembering how she'd frozen, the sheer terror in her eyes? I wasn't entirely sure she'd be able to. "You're right, Dot," I said. "We should call the cops. Maybe see if Lon can log it as an anonymous tip."

"Okay. Yes, good," Dot said. "I just hope Grace is okay."

"Who's Grace?" Skeeter asked.

"That hot blonde from the other day," Portia explained. "You sure she needs your help? Seemed like she could handle herself."

"I'm sure she thinks so. Still, looping in the cops can't hurt."

"We can't let that monster get away," Dot said decisively.

"Exactly." While Dot stepped away to call, I leaned against the dumpster. Which was gross, but I didn't fully trust my legs yet. As I waited, I reviewed everything again in my mind.

Especially what Grace had said about Kat. The more I thought about it, the more it made sense. It was like turning around a pair of binoculars and seeing the same thing in an entirely different way.

And here's what was clear: Kat could have been waiting for me that night in the bar. Maybe she'd been following me for weeks, looking for an opportunity to introduce herself. I'd been sloppy in San Francisco—after all, I had no reason to look over my shoulder anymore. So I'd established routines, including drinking at least three nights a week in that particular watering hole. Which made it the perfect place to lay a trap custom-tailored for me: a pretty girl, crying in a bathroom stall. If I hadn't responded, Kat could've tried something else—spilling a drink on me maybe. Or just coming right out and hitting on me.

The crying was genius, though, because it made me think I'd instigated the encounter. Which was precisely how a pro handled a mark. *Make them work for it, and they fall every time*, I heard my mother's voice say in my head.

And I *had* fallen for it, hook, line, and sinker. This would explain why Kat never seemed to have cash available, why she put everything on a credit card (probably a stolen one; I'd never noticed if she alternated cards, but I would in her position). And nine times out of ten, I paid for everything.

I pictured Kat going through my stuff when I was out, trying to get the access codes for my bank accounts. Convincing me to sign on with her (fake) fancy money guy. Maybe even stealing checks. All the shit that my parents had taught me growing up. Thank God I'd transferred the money off that electronic wallet Grace had given me; otherwise, Kat might've gotten her hands on it months ago.

As for my parents, meeting up with us in Vegas? They'd probably grown frustrated that the con was taking such a long time. So they decided to go for one big score, with all three players working the mark.

Working me.

I wondered if Kat was even gay, or if that had been part of the act. I flashed on her kissing me, holding me . . . was it all just for show?

"I really thought she loved me."

"What?" Portia asked, a vape pen paused halfway to her mouth.

"Nothing," I mumbled. I was spinning out. It felt like the whole world had shifted when I wasn't looking.

And then Dot gasped into the phone, "What?"

I squeezed my eyes shut, hoping that when I opened them, I'd be back in my bed—any bed, really. Ideally, one very far away from all of this. "What now?" I asked wearily.

"Okay, thanks, Lon," Dot said faintly. Hanging up, she turned to us, eyes wide. "So I told them that Gregory Grimes was alive and had kidnapped his daughter."

"Let me guess," I sighed. "They didn't believe you."

"It's worse than that!" Dot said, her voice pitching up an octave. "Gina was the victim at the motel."

"Oh no." I winced, remembering the girl sobbing in Dot's office.

"Poor kid," Skeeter said, crossing themselves.

"It gets worse." Dot sounded breathless again. "An anonymous tip came in about the killer. Apparently, the caller told them that Grace Grimes bought the motel where her brother had been staying. They said there was evidence of two other murders hidden inside, women killed in Arizona and Colorado over the past couple days." Dot drew a deep breath and said, "The cops think Grace killed them. There's a SWAT team heading to the Buggy right now."

— — —

"Holy shit. He put a target on her back," I said slowly. "Cut off her options and made it so Grace has to leave everything behind."

"So what do we do?" Dot asked.

"You said she texted you," I said. "But she's with him. Did he not take her phone?"

Dot shrugged. "Maybe not? He went to prison decades ago; he's probably never seen a smartphone. And she's so good with computers, I'm sure she figured something out."

"Should we try to call her?"

"Already did," Dot said, waving her phone. "No answer."

"Shit." I looked at her helplessly. "I don't know."

We stared at each other for a minute. I really needed to lie down and try to sort through everything. My head was still thick from the drugs, making every thought feel like it was happening in slow motion.

"Well, this has been fun and all, chickadees," Portia finally said, sounding bored. "But I've got a client to punish, so unless you need me, I'm heading out."

"I have work, too," Skeeter said apologetically. "But I can call in sick, Dottie, if you need help? You just let me know."

I straightened. "It's cool. You two can go. Thanks for helping."

"You sure?" Portia asked skeptically.

"Yeah, we got this." I motioned with my head. "I'd really like to get out of this alley, though."

"A-fucking-men to that," Portia said, frowning down at her outfit. "All of this is getting dry-cleaned. I can't risk my dungeon smelling like a White Castle dumpster."

The four of us walked (well, for me it was more of a stagger) back to the parking garage. Portia and Skeeter got off the elevator a floor below ours. Portia offered a little wave over her shoulder as the doors were closing, calling out, "You bitches better call if it gets exciting!"

"I'm okay to drive this time, kiddo," Dot offered as we approached the car. "You're still looking a little green around the gills."

"Oh, I insist," I said, handing her the keys. I collapsed in the passenger seat and leaned against the headrest. It was taking considerable effort to keep my eyes open, but I worried that if I closed them again, I'd be out for the rest of the night.

Dot didn't start the car right away. Staring out the windshield blankly, she finally said, "Grace is going to try to deal with him herself, isn't she?"

I nodded. "Yeah, I think so. That's her MO."

"Do you think she can?" Dot asked, turning to face me.

I shook my head. "I kind of doubt it. The thing is, she had him in that alley, but she froze. I don't know if she'll be able to go through with it."

"So we'll help her," Dot said, sounding surprisingly calm.

"Dot, no. You're getting married. You can't be dealing with this right now—"

Dot waved me silent. "Did you know that when my dad died, it was three days before anyone told me? He'd left me in the motel room by myself—room twelve, actually, at the Getaway. The rule was, I wasn't allowed to leave the room alone. So every morning I'd make the bed, drink a little water, and then sit there all day, waiting for him to come home. Jessie finally heard through the grapevine that he'd passed and came to check on me. I was starving by then."

"Oh, Dot," I said, laying a hand on her arm. Jessie had told me that Dot's dad was a gambler who drank himself to death, but she'd left out this part. "I'm so sorry."

"Yes, well." Dot blinked, as if forcing back tears. "I was eight years old. And you know what that taught me?"

"What?" I asked.

"That you can't get through life without help. The key is more people, not less. You need to build yourself a net of folks who will come running if you're in trouble."

"It's funny," I said. "I kind of think that now, too, thanks to you."

"That's sweet, kiddo." Dot managed a wan smile. "Now, the thing about our Grace is that she's still sitting on that bed, waiting for someone. She doesn't think she has a net because she lived without one for so long. But she's wrong. She has us. And we're going to save her."

I stared at her. "Are you sure?"

"Of course. After all, she's basically family, right?" Dot put her hand on top of mine and squeezed. "So let's go get our girl, okay?"

"Yeah," I said. "You're right."

"So where to?" Dot asked, starting the ignition.

I didn't have a clue. But I did know Dot was right—whatever we came up with, we'd need help.

And I had a score to settle.

"Back to the Mayhem," I said decisively. "Tell Marcella to meet us there, if she's up for it."

"She will be," Dot said.

"It's cool if she's not. I know she's never been a huge fan of Grace."

"But she's a fan of us, and that should be enough. Should I rally the rest of the Fatal Femmes, too?" Dot asked, backing out of the space.

"Definitely." The seeds of a plan were starting to take shape in my mind. "We're going to need everyone."

Dot nodded briskly. "Okay, then. Let's go assemble our net."

— — —

"Tell me again why we're doing this?" Marcella asked.

"Because Grace needs us, and she's our friend," Dot said. Off Marcella's look, she amended, "Well, my friend. And her dad killed Gina, so if nothing else, you should be raring for some payback."

"I'd love payback, but I also don't want to end up dead." Marcella leaned against the desk in Dot's back office at the Mayhem. We'd spent the past ten minutes explaining the plan I'd come up with, and she was turning out to be a far more skeptical audience than Dot. She must have showered right before coming over because her curls were still damp and she wasn't wearing any makeup.

I, on the other hand, was exuding a very pungent "eau de dumpster."

"Seriously," Marcella said, making a waving motion with her hand. "Take another step back. You reek so bad it's making my eyes burn."

"Sorry," I mumbled. "I would've changed, but the woman who pretended to be my girlfriend while helping my parents con me is probably still in my room."

Marcella said, "Wait, what?"

"Oh, honey, is that true?" Dot exclaimed.

"Right," I said, rubbing my forehead with one hand. "I must've forgotten to mention that. Grace told me, right before she pumped me full of downers. Although I kind of already knew. Just hadn't been able to admit it to myself." Looking back, it was so obvious. The way Kat had come up with that scavenger hunt story in the cab. Pushing me to invest with her mysterious "money manager." Even the small gifts, like the (probably fake) Rolex, stuff that would sell me on her rich-girl backstory—classic con move. And I'd fallen for it.

"That bitch," Marcella said, pushing off the desk. "I *knew* there was something off about her. I'll go kick her out right now."

"It's okay," I said, holding up a hand. "I'll handle Kat later. Right now I'm more worried about Grace."

"You really think Grimes would hurt his own kid?" Dot asked.

I shrugged. "I don't know. But Grace told me her mom turned him in, and she hasn't had contact with him since she was ten, so he might not be feeling particularly familial."

"His own wife turned him in? That's pretty boss," Marcella said.

"Yeah, it is," I said slowly. Something had occurred to me that might help the plan, but I wanted to turn it over in my mind before sharing it.

"You sure Grace even wants our help?" Marcella said skeptically. "I mean, isn't this kind of her thing?"

"We're her net," Dot said, crossing her arms.

"Her what?"

"Her safety net, basically," I explained. "You're right, Grace probably thinks she can handle this herself. But I'm not so sure. I think family is her blind spot."

"Ain't that true for everybody?" Dot nodded.

Marcella bit her lip. "Just how dangerous is this guy? Because his son was fucking terrifying."

"I hate to say it, but Gregory Grimes might be worse," Dot replied hesitantly.

I threw Dot a look; maybe it wasn't the best idea to share all the gory details? I for one wasn't entirely sure I wanted to hear them.

"Anyone who helps should know," Dot said decisively, meeting my eyes. "That's only fair, right?"

"Right," I reluctantly agreed.

"Okay, then. They called him 'gruesome' for a reason. Grimes was a medical supplies salesman, so he spent a good chunk of the year on the road. He would capture a woman—usually a sex worker—"

"Of course," Marcella snorted. "Asshole."

"And then he'd keep them wherever he was staying. One young woman was saved by firefighters when the cabin Grimes was using had an electrical fire."

"I didn't know there were any survivors," I said, surprised.

"Probably because there weren't, really," Dot said grimly. "Poor thing had been kept in that bathtub for weeks. Every night he'd come back and, well . . ."

"Well, what?" I finally asked, feeling pretty damn sure I didn't want to hear the answer. If I was going up against this monster, though, I should probably know as much as possible about him.

"Why is it always a bathtub?" Marcella muttered.

I threw her an empathetic look as Dot continued. "When they rescued her, they said she barely looked human anymore. Her ears, eyeballs, fingers . . . most of her, really, had been carved off. Grimes was keeping the parts in the freezer. He'd cauterize the wounds and keep her packed in ice with IV fluids while he went to work. She ended up killing herself shortly after being saved. Just didn't want to go on like that."

"Jesus," Marcella breathed. "That is some fucked-up shit."

I swallowed hard. "I'm guessing I don't want to know why he was keeping her body parts in the freezer?"

Dot shook her head vigorously. "You really don't. The worst part is, she was the only one they found, so they didn't even realize he was a serial killer. Not until the FBI got that tip—from Grace's mom, apparently—about the bodies in their backyard. I guess Grimes would bring home whatever was left of those poor girls, then bury them."

We sat there for a minute, processing. "Well. That's fucking terrifying," I finally said. My stomach lurched again as I remembered his breath hot on my neck. I swallowed hard against the bile rising up my throat.

"So why don't we just let Grace handle this?" Marcella said dubiously. "I mean, no offense, but he sounds pretty fucking dangerous."

"Tough to handle things as his prisoner," I said.

"And we can't bet on her being able to get away. I'm not just gonna stand by and let her take all the risk," Dot said firmly. "Wouldn't be able to live with myself, to tell the truth."

"Me either," I agreed. "Besides, when else am I going to have the opportunity to execute one of my brilliant plans?"

"You two are nuts, you know that?" Marcella sighed.

"You want to sit this one out, we can make it work," I said.

"And miss all the fun? Screw that." Marcella squared her shoulders.

"Good girl," Dot said, giving her a quick squeeze. "Now I gotta start making calls to set everything up. I've got the perfect spot in mind, and the owner owes me a favor."

I held up my wallet, offering it to her. "Anything you need, put it on my card, okay?"

"You got it, kiddo," Dot said, taking the wallet before going out to the reception area.

Which left me and Marcella. I cleared my throat and said, "This is turning out to be a hell of a bridal week, huh?"

Marcella shrugged. "I've seen worse."

I laughed. "I call bullshit on that. But let's make sure this murderous bastard doesn't ruin Dot's wedding. Yeah?"

"Damn straight," Marcella said. "But just so we're clear, this is the last time I help catch a murdering fuckhead."

"Never say never," I joked weakly. Seeing her expression, I asked, "What?"

She shook her head. "About what I said earlier . . . it came out wrong."

"It's cool," I said. "I figured you didn't mean it."

"Oh, I meant it," she corrected. "I know it's not your fault, Amber, but I can't stop thinking that you attract this shit."

I opened my mouth to retort, but she wasn't wrong. So instead I shrugged. "I get it. I'm starting to think that, too."

We were standing in silence when Dot swept back into the room, looking much perkier. "All set! I got the perfect setup—you're gonna love it."

"That's great, Dot," I said, struggling to insert enthusiasm into my voice.

"Lots to do, though." She bit her lip. "I better get my clipboard. We're going to meet there in an hour."

I checked the clock. "You think we'll have enough time?"

"Might have to pull an all-nighter, but we'll make it happen." Dot handed me a key. "Go get cleaned up in my place."

"That's okay," I said, deciding something. "I'll go back to my room."

"You sure?" Marcella said.

"Yeah, hon. Might not be the best time to deal with those a-holes," Dot said with concern.

"It's actually the perfect time," I said resolutely. "Because those a-holes are going to help us."

CHAPTER TWENTY-SIX

HUNT THE MAN DOWN

My parents stared at me. They were seated side by side on the bed in their Mayhem motel room—the room that technically they should have vacated already. But it had been such a relief to find them there, I'd opted not to point that out. I'd spent the past few minutes laying out my plan, which, when I said it out loud, did sound kind of insane. Still, I kept up the front I'd walked in with, that everything was under control. "Any questions?"

My mom actually raised her hand and said, "Emily, honey, what on earth have you been doing? You smell positively ghastly."

"Like low tide," my dad agreed.

"That's a long story that's frankly none of your damn business," I said impatiently. "I meant, do you have any questions about the plan?"

"Will you be showering first? Because it sounds like we'll be in close quarters for this, and you know how sensitive I am to odors—"

"Yes, Mom. I will shower and change before we go." Exasperated, I threw up my hands. "You were listening to the rest of it, right?"

They exchanged a look, then shifted their attention back to me. "I'm sorry, Emily, I'm confused," my dad said. "You want us to do what now?"

"It's a con." Despite what Dot had said, I'd decided against filling them in on all the details. Even if they were desperate enough to participate in a swoop and squat, that was still a far cry from messing with a serial killer. And also, fuck them for trying to con me. So I'd only provided the broad strokes of what they'd be responsible for. "Classic Joliet ragtime setup."

"You said you weren't on the grift anymore," my mother said, eyeing me.

"Yeah, well, I lied." I didn't feel like going into the whole thing; better if they just bought that. It was what they were most likely to believe anyway.

"I must say, Emily—"

"Amber," I said, fighting a wave of impatience as I glanced at my watch again; the minutes were flying by, and I could practically feel our window of opportunity slipping away. For all I knew, Grimes had Grace miles away by now. Or worse, she was stowed in a bathtub. I repressed a shudder and said, "I go by Amber now."

"Well, *Amber*," my mother said, making it clear what she thought of my new name, "why would you come to us, after claiming to have washed your hands of your only family?"

"Nice," I said. "Really love the tremor in your voice. That definitely helped sell it."

"If you're going to be like that—" my mother sniffed.

"Honey, don't hurt your mother's feelings," my dad chided, wrapping an arm around her. I noted that he was no longer wearing a cast on his arm, so apparently that injury had been a lie, too.

"Look." I gritted my teeth; this was harder than I'd imagined, and I'd pictured it being pretty awful. "I need some of your special skills to pull this off." Which was true. I didn't have time to enlist anyone else; right now, they were my best shot for the plan to work.

"I think we'll pass, dear," my mom said curtly.

My father appeared ready to argue, but she threw him a look and he clamped his mouth shut. My mom patted his knee and added, "After all, your father needs to rest. He's still healing."

"Is he?" I said, crossing my arms. "Then where's the cast?"

"He took it off to shower," my mother said smoothly. "He was just about to put it back on when you showed up. Isn't that true, dear?"

My dad smiled weakly and got off the bed, grabbing the air cast from the bureau. He made a big show of wincing as he eased it back on, saying, "Yup. Had to get that hospital smell off me."

"It wasn't a hospital, it was an urgent care clinic," I said. "You know, I've got a friend who can access hospital records. Should I have her check into yours?"

"Go ahead," my mother said, also crossing her arms. "I swear, the utter lack of trust. And here you are, asking for a favor?"

"Not a favor," I said, holding up a finger. "I'm paying you, remember? And you need the money, unless you were lying about that, too."

"How much?" my mother said cagily.

"You mean, on top of what you've already managed to steal from me?" I said, cocking an eyebrow.

"What? Why, I never!" my mother gasped, clutching her literal pearls.

There was a knock at the door. "Oh, good," I said. "I was beginning to worry."

My parents exchanged a glance. "Who's that?" my mother asked guardedly.

"I need another warm body for this to work," I said, going to the door. "So I guess it's lucky there are so many pros in town." I threw it open to find Kat standing there, fist raised to knock again.

Seeing me, she broke into a wide grin. "Amber! I am so delighted—"

"Cut the shit, Kat," I said. "Or whatever your name is. Come in, we don't have much time."

Kat froze, mouth open. Which I would've enjoyed if I hadn't been seething inside. What I really wanted to do was scream at all of them. Maybe pummel them with my fists, give them a good jab with a cattle prod, or cover them with honey and stick them on an anthill.

Because the more I thought about it, the more betrayed and violated I felt.

"What are you talking about?" Kat finally managed.

I waved her inside. "Get on the bed, next to your idiot partners. I've got a new gig for you."

"A gig? What is—"

"Seriously, stop playing. I know you've all been working together for months." I drew a deep breath and said the most difficult words that have ever come out of my mouth: "And I'm the mark."

My dad, at least, had the good grace to look discomfited. Kat was aghast. "But—"

"Sit." I pointed at the bed. Mutely, Kat went over and plonked down beside my parents. I planted myself in front of them, hands on my hips. "You've been siphoning money out of my bank account for months—small amounts so I wouldn't notice. I'm guessing all the crap you've pulled here was to try to get the rest in one fell swoop. And believe me, I have more than enough evidence to prove it." That last bit was a lie, but what the hell; as long as it convinced them.

A moment of silence as they all stared at me. Then Kat sighed and said without a trace of an accent, "Well, shit. Who told you?"

"Does it matter?" I glared at her. Finding out my parents had tried to con me was bad enough. That's who they were; they couldn't help themselves.

But I'd really thought that Kat loved me. I felt a tremor in my heart and locked it down, hard. I couldn't let those feelings come, not now. I'd deal with them later. For Grace's sake, I had to focus.

Sniffing, my mother said, "What an absurd accusation, Emily. Honestly, I don't know what's gotten into you."

"Like I said, enough." I gritted my teeth, determined not to rise to the bait. "I'll give you another fifty grand if you help with this."

"A hundred," my mother said without missing a beat.

"Really?" I rolled my eyes. "Maybe I just hand those files over to the cops. Out of curiosity, how many outstanding warrants do the three of you have?"

"You'd send your own parents to jail?" my mother asked.

"In a fucking heartbeat," I snarled. "But I'd rather have you help voluntarily. So I'm willing to pay."

"Honey," my dad said, looking aggrieved. "I'm so sorry, but we were in quite a pinch."

"I don't care," I said. "Fifty. Take it or leave it."

"Seventy-five," my mother said.

I hesitated, which was largely a feint. A significant chunk of my childhood was spent watching my mother haggle for everything; she'd regularly gotten restaurant tabs discounted or completely covered by claiming there was a hair (plucked from her own head) in the food. But I couldn't afford to waste time. "Sixty," I said. "Best offer."

I watched as they all held a silent conversation. One thing about my parents, they were quite a team. Decades of pulling cons together meant they could basically read each other's minds.

But then, I'd spent plenty of time doing the same. And I already knew their answer was a foregone conclusion. After all, my innate greed and proclivity for unnecessary risks hadn't come out of nowhere. Seeing Kat engaged in that silent chat with them sparked another feeling, though: jealousy. It was like she was their kid and I was an outsider.

I was definitely going to need a ton of therapy if I survived this. I sighed heavily and got to my feet. Palms up, I said, "Oh well, your loss. I'll find someone else."

"Fine," my mother said, in the same moment my father said, "Of course we'll help you, dear."

"Money up front," my mother added quickly.

"Yeah, right!" I laughed. "Who do you think raised me? I pay when the gig is over."

"How do we know you'll pay?"

"You don't," I said curtly. "Take it or leave it. Worst-case scenario, you'll have what you already got off me."

"And the files?"

"And the files." I avoided Kat's eyes as they held another silent conversation.

"Fine," my mother said wearily, as if this was all a huge imposition. "I suppose you leave us no choice."

"Looks like the band is getting back together!" my dad exclaimed, jovially clapping his hands.

Kat didn't say anything. She still hadn't met my eyes, which kind of pissed me off. But then again, there really wasn't anything she could say. Except sorry. And no amount of sorry would ever make up for what she'd done to me.

I glanced at my Rolex, which I fully intended to throw into a volcano when all this was over. Grimes had grabbed Grace a couple hours ago, and I could practically hear a clock ticking in my mind.

"I'll text a list of what to bring. If you don't have something, let me know and I'll see what I can do. Or hell, just steal it, the way you usually do."

"Really, Amber," my mother sniffed. "And might I ask when this is happening?"

"Meet me in the parking lot tomorrow morning at six a.m."

"Six a.m.!" my mom exclaimed. "Does it have to be so early?"

"Yeah, it does. And if you're not there?" I leveled a stern gaze at each of them in turn. "I set the cops on you. Got it?"

"We won't let you down, honey," my dad said, offering a salute.

"Well, that would be a first," I scoffed.

"Will you be coming back to the room?" Kat asked.

"Stay here for fifteen minutes while I shower and get my stuff," I said coldly. "Then it's all yours. I probably won't sleep tonight anyway."

"Amber—"

"I'm having the locks changed in San Francisco, too," I said, cutting her off. "Hopefully there's nothing there you give a shit about because as soon as I get back, it all goes out on the street."

I turned on my heel and left the room before she could answer.

— — —

I would've loved a long, luxurious shower, but there wasn't time for that. So instead, I soaped up and rinsed off as quickly as possible, hopefully enough to eliminate the dumpster stink. The entire time, I carried on a conversation with an imaginary Grace in my head. True to form, she shot down every aspect of my plan.

It was weirdly comforting and kept me from ruminating obsessively about Kat and my parents.

Despite how little she'd shared, I'd gleaned that Grace's dad was her own personal bogeyman: the scary, authoritarian monster who had dominated her childhood. Of course she couldn't see him clearly. To her, he probably seemed preternaturally powerful.

And yeah, he was scary, but also old and out of touch. And I could use that. To pull a successful con, you had to know your mark, and I had a pretty good sense of who this murderous sociopath was. So in my head, I explained to Grace, *Listen. Your dad came to Vegas so he could find out what happened to Gunnar, right? And to try to track down you and your mom.*

Imaginary Grace inclined her head in acknowledgment.

So there's no way he could've had a plan yet.

He's had a couple days to come up with one, she pointed out.

Sure, but when you were growing up, was everything planned out in detail? Based on what I knew about his kids—and about serial killers in general—they tended to be hard-core control freaks. So Gregory Grimes had to be feeling seriously off kilter and out of his element.

Father was definitely a planner, she conceded.

Exactly. And right now he's in a world filled with tech he doesn't understand, and he's older, and weaker, and doesn't have anyone or anything.

He has me.

Not really, because I'm guessing you've probably already tried to kill him, I scoffed.

If you're right, that doesn't bode well for me, imaginary Grace said.

I know, which is why we have to give him the illusion of control to keep him calm. Out loud, I added, "This plan will work. I know it will."

I turned off the shower and toweled dry, trying not to look at Kat's stuff spread across the counter. Catching my reflection in the mirror, I almost startled. I looked worn and far older than my twenty-four years. Which wasn't really surprising, considering the fact that I hadn't had an easy life, was sleep-deprived, and was still coming off a pretty hefty dose of sedatives.

I was tired of getting pushed around, tired of living in fear, tired of people thinking they could shave me, drug me, con me, and hold a knife to my back. I was officially pissed off and ready to make some-one pay.

And worst-case scenario, if we failed and Grimes killed me, at least I'd never have to face Kat or my parents again. Which was a special kind of silver lining.

A knock on the door and then Dot called out, "You ready, kiddo? We got everything set up in my office."

"Coming!" I called back. Giving myself one final look, I leaned in and said, "Let's get this motherfucker."

— — —

Too nervous to sit, I stood behind the desk chair in Dot's office, my hair still wet from the shower. For this part of the plan, I needed help. After all, I was supposed to be dead. And if Grimes believed otherwise, it would only make things worse for Grace.

Dot sat on the edge of her chair, looking pale and nervous. Mar-cella was perched on the desk, glowering down at the phone set between us. "You sure you're up for this?" I asked again.

Dot smiled weakly at me. "You questioning my acting ability, toots?"

"No, it's just . . . I don't know. He's pretty scary."

"He's just a man, like any other." Dot waved her hand dismis-sively. "Thinks far too highly of himself and believes whatever he wants is his to take. Don't you worry. I got this."

"Okay. Here we go." I drew a deep breath and dialed Grace on the speakerphone.

It rang three times and then went to voicemail. True to form, Grace used the default robot that told you to leave a message. I gritted my teeth and dialed again.

It was answered almost immediately, but there was nothing but silence on the other end of the line. Dot cleared her throat and said, "Hello?"

"Who is this?"

Dot threw me a glance; I shook my head. I'd rather not give him any more information than necessary. "A friend of Grace's," she said. "May I please speak with her?"

"My, don't you have lovely manners," he said approvingly. "Am I to assume this is Dot, renowned owner of the Mayhem and Getaway motels?"

Dot sucked in her breath sharply, and the remaining color drained from her face. I mouthed, "Are you okay?"

She closed her eyes, nodded once, and then said in a level voice, "Speaking. Would it be possible for me to talk to Grace, please?"

A low chuckle emanated from the receiver; it made all the hairs on my arms stand up. "I'm afraid Grace can't come to the phone right now."

Marcella swore under her breath. I felt a chill; had he killed her? Were we already too late?

"May I ask when she'll be available?" Dot said smoothly.

A long pause. I clenched my hands together in front of my chin. If he'd killed her, I would hunt him down.

"I really couldn't say. She's indisposed at the moment."

I scribbled something on the desk pad and spun it around. Dot read it and then nodded. "Oh, that's a shame. I was really hoping to give her the good news about her mother."

"Mother?" he said suspiciously. "It was my understanding that Mother had passed."

"Oh, no, of course not!" Dot's laugh sounded forced, but the fact that she'd managed one at all was impressive. "The nursing home called, and a room opened up for her after all. I wanted to make sure Grace was aware."

"I see. And why would this facility have contacted you, in lieu of my daughter?"

"When they couldn't get ahold of her, they rang me." I gave her a thumbs-up. She nodded and continued. "She travels quite a bit, and since we're neighbors, I'm kind of her doorman. Sign for packages, take messages, that sort of thing."

"A care facility, you say?"

"Yessir. But they said it's very important that Grace call back as soon as possible. These rooms don't come available very often, and they go quickly."

"Hm. And where would Mother be moving from?"

"Well, now, I'm not sure I feel right providing that information to a total stranger. Would you please pass along the message for me?"

"Certainly."

The line disconnected.

We stared at each other. "Goddamn, Dottie," Marcella finally said. "You deserve an Oscar."

"Yes, I might've missed my calling," she said, blushing slightly. "Do you think it worked?"

"I hope so." I checked my watch and then went to the door to peer out the plate-glass window that overlooked the parking lot. My parents and Kat stood beside my car; based on their body language, they were having some sort of argument. Hopefully not about leaving, because if they called my bluff, there was nothing I could do about it. Worst-case scenario, I could make the plan work without them, but it would be much riskier for everyone involved.

I was debating going outside to put the fear of God in them when the phone on the desk rang. I looked at Dot. "Ready?"

"Oh, yeah," she said, hitting the button to pick up. "Hello?"

"What are you doing?" Grace snapped. She sounded angry—and very much alive, which was a relief.

"A space has opened up in the facility you were hoping to get your mother into. However, she would need to be checked in tomorrow morning, and you would have to be there personally to fill out the paperwork. What would you like me to tell them?"

A long silence, until I wondered if the connection had been broken. Finally, Grace said, "I would not want to put Mother at risk."

"Oh, no, dear, she would be just fine," Dot said. "You know they wouldn't let anything bad happen to her there."

Hopefully, that was clear enough for Grace to grasp, but oblique enough to slide past Grimes.

"And I have to be the one to sign the paperwork?"

"Oh, yes. You have power of attorney, so it absolutely has to be you. They were very clear on that."

Hushed voices on the other end. I crossed my fingers and prayed that he took the bait. Finally, Grace came back on and said, "What time?"

"Well, they're hoping to get her in as soon as possible. Ideally tomorrow morning around eight?"

Another pause. We waited, straining to hear what was being said in the background. Finally, Grace came back on and said, "We can meet you there."

"We?" Dot said innocently.

"Yes. Father will be coming as well." A beat, then she added, "I wish you wouldn't involve yourself with this, Dot. I know you must be busy."

"No trouble at all, dear. I have plenty of help," Dot said. "I will collect your mother, and we will see you at eight a.m. I'll text you the address."

"All right. And Dot?"

"Yes, dear?"

"I'm sorry about Amber." A click as the line disconnected.

"Well, now. That went much better than expected," Dot said.

"You're a champ," I said, feeling genuinely awed. "That was amazing."

"That was the easy part," Marcella said. "Now comes the hard shit."

She wasn't wrong. "You both know what you need to do?" They nodded. "Okay, then. Let's go set it up."

CHAPTER TWENTY-SEVEN

BLIND SPOT

Dot had been right about pulling an all-nighter: it took a significant chunk of the next twelve hours to get everything ready. Maybe this was a more elaborate plan than the situation required. But I'd pulled off something similar back in Kansas City when I was eighteen, and took comfort in the familiarity. Plus, it was straight out of my parents' playbook, which would help them do their part.

At least, I hoped so.

Regardless, Dot came through smashingly, as always. She'd managed to wrangle not only her Fatal Femmes group, but also a wide assortment of other Vegas folks, mostly set designers, theater techs, and performers. Her extensive network of friends and contacts never ceased to amaze.

Toni showed up around two a.m., wheeling a rack of costumes. They were immediately descended upon by everyone who had agreed to help out. She came over to where Marcella and I were setting up the tables that had been loaned by a caterer. "Hot damn, ladies," she said approvingly, hands on her hips. "This is something else!"

"Thanks for the costumes, Toni," I said, trying not to react as Marcella wrapped her arms around Toni's neck and gave her a deep kiss.

"It was nothing," she said dismissively. "Had this rack in storage from a show last year, just glad I hadn't already donated them. You need anything else?"

"Nah, I think we're almost done." I scanned the room. The majority of people had grabbed their outfits and were drifting away, saying goodbye to Dot, who stood by the door supervising.

"Well, you two better be careful," Toni said. "I don't know that I approve of any of this."

"I'll be fine, baby," Marcella said, wrapping an arm around Toni's waist. "You know I can handle myself."

Toni still wore a look of concern. Turning to me, she said, "You watch out for her, yeah?"

"I promise," I said. "She's not going to be in any danger." Which wasn't entirely true, but Marcella had insisted we tell Toni only the bare minimum.

Toni nodded. "All right then. I'm supposed to fly to L.A. in the morning to source some fabric, but if you need me here, I can cancel."

Marcella nuzzled her shoulder. "Nah. We got this."

"If you say so." Toni sighed, still looking uncertain. "You coming home with me tonight?"

Marcella glanced at me and then said, "I gotta help finish up. Probably better if I crash at my place so I don't wake you."

"Then I'll see you tomorrow night. Call to let me know how it goes, 'kay, babe?"

Marcella nodded, and they kissed again. I turned away, trying to ignore the pit that had yawned open inside me. It had been hard enough watching them canoodle when I still thought I had a girlfriend. Now, knowing I'd just been a mark, well . . . it was a hundred times worse. Plus, things had felt stilted since our conversation in the back office. I could tell that something had shifted for Marcella. Whenever she spoke to me now, it felt like chatting with an acquaintance, not a friend.

To give them some privacy, I went over to where Dot was directing people to hang a series of framed watercolors she'd produced out of nowhere. "Wow," I said. "It's really coming together. Thanks again, Dot. This is incredible. I can't believe it was an empty space a few hours ago."

"Right? Paco's the best. Won a Tony a few years back for set design. We're lucky he was in town for the latest Cirque revamp," she said. "Couple more weeks, this whole place will be booked up, so we got in under the wire. Skeeter, hang that a little lower, hon."

Skeeter nodded, moved the nail down a few inches, and hammered it in while we watched. Dot crossed off another item on her clipboard and said, "Almost done. We might get out of here earlier than I thought, not that I'll be sleeping tonight. I just can't stop worrying about poor Grace."

"She'll be fine," I said with more confidence than I felt. "I think Grimes wants her mom more than anything. And he knows he needs Grace in one piece to get to her. He won't hurt her before tomorrow."

Dot shook her head. "Well, I just hope you're right, kiddo."

"What does Jim think?" I asked.

Dot hesitated, then said, "I haven't told him. Didn't want to worry him, 'cuz if he knew, he'd rush back."

"He's lucky to have you," I said, then added awkwardly, "By the way, I'm really sorry. I kind of flaked on all the traditional bridesmaid stuff."

Dot laughed. "Are you kidding, hon? It's like I said the other night. I'm not a traditional bride, and we're not traditional people.

Catching two bad guys in one week? Hell, that's the best wedding gift ever. Besides, the wedding planning was done and dusted weeks back. My gal Steph handled it for me."

"That's good," I said. "Still. I feel bad."

"Don't you dare," Dot admonished me. "I'm just sorry you're having such a terrible week. You need anything else, you let me know."

"My offer still stands," Marcella said, coming over. "I'll go kick her teeth out right now."

"Tempting, but we need Kat to be presentable for tomorrow," I said grimly.

"You sure involving them is a good idea?" Dot asked worriedly.

I nodded. "Yeah. They're awful people, but that's what makes them good at stuff like this. I trust them to pull this off."

"And if they don't show?" Marcella asked.

"Then I'll handle it." I was really hoping that wouldn't be the case, though. One of the few advantages we had was that Grimes thought I was dead. Maintaining that misconception was a critical element of the plan. I checked my watch: almost two-thirty a.m. It was starting to feel like I'd never sleep a full night again. "So what do you think? Should we crash out for a couple hours?"

"I'm definitely gonna try," Dot said. "Don't want to look like death warmed over when Jim gets back tomorrow afternoon, that might give him a reason to reconsider."

"Never happen," I said. "And you know it."

"Still, I'm wiped. See you gals tomorrow." She gave us each a hug and then went to say goodbye to the few folks who remained.

Marcella and I stood there for a minute. "Want to grab a drink?" I offered awkwardly.

Marcella shrugged. "Sure. Might be our last chance for a buzz, if this asshole murders us tomorrow."

"Thanks for the vote of confidence," I muttered.

"You know me, always an optimist. There's a place right around the corner."

We walked there in silence. The crowd was sparse due to the late hour, and we managed to score a table by a giant fern. I stirred my margarita and took a sip; it wasn't bad, for a casino drink.

Marcella had ordered the same. "Cheers," she said, raising her glass.

"To not dating grifter assholes," I said.

She threw me a rueful smile and clinked, saying, "To not dating grifter assholes." She took a sip and then said, "We're not counting you, right?"

"I mean, I'm a grifter, but hopefully not an asshole."

"Hm," she said, eyeing me. "Jury's still out on that."

"Fair enough." I pretended to think for a second, then said, "To not dating five-foot-eight blonde fake-German grifting assholes."

"Now that I can get on board with," Marcella said approvingly. We clinked again, and she said, "I really am sorry about earlier. Didn't mean to hurt your feelings."

"Don't be," I said. "You're not wrong. I don't know why bad shit keeps happening to me, but it does. And the people around me always get pulled in."

"Still. It was a shitty thing to say."

"A little, yeah." After a second, I added, "Sorry about kissing you earlier."

"Are you?" She raised an eyebrow. "Why? It was a good kiss."

"Yeah, but . . . you and Toni seem really happy."

"We are," Marcella said. "I don't think she'd mind, to be honest. Neither of us is possessive like that."

"Must be nice," I muttered into my margarita.

"Fuck Kat. You deserve better."

"I don't know about that," I mumbled.

"Amber, look at me." Obediently, I raised my eyes to meet hers. Taking my hand, she said, "You're a good person. I mean, you're trying to help Grace even though we both know she's a stone-cold bitch. Trust me. You deserve someone great."

"Thanks." I hesitated, then said, "I'm glad you found Toni. She seems great."

"She is." Marcella released my hands and shifted back slightly. "She's helped a lot with my recovery."

"That's good." I realized I was nodding dumbly and made myself stop. "I wouldn't want to mess with that."

"Oh, you couldn't."

"Gee, thanks."

"I don't mean it like that," Marcella said earnestly. "Really. The thing about you and me is, we're too alike. I was so pissed and hurt after you left. I kind of thought we were meant to be. I know how dumb that sounds, but it just felt like we clicked, y'know?"

"Yeah, I know," I said. "I felt the same way."

"Then why'd you just take off?"

"I don't know," I admitted. "I guess maybe I got a little freaked out? I mean, I told myself I was just trying to keep you safe—"

"Which was bullshit," Marcella interjected pointedly.

"Yeah," I said. "It was."

"And deep down, I knew that." Marcella leaned forward again. "Going into treatment made me realize that we were both attracted to the damage in each other. That's what we recognized. That's why it felt so right. Because we have the same broken bits inside us."

I squirmed; that felt a little too on the nose. Uncomfortably, I joked, "Sure that *you're* not the therapist in training?"

She laughed. "Oh hell no." After a long beat, she added, "You probably don't want to hear this, but I don't think that's what you're cut out for either."

My hackles rose at that. I snapped, "Why not?"

"I'm not saying never, Amber. It's just . . . I don't know if you've sorted through all of your shit yet. And shouldn't that happen before you try to help other people sort through theirs?"

I hated to admit it, but she had a point. And if I were a bigger person, I'd be able to say so. Instead, I took a big gulp, polishing off the last of my drink. Getting to my feet, I said, "We should get some sleep. Tomorrow's a big day."

"Yeah, sure." Looking wounded, Marcella sucked on her straw. Still focused on her drink, she asked, "So do you really think we can pull it off?"

"Absolutely," I said, trying to sound more certain than I felt.

— — —

Unsurprisingly, I did not sleep. Based on a thorough sweep, Gregory Grimes hadn't left anything in the motel room (although I found an old condom wrapper under the bed that I could have lived without seeing). So I swallowed my discomfort, double-bolted the door, and jammed a chair under the knob for good measure.

Then I lay on the bed, staring at the ceiling and reviewing the plan over and over in my mind. An hour in I considered going out to run sprints, but figured it wouldn't be smart to waste my energy. So instead I spent the remainder of the night spinning out over every detail of my last few months with Kat. I reexamined every conversation, every moment of our relationship, looking for the clues that I'd missed.

Which actually turned out to be more exhausting than running sprints. I finally crawled out of bed at five a.m. and made my way to the dining area, where I downed three espressos, one after another.

Then I went back to my room and sat on the bed until it was time to meet the assholes.

The early morning air was frigid; I shivered as I walked to the parking lot. When I got there, it was empty. My heart sank. Swearing to myself, I stormed to my parents' room and banged on the door, calling out, "You better be in there!"

The door popped open, and my dad beamed at me. "Morning, sunshine! How'd you sleep?"

"I didn't," I said, leaning to see past him. My mom was staring into the mirror over the bureau, adjusting her wig. Kat sat on the bed, already dressed in scrubs. The wave of relief I felt was quickly supplanted by the sourness of seeing them again. I nodded briskly and said, "Let's go."

They followed me to the car in silence. My mom took the front passenger seat while Kat and my dad got in the back. "I hope it's not far," my mother said. "My back has been acting up. These mattresses are awful, frankly. I was going to have a word with the front desk about it."

"You will do no such thing," I snapped. "Just be grateful you're not sleeping in your car. Unless that was bullshit, too?"

None of them answered. I glanced at Kat in the rearview mirror; she was staring out at the passing landscape as if strip malls and pawn shops were fascinating.

Which just pissed me off more. I snapped, "What's your real name, anyway?"

After a beat, she said in a small voice, "Kate. Kate Merritt."

Her accent had vanished entirely. I wanted to kick myself for being such an idiot. "So my parents recruited you to seduce me? Because that's pretty fucking creepy on a lot of levels."

"It wasn't like that," Kat/Kate protested. "I didn't even know you were their kid at the beginning."

"Jesus." Turning to my mom, I said, "How'd you find out about the money?"

"Well, if you must know, Roger saw you at some fancy restaurant in San Francisco," she said. "You remember Roger? Specialized in widows? Anyway, he was sure it was you. You apparently were making a bit of a scene, and they were asking you to pay for damages. You claimed you could buy the place if you wanted."

I winced, vaguely remembering getting banned from a Michelin-starred restaurant my first week in town. Not my finest hour for sure.

"Anyway, Roger charmed the hostess into providing your new name, and from there, we tracked you down."

"Right." I remembered Roger as a particularly oily character my parents had pulled three gigs with. I also remembered them telling me to make sure I was never alone in a room with him, so, yeah—real prince of a guy. "And how do you all know each other?"

They exchanged a glance and then my mother said, "Kate is Jen Merritt's girl. Remember her? Actually, the funny thing is you two did a job together when you were little! Of course you won't remember, but still. Isn't that something?"

"It sure is something," I growled, throwing Kate a dirty look. She avoided my eyes.

"I'm curious, Emily," my mom said innocently. "Where *did* you get all that money?"

Based on her expression, this had been driving her particularly crazy. Which gave me no small measure of satisfaction. Loftily, I said, "Won the lottery."

"Really! Which one?"

I snapped my fingers and said, "No, wait . . . it was an insurance settlement. Actually, now I remember, I inherited it from a distant relative."

"If you don't want to tell us, just say so," my mom sniffed.

"Great. Because it's none of your damn business."

"Rude," my mom said.

"The thing is, sweetheart, we really are in the hole to some scary people," my dad said apologetically from his seat in the back.

"I'll bet," I muttered, turning right. "Story of your life, isn't it?"

"And you wonder why we left you," my mother said quietly.

"What?" I spat, whirling on her. She stared back at me, a challenge in her eyes.

From the back seat, my dad piped up nervously, "Girls? Can we all just try to get along?"

I glared at my mother, who regarded me placidly. But fighting with her now wouldn't accomplish anything. And knowing her, she was just fishing for an excuse to bail on the job. So I gritted my teeth and said, "Sure, Dad. You know, you could've just asked me for a loan."

"Right," my mom scoffed. "As if you would've given us one."

"Well, you could've tried." My hands tightened on the steering wheel. We were getting close to the site, and there was one more thing I wanted to say before we shifted into the mindset for the con. "Out of curiosity, Kate, was any of it real?"

She had the decency to look wretched. "Of course it was real."

"Right." I replied. "I bet you're not even really gay."

"Perhaps we should put a pin in all this," my mother said primly. "You know how I like to get into character."

"Great idea," I muttered. "Do you need me to go over it with you again?"

"Please, Emily. We practically invented this con."

"You definitely didn't."

"Well, we put our own spin on it at least."

"None of that today," I said forcefully. "I mean it. No ad-libbing, no extra theatrics. Just follow the script to the letter. Got it?"

"If you insist," she sniffed. "Although I much prefer to riff."

"Your mom is one heckuva improviser," Dad chimed in from the back seat.

"Knock yourself out on your next job," I said. "But if you want to get paid, you do it *exactly* the way I said."

My mom sighed heavily. "I'm really not sure where you get this bossiness from."

"Gee, I wonder," I muttered, turning into the parking lot. It was already full of cars: Dot's crew, right on time. I eased into a spot at the far end behind a van on the off chance that Grimes might recognize my Audi.

"We're doing it here?" my mom asked, craning her head forward.

"Yes, Mom, we're doing it here." I turned off the car and shifted to face my dad and Kate. "Hopefully we have a couple hours before the mark shows up. But if he gets here early, we need to be ready."

"And who is he again?"

"Not important," I said briskly. In spite of everything, I felt a slight pang; was it truly awful of me not to tell them who they were going up against? Of course, if I did, they were sure to bail. And even though they were all great actors (as evidenced by Kate making me believe she loved me), I didn't trust them to maintain their poise if they knew they would be facing off against Gregory "Gruesome" Grimes.

"If you say so," my mom said. "Although I simply cannot understand all the mystery. Is it someone famous?"

"No, mom, it's no one famous. All you need to know is that he thinks you're his wife who suffers from dementia and who he hasn't seen in a really long time. Okay?"

"I suppose."

"He better not get handsy!" my dad chirped.

"Can we talk, Amber?" Kate asked, her voice pleading. "Just, really quick?"

"Her name is Emily," my mom scoffed. "Honestly, can we please just call her that, now that everything is out in the open?"

"I prefer Amber. And there's nothing to talk about." Across the lot, I spotted Marcella sauntering toward the entrance. "Let's get going. There's still a lot to do."

We all climbed out in silence. I felt jittery, infused with caffeine and the adrenaline rush that kicked in at the start of a job. The sun had fully risen, but it was overcast and cold. I shivered in my thin jacket and tightened the scarf knotted at my throat.

Kate grabbed my elbow, stopping me. Her eyes were full, and she looked pale, like she hadn't slept much either. There was a catch in her voice as she said, "Amber—"

"I can't," I said forcefully, shaking her off. "Not now. I need to focus and so do you. Okay?"

"Sure," she said in a small voice. "I just wanted to say I'm sorry."

"Sorry doesn't help me," I said. "Doing your job will. So c'mon."

- - -

A painted sign above the door read **SUNSET LIVING** in elaborate script, surrounded by olive leaves.

"Is this a theater?" my mom asked, squinting up at the sign.

"Usually," I said.

"Won't that make the mark suspicious?"

I shook my head. "I don't think so. A lot of buildings get repurposed, and the inside should convince him." At least, that's what I was counting on. Because if Grimes picked up on the ruse, my plan would be over before it started.

"Well, it sure looks like a nice place," my dad commented.

"Wouldn't mind ending up somewhere like this in our old age, don't you think, pet?"

"If only we had a daughter who would pay for it," my mom said, shaking her head. "Sadly, we'll probably be living on the streets."

"Who knows," I said. "Maybe Kate will cover it. She's a baroness, you know. Primeval nobility, apparently."

Kate threw me a look, which I met with a stony gaze. I pulled open the door and waved them inside. "Now let's go."

We stepped into a fancy lobby bustling with activity. It looked every inch the posh retirement facility, which was particularly impressive considering the fact that last night it had been a giant empty room.

"My," my mother said approvingly. "This is nice."

"Love the verisimilitude," my dad agreed. "If I didn't know better, I'd think this was the real deal."

"That's the idea," I said. It was a relief to see that in daylight, it looked even better than it had the night before. I'd worried that we wouldn't be able to pull it together in time, but Dot had come through yet again.

Speaking of which, she was currently standing across the room, clipboard in hand, emanating a frenetic energy as she barked orders. "Portia, hon, you gotta wear the scrubs."

Portia was standing in front of her, wearing an ensemble that had definitely been marketed as a "naughty nurse" costume. She propped a hand on her hip and said, "Why? I use this in the dungeon all the time. It's authentic."

"I'm sure, but we need folks to fade into the background, and this—" Dot swept a hand over her. "I mean, c'mon, Portia. You're all he's going to see."

"Fair point," Portia conceded. "Fine, I'll change. Those scrubs do nothing for my ass, though."

"Great. Oh, and make sure to tell BJ to double-check the camera feeds. Thanks, toots." Spotting us, Dot waved me over. "Thank God, Amber, I was starting to worry." She hugged me with her free arm and then turned to my parents and Kate. Jutting her chin up, she said, "Just so y'all know, if I had my way, you'd be strung up by the heels from the top of the Strat. Shame on you."

"Well, I never," my mother gasped.

I motioned for her to shush and said, "Thanks Dot, but it's fine. They feel terrible and are eager to help. Aren't you?" I asked them pointedly.

"Well, of course," my mother said stiffly. "She is *our* daughter, after all."

"You sure as hell don't deserve her," Dot said. "Kat—or whoever the heck you are—you're going to be right here." She pointed to the giant mahogany desk set behind us. "And you two will be stationed in the common room. Amber can take you there, 'cuz if I'm alone with you, I might not be able to keep from saying a few choice words."

My dad had the good sense to look abashed. But judging by the expression on my mom's face, she was ready to throw down. I intervened, taking her arm and saying, "C'mon, Mom. You wanted to get into character, right?"

My mother nodded stiffly, saying loudly as I escorted her from the room, "I must say, Emily, some of your friends are *very* rude."

I gritted my teeth and led her through an arched doorway, down a short hallway, and into an enormous common room. It was filled with round tables draped with expensive-looking linens. Elderly folks were seated everywhere, working on puzzles, playing cards, and eating pudding. Paintings hung along the walls at regularly spaced intervals, and a small café counter set against the rear wall featured a coffee and juice menu. Ambient classical music was being piped through the speakers tucked discreetly in the corners behind potted plants.

"It's perfect," I said, feeling somewhat awed.

"Impressive," my dad said, nodding approvingly.

"I don't know," my mom said with a sniff. "I still think our setup in Columbus was better."

Choosing to ignore her, I guided them to a table by the café counter. Motioning to the chairs that faced the back wall, I said, "Those are for you."

"Make him work for it," my dad said with a nod. "Smart."

"Gee, thanks," I muttered. He was right, though. This way Grimes would have to navigate the entire room before getting close enough to see my mom, which was a critical aspect of the plan.

Just as I was getting them settled, the door beside the café counter opened and Marcella emerged, carrying a bakery box. She tilted her chin at me and started putting muffins into the display case. I nodded back and said to my parents, "Now just stay here, okay? When it's time, Marcella will signal you."

"Who's Marcella?" my mom asked, craning her neck and peering around the room. "My, there are an awful lot of people. Not all getting a cut, are they?"

"Nope. Everyone else is helping out of the goodness of their hearts." Pointing, I added, "That's Marcella behind the coffee counter."

"Oh, is there coffee?" my mother said, perking up. "Your father and I are ravenous. The breakfast buffet at your friend's motel is just disgraceful."

"I could murder a muffin," my dad agreed.

"And perhaps a scone? Or if there's hot food, an omelet would be even better." My mother tugged at her wig of tight gray curls.

"Stop messing with it," I said, annoyed. "It looks fine."

"Honestly, I don't know why this is necessary," my mom complained. "Plenty of older women dye their hair. Who am I supposed to be again?"

"Someone with that color hair," I said pointedly. "All you have to do is sit there and look like you have dementia."

My mom eyed me. "You said this was a Joliet ragtime."

"It is, with a little pig in the poke thrown in," I said. "Okay?"

"I don't see why this is so complicated," she grumbled. "Or why I can't talk. We all know that patter is my greatest gift."

"She is a true siren," my dad chimed in.

"Thank you, sweetheart," my mom said. "Now listen, Emily, what if I tell him that I'm an heiress, and—"

"Just do what I tell you to, okay?" I snapped. "For once in your life?"

"Well. There's no need to get snippy." My mom settled into the chair and crossed her arms. "I am a professional, after all."

"Yeah, I know. Thank you." I clenched my hands into fists to keep from wrapping them around her throat and strangling her. I needed all of them to go along with the plan, and for that, my mother had to be kept placated. "Now hang tight, and I'll get you something to eat."

Pushing back from the table, I stomped to the café counter and braced myself against it with both hands.

"You okay?" Marcella asked with concern.

"Not really," I said. "I need a couple muffins for my pain-in-the-ass parents, preferably with arsenic sprinkled on top."

"Two arsenic muffins, coming right up," Marcella smirked. As she set them on plates, she continued, "So those are your parents."

"Yup."

"Explains a lot."

"Thanks. Grimes better hurry up and get here before I kill them myself," I muttered.

"What are we talking about?" my mom said brightly, popping up in the space between us.

"None of your damn business," I said.

"No need to be rude," my mom said with a frown. "I appreciate a little levity before a job as much as the next person."

"Get back to your place, Mom," I snapped. "He could be here at any minute."

"I just wanted to see why the muffins are taking so long," my mother said plaintively. "Your father is feeling faint."

"Here," Marcella said, shoving the two plates across the counter. "Hope you choke on it."

"Everyone here is so unpleasant," my mother said, taking the plates. "I never would've agreed to help if I'd known how poorly I'd be treated."

"Take comfort in the thought of all the money I'm paying you."

She rolled her eyes at me and walked away regally.

Marcella was smirking at me. "What?" I demanded.

"The way she rolled her eyes was kinda familiar."

"Don't start."

A walkie-talkie crackled behind the counter. We exchanged a look, then Marcella held it to her mouth and pushed the talk button. "Yeah?"

Dot's voice was shrill with nerves and excitement. "Bambi just saw them pull in!"

I checked my watch: seven-thirty a.m. They were early, just as I'd expected. Good thing we'd planned for that. I reached for the walkie, and Marcella passed it to me. Clicking the button, I said, "I'll meet you in the security room."

"You got it, kiddo. Good luck."

"Thanks, Dot."

A beat, then she added, "This is going to work."

I couldn't tell from her tone if it was a statement or a question, but I repeated firmly, "This is going to work."

Handing back the walkie, I said, "All right. I guess we're doing this."

"Guess we are," Marcella agreed. Then she held her hands up to her mouth and called out, "Okay, everyone, get your shit together. It's time!"

The energy in the room ticked up a notch. I turned to go, but Marcella caught my arm and pulled me in to her.

"What—" But before I could finish the question, she'd grabbed my face in both hands and kissed me, long and deep. I was gasping for breath when she pulled back and said, "For luck."

"Thanks," I said weakly, still buzzing. Then I staggered back to my parents' table. My dad had already finished his muffin, and my mom was picking at hers like a bird. "My," she said archly. "*That* certainly was friendly. It's a good thing Kate wasn't here to see it."

"Go to hell, Mom," I said, shaking it off. I drew a deep breath and shifted my attention to my dad. "You all set?"

"All set, sweetheart." My dad threw me a salute, adding, "See you on the other side!"

I felt a surge of emotion; that's what he'd always said before a con. It should've made me feel dirty, or angry, but instead it spurred an unexpected wave of nostalgia. I nodded and said, "See you on the other side."

CHAPTER TWENTY-EIGHT

A LIFE AT STAKE

As I watched, Gregory Grimes opened the front door and held it for Grace. From this angle, we mainly had a view of the tops of their heads. Grace was limping slightly, but otherwise appeared okay.

"He just looks so darn harmless, doesn't he?" Dot said from where she stood beside me.

"Probably how he got away with it for so long," I muttered. We were ensconced in a tiny security room, in front of an array of monitors set up by, of all people, BJ. Apparently he was somewhat of an expert at discreet surveillance, the implications of which I definitely did not want to consider. It looked like all the rooms were covered. Nervously, I asked, "These are set to record, right? We might need that, if it comes down to it."

"Don't worry, we tested it. Now here we go," Dot breathed as Grace and her father walked to the desk where Kate was sitting.

Kate was placidly flipping through a magazine. As they approached, she threw them the same smile that had captivated me on the night we met. I felt my heart lurch and tried to cover it with a frown. "She really is beautiful, hon," Dot said, patting my arm reassuringly. "Hell, I might've fallen for her, too, if I swung that way."

"Won't be making that mistake again," I mumbled.

We could hear Kate's voice surprisingly clearly as she said, "Can I help you?"

"Why yes." Grimes stepped to the desk. His smile was broad and toothy, the rictal grin of a shark. "We understand that there's some paperwork to fill out for my wife, Marjorie?"

"Ah yes, of course," Kate said smoothly. "We're so thrilled to have Mrs. Cabot joining us."

"Cabot?" Grimes's face darkened. "There's been a mistake. Her surname is—"

"Cabot, Father," Grace said with annoyance. I was heartened to see that she appeared unharmed, at least as far as I could tell from this vantage point. And her attitude certainly hadn't been affected; she sounded like her usual cantankerous self. "I have power of attorney."

"That's what we heard from Ms. Roux," Kate said. I had to hand it to her, she was playing the part beautifully. But then, pretending to be someone else was definitely in her wheelhouse. "Ms. Cabot, if you'd please go with Portia to the back office, she can get you sorted."

Portia, who thankfully had changed into standard nursing scrubs and tucked her hair into a bun, stepped around the desk and motioned for Grace to follow. When Grimes started to join, Kate stopped him and said, "Mr. Cabot, if you'd like to go straight to your wife, we've got her settled in our common room with some of the other residents. Her room should be ready shortly."

Grimes hesitated, clearly torn. I held my breath, and Dot reached for my hand and clutched it. This was the moment of truth. Separating

Grace from her dad was a key part of the plan. If he refused, we were up a creek. I was counting on the fact that his desire to enact revenge on his wife would outweigh whatever he wanted from Grace. Plus, someone that mannerly would have trouble going against social norms in a public environment; it would seem rude. And I was betting that even though he was a murdering psychopath, Gregory Grimes was never impolite.

Finally, he nodded and boomed, "Of course! Where did you say I could find my wife?"

"I can show you." Kate gestured toward the archway and added, "They're serving breakfast right now if you're hungry."

"Fabulous!" He clapped his hands together, exuding the bravado of a game show host. It was creepy as fuck, like he was an alien attempting to mimic human behavior without actually understanding it. "Lead the way, young lady!"

I watched as they shifted frames, moving to the monitor that showed the hallway.

"That's my cue," I said, fighting a sudden rush of nerves.

"You got this, toots," Dot said, pulling me into a tight embrace.

I wished I shared her confidence. "Remember," I said. "If I give the signal, we go to plan B. Get everyone out safely, and don't worry about me. Right?"

Dot hesitated but then nodded. "It won't come to that. But don't worry, I got you."

"I know you do." Overcome with emotion, I squeezed her again and said, "You're the best friend I ever had, Dot."

"Aw, I love you, too, hon," Dot said, dabbing at her eyes. "Now don't go getting yourself killed. It's too late for me to find a bridesmaid who fits that dress."

"I'll do my best." Turning away, I squared my shoulders and said, "How do I look?"

"Like a hot old lady," Dot said approvingly. "Now go out there and get him."

The door to the room suddenly popped open, and Portia and Grace walked in.

"What kind of absurd charade is this, Amber?" Grace said, crossing her arms in front of her chest.

"No time to explain," I said. "And you're welcome, by the way."

Grace leaned in and peered at the monitors. "Are those your parents?"

"Dot will fill you in," I said. "Now just sit tight and let me do my thing."

"'Your thing'?" Grace cocked an eyebrow. "I would have preferred that you stay out of this. I am perfectly capable of handling my father."

"Too late," I said, trying not to let her shake my already quavering confidence. "So just buckle up and come along for the ride."

"You ready, toots?" Dot asked in a low voice.

I nodded, tightening my grip on the gun. She held up a finger and counted:

One . . .

Two . . .

On *three,* she threw open the door and I charged out.

— — —

When I reached the archway that led to the common room, I paused and drew a deep breath. My nerves were already subsiding, the way they always did when a con got underway. I suspect it's kind of like stepping onstage for an actor; once the proverbial curtain rose, I felt nothing but calm.

After all, I was a pro, too.

Over the low chatter in the room, I heard Kate say, "Can I interest you in something to eat or drink, Mr. Cabot? They make a lovely avocado toast here."

"Well, aren't you a sweetheart!" Grimes boomed. "And so polite. I do appreciate that in a young lady."

The way he said it made my skin crawl. There was a disconcerting hunger underlying his words. And in spite of how angry and upset I was with Kate, my protective instincts spiked. Gritting my teeth, I shuffled toward them, careful to keep my pace slow.

I was halfway across the room by the time they reached the table occupied by my parents. Right on cue, my dad got to his feet, staggered, and caught himself on Grimes. Grimes reacted fast, shoving him off. My dad's arms pinwheeled, but he didn't fall. He protested, "Watch yourself, young man!"

"I'm so sorry," Kate said quickly. "Mr. Lawson has vertigo, and his balance isn't what it should be. Mr. Lawson, can I help you back to your room?"

I saw my dad nod weakly, grumbling to himself. Kate took his elbow and said, "Apologies again, Mr. Cabot. I'll send your daughter back as soon as she's done with the paperwork."

"Yes, of course," Grimes said. He was motionless, staring at the back of my mother's head.

Kate guided my dad toward me. She met my eyes and gave me a curt nod that I returned. As they passed, my dad said in a low voice, "He's unarmed."

"Got it," I murmured back. "Great job."

He reached out and subtly squeezed my hand. "Good luck, sweetheart. Love you."

I felt another rush of emotion that I quickly quashed. It was taking an eternity to cross the room, and the desire to simply drop the act and bolt was nearly overwhelming. But I forced myself to edge forward even more slowly.

Fifteen feet.

Ten.

As I watched, Gregory Grimes pulled out the chair next to my mother and sat down.

I sucked in a deep breath, fear suddenly clenching my stomach. *Will he buy it?*

Grimes leaned in, squinting at her. I was ten feet away when he sat back, looking pensive. "My, Marjorie," I overheard him say. "Didn't you get old."

My shoulders sagged. He'd bought it, at least for the moment. Now it was up to my mom. I shifted left, circling around as if headed to the café counter. "I am so sorry, dear," my mother said in a thin, quivering voice. "Do I know you?"

"Oh, yes," Grimes intoned menacingly. "You are my Judas, my Brutus. My most trusted companion, and my betrayer."

Five feet. I was nearly there.

I lifted my head to exchange a quick glance with Marcella, who stood stiffly behind the café counter. It was a good thing Grimes wasn't looking at her because her eyes were wide with terror, her breathing shallow. I mouthed, "It's okay," and she nodded.

"I don't think I know a Brutus," my mother said doubtfully. "And what was the other name you mentioned?"

She raised her head. In profile, I saw her eyes widen. Her voice had changed entirely as she gasped, "You're Gregory Grimes!"

Grimes leaned in closer to examine her, his face inches away. My mother shrank back with a cry as he growled, "You're not my Marjorie."

He half stood, fists clenched.

But before he could do anything else, I was there. Jamming the muzzle of the gun to the base of his neck, I said, "Remember me?"

CHAPTER TWENTY-NINE

EACH DAWN I DIE

Grimes froze. My mother pushed back her chair and staggered to her feet. Her voice pitched an octave higher than normal as she exclaimed, "What's happening, Emily? Why is Gregory Grimes here?"

"Get out of here, Mom," I said. "I'll see you after."

"After what?" Fists clenched, she cried, "Emily, I demand to know what's happening!"

"You have just made a terrible mistake, young lady," Grimes growled, his voice low and menacing. Around us, the rest of the crowd had risen to their feet. People were pulling out canisters of pepper spray and tasers. The crowd of elderly folks scattered throughout the room turned out to be a more motley assortment of ages, made up to appear older. They formed a rough semicircle around us, blocking the main exit.

"It's funny," I said. "That's almost exactly what Gunnar said right before we killed him."

Grimes fell still. "What did you say?"

"You killed someone?" my mom gasped.

"Seriously, Mom, get out of here!" I snarled. To Grimes, I said, "That's right, fuckwad, I killed your son. And now I'm going to kill you."

"You most certainly will not."

Shit. I turned my head slightly to see Grace standing in the archway, hands on her hips. "I told you to stay out of this."

"He's my father." Grace walked toward us, limping slightly. As she reached the people on the outer edge of the circle, they shifted to let her pass. "And I will handle him."

"Yeah, well, hell of a job you were doing," I said. "Because it seemed more like you were about to become his next victim."

"I would never hurt my own daughter," Grimes said. "I was merely going to teach her a lesson."

"I would have stopped him," Grace insisted. "In my own way."

"We didn't have seventeen years to spare," I scoffed. "I've got a wedding to get to."

"Give me the gun, Amber," Grace said, reaching for it. "Then get everyone out of here and call the police. I will make sure Father ends up in custody."

I hesitated. "That's not the plan."

"It is now."

Grace stood a couple feet away, arm extended. She looked exhausted. The dark circles under her eyes had deepened, and her pallor was even worse than it had been yesterday. Whatever her dad had subjected her to had clearly taken a toll.

But she also had determination in her eyes, without even a twinge of fear. So maybe she'd overcome her terror. Maybe she could actually handle him. "Okay," I said, relenting and offering the gun. "But be—"

Grimes moved swiftly, like a snake. Before Grace could grab it, he snatched the gun from my palm and turned it on me.

— — —

"Emily!" my mother shrieked from the archway.

I couldn't answer, staring down the barrel. Grace had frozen as well. Arms out, she said, "Don't do it, Father."

"Plan B!" I shouted, watching Grimes's finger tighten on the trigger. As I raised my hands defensively, colored balls flew toward us. Grimes's eyes widened as the air around us suddenly erupted in technicolor smoke.

"Everyone, run!" I screamed, ducking down. The gun went off, too close. Coughing, I pulled my silk neck scarf over my mouth and fumbled for the café counter behind me. Finding it, I groped my way along to the door that led to a service hallway. As I opened it, I felt someone at my shoulder: Grace.

"Where on earth are you going?" Grace demanded. "We need to stop him!"

"With what?" I said, grabbing her hand. "Don't be an idiot. C'mon!"

I dragged her down a utilitarian back hallway. At the very end was a set of double doors. We'd nearly reached them when the service door popped open behind us. Glancing back, I saw Grimes storming toward us, his face a furious mask. He raised the gun again, aiming at me.

"I can stop him," Grace insisted, trying to yank free.

"The hell you can!" I retorted. "You're a lot of things, but none of them is bulletproof." I threw open the door at the end of the hallway and physically hauled her into the small room beyond it.

Automatic lights flickered on overhead. Grace swore, then spun on me. "Well, I hope you're happy. You've led us into a dead end."

I swallowed hard—she was right. We were standing in a small rectangular storeroom the size and shape of a shipping container that was filled with boxes of cleaning supplies stacked on shelving.

The only way out was the door we'd entered through. The same door that now was slowly opening. I shrank back against the far wall as Grimes stepped inside. He grinned at us and said, "Well, now, girls. Time to teach you some manners."

CHAPTER THIRTY

THE BIG GAMBLE

Let Amber go," Grace said, placing herself between us and crossing her arms over her chest. "I'll come with you and do whatever you want."

"You're saying you'll join the hunt after all?" Grimes cocked an eyebrow.

"Yes," Grace said curtly. "But only if she is unharmed."

Grimes chuckled. "Oh, Gracie. Do you really expect me to fall for that again? Besides"—he gestured at me with the gun—"your little friend confessed to killing your brother. She certainly needs to be punished for that. Step aside, please."

"Quick question for you, Gregory Grimes. What kind of father frames his own kid for murders he committed?" I said, interrupting him. "That seems like something a coward would do."

Grimes's face darkened. "How I choose to discipline my children is none of your concern, young lady."

"Discipline?" I scoffed. "You know, my parents are assholes, but at least they never set the cops on me for stuff they did. You're a selfish, narcissistic psychopath. Rotting behind bars was too good for you."

Grace turned to me and hissed, "Could you please stop antagonizing Father? I'm trying to save your life."

"And I'm trying to save yours," I retorted. "And clear your name. It's not your fault your dad and brother turned out to be serial killers. Don't let him make you think you're like him. You're not. You're nothing like him."

Grace's eyes softened. "Thank you, Amber."

"I think I'll start by cutting out your tongue," Grimes said, coming closer. "Perhaps that will teach you the cost of impudence."

Grace shifted between us again, but he snapped at her, "Grace Anne Grimes, step aside."

"I won't," she said, her voice shakier than normal. "If you want to get to her, Father, you'll have to go through me."

"You dare challenge me, young lady? Did you not learn your lesson last night?"

"You know what, Dad? Go fuck yourself." Grace jutted her chin up. "I'm not afraid of you anymore."

"Yeah," I said, crossing my arms. "Go fuck yourself, you misogynistic asshole."

"Perhaps I'll just shoot you both right here," he said.

"Go ahead," I snorted. "There's nothing but blanks in that gun anyway."

Grimes's eyes narrowed. He squeezed the trigger.

The roar of the gun was deafening in the tiny space. I flinched in spite of myself, then straightened. Drawing a deep breath in, I said, "See?"

Grimes examined the gun, frowning. "Blanks?"

"Yeah, blanks. Try to keep up. And if you liked that, you're going to love my next trick. Abra-fucking-cadabra," I said, raising my hands high above my head and clapping them together loudly.

The lights went out.

It was pitch black, a profound and oppressive darkness. There was a giant *BOOM!* Then another, and another . . .

"What's happening?" Grimes cried out as a spotlight flared, pinning him in place. As he raised a hand to shield his eyes, I grabbed Grace's arm and dragged her back a few feet.

"What's going on, Amber?" Grace demanded, trying to shake free.

"Plan B," I said. "Now shut up and follow my lead."

As my eyes adjusted, our surroundings became clear. The loud bangs had been the sides of the "storage room" falling outward, as constructed by Tony Award–winning set designer Paco. Now, we were revealed to be standing on a stage in the middle of a theater in the round. And completely encircling us was a full SWAT team. They gaped at us, automatic rifles aimed at Grimes. Then someone yelled, "Freeze! LVPD SWAT! Drop the gun!"

I raised my hands and motioned for Grace to follow suit. In a low voice she said, "So your plan was for us to get captured by the police?"

Grimes was hesitating, the gun still pointed at us.

"Drop it! Now!" a cop boomed from the shadows.

Grimacing, Grimes slowly started to lower the gun. I edged back a few inches and hissed, "Grace! This way!"

"Stay where you are, all of you!" the cop ordered.

"Sorry," I called back, stomping my foot twice. "But I got places to be."

Grace let out a yelp as the floor suddenly disappeared beneath us and we fell into a dark hole.

— — —

We landed hard on a mat. Even though I'd been expecting it, the wind was knocked out of me. Probably because Grace had fallen on top of me.

Making a strangled noise, she rolled off, snarling, "What on earth is happening?"

"Are you two okay?" Dot asked anxiously. The trapdoor above us had already swung shut, and I heard the pounding of boots overhead as I did a quick body scan: Everything felt bruised, but nothing felt broken. Hopefully the same was true for Grace.

"We gotta move," Marcella said, stepping forward. "Before they figure out how to get down here."

"Yeah, totally," I agreed. Dot extended a hand and helped me to my feet. Grace had already stood and was glaring at all of us. "So this was the plan all along?"

"More or less," I said. "But we're not out of the woods yet. Let's move. I can explain when we get some air between us and the cops."

I could tell by Grace's face that she wanted to argue but thankfully seemed to think better of it. I fell in step behind Marcella as she guided us through the labyrinth beneath the stage. She motioned to a coil of rope on the floor and said, "Careful, don't trip on that."

"How are my parents?" I asked in a low voice.

"Still assholes, but they're safe." Glancing back at me, she added, "Your girl, too."

"She's not my girl anymore," I muttered.

"Is there an end to this maze?" Grace protested from behind me.

"Shh!" Dot said. "Keep your pants on, we're almost out. But we gotta hustle."

Obediently, we stepped up the pace.

"Looks like your good luck kiss worked," I said casually to Marcella as we approached another door.

"They always do," she smirked, rapping on it lightly with her knuckles.

Grace asked, "Why are we—"

"Shut it!" Marcella barked, glaring at her.

A second later the door popped open, letting in a dazzling beam of sunlight. Deputy Riggs waved us forward. "Better hurry. I told them I'd cover this end, but based on the radio chatter, you got about a dozen pissed-off SWAT headed this way."

"Thanks again, Lon. We've got a recording of him admitting that Grace had nothing to do with it, if it helps."

"Perfect, send it along. And thanks for the tip; this'll make me a shoo-in for a promotion. Now go. I'll call later with an update."

We hurried past Riggs into the empty parking lot behind the theater. I could hear the chirp of walkie-talkies and sirens from the opposite end of the building. "Shit," I said. "Did the others make it out?"

"Don't you worry, kiddo. Portia already texted that they all got clear," Dot said reassuringly.

"They're waiting at the Tiki Hut," Marcella said. "Everyone's grabbing drinks there to celebrate."

"It's not even nine in the morning," Grace said. "Isn't that a bit early to start drinking?"

"It's Vegas, baby," I said, chucking her on the shoulder. "No such thing as too early. Now c'mon, first round's on me."

— — —

The celebration at the Tiki Hut was already in full swing by the time we got there. Most of the crowd was still wearing their leisure suits and wigs, which gave it the general vibe of a *Golden Girls* convention. As we entered, everyone broke into applause. Dot raised both arms and then gestured to us, saying, "Let's hear it for the ladies of the hour!"

I blushed, discomfited by the attention. "Actually," I said, raising my voice, "This was all Dot. So raise a glass to the bride-to-be!"

"To Dot!" the crowd roared.

Amid the clinking of glasses, Dot leaned in and pecked me on the cheek. "I'm just so chuffed that it worked out, kiddo. I gotta be honest: I had my doubts for a minute there."

"You and me both." Hugging her back, I added, "I mean it, though. I couldn't have done it without you."

"Is this bad luck?" a low voice drawled behind us. Past Dot's shoulder, I spotted Jim. A former Marine with a black belt, he looked like a six-five, pre-bloat Elvis, sideburns and all. Dot's eyes went wide and she squealed, "You're early!"

"Couldn't wait to get back and see my girl," he said, sweeping her up in his arms.

While they exchanged a deep kiss, I motioned to the bar and said, "Um, I'm gonna grab a drink."

"I'll join you," Grace said, wrinkling her nose. "Public displays of affection always make me uncomfortable."

"Shocking," I said. "I never would've guessed that."

"Yes, well. Your brother didn't murder your first boyfriend," she said wryly. "Discretion seemed wise after that."

"True. I mean, we didn't even kiss, and he came after me." Off Grace's look, I said, "What? I'm not wrong."

The crowd parted to let us through, nearly everyone offering congratulations, a handshake, or a word of encouragement. I hardly knew how to handle all the attention, and it made me extremely self-conscious. The thing about con artists is that we generally exist in the shadows; if you notice us, we aren't doing our job very well. So this kind of post-gig validation was new.

Marcella had already found a seat at the bar. I squeezed in beside her and said, "Order me a margarita?"

"Only if you promise to dance on the bar again," she shot back.

"Not today. Still too sore from dropping through the floor," I said, pulling off my wig.

"There's a bag in the corner for those," Marcella said with a nod. "But you might want to keep it. You make a pretty hot old lady."

I blushed.

"Are we going to discuss what happened?" Grace said from behind me.

"I mean, I think it's pretty obvious," I said. "But I can explain it in smaller words if that helps."

Grace's frown deepened. "So the trapdoor was your plan all along?" she said.

"Yeah, basically," I said.

A small part of me was expecting her to be impressed. Maybe even to tell me so. But this was Grace, after all, so she said, "That entire scheme was ridiculously elaborate and could have gone horribly wrong."

"Gee, thanks."

"Saved your ass, didn't it?" Marcella said, crossing her arms.

"I was hardly in need of saving," Grace said.

"Then why are you limping?" I pointed out. Grace didn't answer. "Yeah, that's what I thought. You know, the least you can do is say thank you."

A beat, then Grace said, "Thank you."

I stared at her. "Holy shit. Really?"

"Yes, Amber." She nodded. "That certainly was not how I would have done it. But despite the rather flamboyant elements, Marcella is correct—the desired outcome was achieved. So thank you."

"You're welcome." A margarita was slid across the bar to me. I picked it up and took a sip, feeling dazed. Over the rim I spotted my parents and Kate sitting awkwardly at a table off to the side, separate from the revelers. Gesturing with my head, I asked, "Out of curiosity, how did you know they were conning me?"

"Your girlfriend mispronounced the name of her boarding school."

I stared at her. "That's it?"

"It was enough to make me suspicious," Grace said. "So I performed a deeper background check and discovered several anomalies."

"Uh-huh. And when was that?"

"That same day. Once I uncovered her true identity, I saw that she'd committed fraud with your parents in Ohio."

I stared at her. "So two days ago, you knew that my parents were colluding with my girlfriend to rip me off. And you didn't say anything?"

Grace looked discomfited. "I intended to tell you in the café, but you were with all of them. And frankly, I wasn't certain you'd believe me. I know how complicated family can be."

She wasn't wrong there. Two days ago, I wouldn't have been willing to hear anything negative about Kat. "Well, next time, just go ahead and tell me."

"I did take precautionary measures. Any significant withdrawals from your bank accounts would have been flagged."

"The *fuck*," Marcella muttered.

"Um, thanks, I guess?" I took a swig of my cocktail. "Which reminds me, we should probably have another chat about boundaries."

"You're welcome," Grace said. "I also strongly advise changing accounts entirely. Perhaps even transferring the money to a new bank."

"I will. I just have to pay them off first," I said, motioning with my drink.

Marcella scoffed. "Screw that. You don't owe them anything."

"I'm tempted to agree, Amber," Grace said. "If you prefer, I could ensure that they're forced to answer for their crimes."

"You mean, set them up?"

"I doubt that would be necessary. They have outstanding warrants in several states. I could anonymously alert the authorities to their location."

My mother suddenly raised her head. Spotting me, she offered a tentative wave.

I sighed. What Grace was offering was tempting. But the one code my parents had instilled that I agreed with was "Never be a rat." So I said, "It's fine. They're shitty people, but they're still family. I'd rather just be done with them."

"What about the baroness?" Grace asked archly.

Kat—Kate, rather—was watching us uncertainly. As our eyes met, she looked away. "Same with her. Life's too short. And I gotta believe karma will catch up with them someday."

"We could make it today," Marcella growled. "I got nothing on my calendar."

"Thanks, both of you. Really. It means a lot." And it did. Feeling surprisingly emotional, I said, "I just want to start clean."

"Again," Grace said with a small smile.

Grinning back at her I said, "Yeah, again."

"Then if you'll excuse me," Grace said, "I need to go check on Mother."

"Give her my best." As she started to limp away, I called after her, "See you at the wedding!"

Grace waved back over her shoulder. I watched as she spoke to Dot and stiffly accepted a hug.

"Damn," Marcella said. "She's kind of growing on me."

"Yeah, she does that," I said, polishing off my drink. "Order me another? I'll be right back."

Drawing a deep breath, I made my way through the crowd to their table.

"You have a lot of explaining to do, young lady!" my mother exclaimed as soon as I got close.

"Putting your mother in danger like that," my dad said disapprovingly. "How could you?"

"He could have killed me!" my mother wailed.

"Well, you're fine," I said curtly. "And I'm not apologizing. Far as I'm concerned, this does not make us even."

"Well," my mother sniffed. "You certainly have changed."

"Yeah, I have. Now, I'm going to pay you in Bitcoin."

"After all that pain and suffering? I certainly intend to renegotiate. I never would've agreed to such a paltry sum if I'd known we'd be dealing with a madman."

"Hazard pay," my dad agreed with a nod.

"Fine," I sighed. "I'll tack another fifty grand on top of it. On one condition." I held up a finger. "I never see you again. And if you see me, you turn and walk the other way. Is that clear?"

"But we're your parents!" my mother said. "How could you—"

"Yeah, you are," I said, cutting her off. "And a part of me will always love you. I can't help that. But I don't like you, and I don't trust you. We don't have a relationship anymore, we haven't since you walked out on me. So take the win. You say another word, that extra fifty grand goes away."

My mom opened her mouth to retort, but my dad laid a hand over hers and nodded. "Okay, kiddo. Love you."

"Love you, too, Dad. Now get the fuck out of here. Oh, and Kate—if I were you, I'd stick with them. No way they're cutting you in otherwise. And you might want to be more careful about who you partner with next time."

"Rude," my mother sniffed.

"Okay," Kate said in a small voice.

"Goodbye, Emily," my mom said, getting to her feet. "I certainly hope you live to regret this."

"Yeah, I won't. Regret it, I mean." I offered a little wave. "Enjoy the rest of your lives."

Without another word, my parents headed for the door.

I have to admit, despite everything, part of me felt a little emotional. The little girl deep inside still wanted to follow, to make them love me, see me.

But if I'd learned anything, it was that they weren't capable of giving me what I needed. They never had been, and that wasn't my fault.

Halfway to the door, Kate hesitated, then hurried back. "It was real, you know. For me. I fell for you."

"Not enough to keep from fucking me over, though. Not enough to tell me what was going on," I said. "Right?"

A tear slid down her cheek. I turned away. Dot was standing at the bar with Marcella and Jim, watching this exchange with concern. She waved for me to join them. Squaring my shoulders, I said, "Goodbye, Kate."

Then I went to join my real family.

CHAPTER THIRTY-ONE

DEADLINE–U.S.A.

BREAKING NEWS:
GREGORY GRIMES FOUND ALIVE, RECAPTURED BY LVPD SWAT

In a stunning turn of events, it was revealed today that Gregory Grimes, who was believed dead when the Coal Creek wildfire overtook his prison transfer bus, survived the incident. LVPD SWAT arrested Grimes in Las Vegas this morning. Details remain scarce, but according to an anonymous source, Grimes is suspected of the brutal murders of three women in Colorado, Arizona, and Las Vegas in the days since his escape. Prison authorities in Colorado have no explanation for why Grimes was mistakenly reported to be among the dead. Warden Roberts has promised a full and thorough investigation.

This is a developing story.

CHAPTER THIRTY-TWO

PLUNDER ROAD

ST. GEORGE, UTAH
BLOOMINGTON MARKET

I still don't know why Emily couldn't just pay us in cash," Sarah grumbled, arms crossed over her chest.

"We're lucky she paid us at all, dear," Perry said. "Now read off those last five numbers."

Squinting at her phone, she slowly read, "Q-7-5-5-3. Honestly, does no one use Western Union anymore?"

"I actually kind of like it," he said. "Keeps us nimble, nothing to lose."

"You better let me hold on to that key, then," she said. "Remember Wichita?"

"Not my fault," he snapped back. "You were supposed to grab the bag."

"This again? I swear, Perry, if you're going to keep beating that dead horse—"

"It's all here," he said. "A hundred-ten K."

"Well, that's a relief." Sarah peered at the screen. "How much can you take out at once?"

He leaned in beside her. "It says fifty, but maybe we should just take out enough to get us back to Akron."

"Yes, that's smart." She straightened and patted her hair. "Five thousand to start."

"I want my cut, too," Kate said, coming out of the aisle behind them, holding a bag of Takis.

"Eager to get rid of us, Kate?" Sarah said.

"Yeah, totally. I never should've agreed to this shit show in the first place."

"Well, if you'd done your part properly, we would have a lot more than a hundred K," the older woman sniffed.

"A hundred ten," Kate said. "Don't think I wasn't paying attention."

As Perry pressed the buttons, a cool female voice above them said, "I'm so glad to see that my algorithm was right."

They all exchanged a glance and then turned as one to face the camera pointing down at them from a corner of the market.

"Goddammit," Kate said with resignation. "I knew it."

"Is there a problem?" Sarah said innocently.

"For me? No. No problem."

The wail of approaching sirens. They all looked at the door, then back to the camera. Sarah's eyes narrowed. "Who is this?"

"As I was saying, I personally don't have a problem with you. But I do object to your poor treatment of your daughter."

"Our agreement is with Emily," Sarah said, hands on her hips. "And I really don't see how this is any of your business, whoever you are."

Her husband caught her eye and inclined his head toward the

service door. Sarah tilted her head slightly in acknowledgment. Edging toward it, she continued, "We earned every penny of that money."

"Debatable," the voice said. "Regardless, I'm a firm believer in people receiving their just deserts. Amber might have let you go, but I did not agree to that. And I should warn you, there are authorities stationed outside that exit as well."

As the doors at the far end of the market slid open and a slew of uniformed police stormed in, Sarah wailed, "Why are you doing this?"

A pause, then the voice said, "Karma."

CHAPTER THIRTY-THREE

PARTY GIRL

Moodily, I sipped champagne. The dance floor was filled, a tribute to the talent of Jim's band. Dot was twenty feet away, looking absolutely stunning in a sapphire gown. She led the conga line as it wove among tables where a handful of other guests were finishing their cake.

She waved for me to join. I held up my glass and shook my head, forcing a smile. I wasn't really in the mood to celebrate.

The wedding had been every bit as incredible as Dot herself. All of Vegas seemed to have turned out for it; valets rubbed elbows with headliners, and a line of showgirls kicked off the reception with a full floor routine. Jim had literally swept Dot off her feet during the tango they performed for their first dance.

I was thrilled for Dot . . . and simultaneously miserable and wallowing in self-pity. I couldn't stop ruminating over how I'd been played for a fool. And also what Marcella had said, about me attracting terrible shit; maybe she was right and I was cursed. Watching her make out with Toni a few tables over wasn't helping either. Even

Sandra had landed on her feet; she and Skeeter were dirty dancing in the far corner.

I went to take another swig, only to discover that my champagne coupe was empty. I eyed the bar, which seemed to have gotten farther away; I wasn't a hundred percent sure I could stagger over there in my heels. I turned to look for a waiter to flag down and found Grace standing right behind me. I startled and put a hand to my chest. "Oh shit. You scared me."

"I'm here to avenge my father," she deadpanned.

"Not bad," I said, slow-clapping. "You're really getting the hang of this joke thing. But seriously, if there are any more serial killers in your family, this would be a great time to let me know. Murderous cousin Bill, maybe? Or slasher Aunt Sally?"

"I sincerely doubt there's ever been a Cabot named Sally," Grace sniffed, making a face. "We do have a few Bills, though. Well, Williams."

"Fan-fucking-tastic," I groaned. "I'll keep an eye out."

Grace sat down beside me and motioned with her hand; seconds later, the waiter who I could've sworn had been avoiding me was refilling my glass. "Perhaps you should also have some water," she said.

"You're not my mother," I retorted, wincing as soon as the words left my mouth. For once, Grace didn't seize the opportunity to make me feel like even more of a chump, which actually had the opposite effect. I sighed. "Thanks again for making sure they didn't rob me blind."

"Of course." Grace paused, then added, "Thank you for making sure Father ended up back in prison."

"Any time." I took another big gulp of champagne and said morosely, "Must've been very validating to see me make such an idiot of myself." I'd had breakups before, but no one had ever made me feel like a mark. It was a serious blow to my ego.

"Amber, stop blaming yourself," Grace said gently. "You could not possibly have known."

"You know what the kicker is?" I said, shaking my head. "I think I vaguely remember Kate from when we were kids. Which would explain why something about her was immediately familiar. I chalked it up to chemistry, but no: She seemed familiar because we'd actually met."

"It was kind of you to give them the money regardless," Grace said.

I shrugged. "It was only a hundred K."

Grace quirked a corner of her mouth. "'Only'?"

"Yeah, I know. You've ruined me." I drained my glass and sighed. Yesterday, I'd changed banks and done a full accounting; Kate had siphoned off nearly forty grand of my money and I hadn't even noticed. Served me right for never checking bank statements; I would not make that mistake again. "Listen, I think I'm gonna head to bed. I'm not really in the mood for a party right now."

"That's understandable." Grace eyed me, then said, "Will you be heading back to San Francisco tomorrow?"

I shrugged. "I don't know. I was thinking of trying someplace else for a bit." In truth, I was dreading going back to my apartment and facing the stuff Kate had left there. Part of me was tempted to just leave everything behind, but I did want to collect my diploma.

"That's a shame," Grace said. "I was planning on visiting."

"Visiting *me*?" I put a hand to my chest. "Seriously?"

"Not you specifically."

"Gee, thanks."

Grace cocked her head to the side. "This morning my algorithm flagged some activity in Alameda that seemed worth checking out. It's only a few miles from San Francisco."

"No shit?" I cocked my head to the side, mirroring her.

Grace smiled thinly at me. "I considered what you said, and perhaps you weren't entirely mistaken."

"Wow, thanks. About what part?"

"I have been somewhat adrift of late. I do have a talent for this. And I could use a change of scenery. Plus, Mother is settled in the facility Chuy recommended, and she seems quite content."

"That's great, really. I'm glad," I said sincerely.

"Thank you." After a beat, she added, "I was thinking that perhaps you might join me."

"Join you?" My eyebrows shot up. "Wait, are you asking me to hunt serial killers with you?"

"Unless you'd rather go to graduate school?" Grace asked.

Someone tapped my shoulder, and I turned to find Marcella standing there. "Dot said if you don't get your ass on the dance floor, she'll make you regret it."

"Well, then I guess I better get out there," I said.

"Damn straight," Toni said. "What are you ladies talking about?"

I looked at Grace. She raised an eyebrow, and I gave her a slow nod. "Alameda, huh?"

"In the general vicinity, yes," Grace said. "Of course, we would have to narrow it down. I'm tweaking the algorithm."

"Of course you are." As I let Marcella and Toni drag me away, I called back over my shoulder, "Count me in. But I'm driving. And bringing the snacks."

ACKNOWLEDGMENTS

So here we go again. It has been a *ride*, my friends.

Turns out that finishing graduate school and starting a full-time associateship are—shockingly—not entirely compatible with writing a sequel. And if you're also raising a family and have way too many dogs? Well, that means you're looking at a solid year without a day off. As a practicing therapist now, this is something I do not recommend. But honestly? Challenging though it was (and yes, I know, these are good problems to have; I am well aware of my privilege), it was worth it to be able to dive back into this fun, campy world filled with characters I adore.

I definitely couldn't have done it alone. So here's a shout-out to everyone who shared the burden, making my life a bit easier along the way. (Brace yourselves, people: It's Oscars speech time again.)

I dedicated this book to my agent, Stephanie Rostan, because without her, this story would not exist outside my head. She's not only the best agent going, she's also a heck of a dining companion, especially when you end up eating pasta with Clive Owen. Well, okay, next to Clive Owen. Close enough. Basically, Steph is the best, and I'm so fortunate to have her representing me.

The whole team at Putnam has been remarkable. Kate Dresser stepped in for the inimitable Danielle Dieterich, taking the reins midstream and guiding us to a release date. I'm thankful to her and the rest of the Putnam team for their efforts. From copyediting to marketing to cover design, they have insured that my motley crew received the star treatment. The folks at United Talent Agency also worked tirelessly to give these characters a chance to appear on-screen: I have so much appreciation for Jasmine Lake and Mirabel Michelson. And I am grateful for the extraordinary guidance and support of my producing partner Loretha Jones of Flavor Unit.

I am also lucky to have a wealth of amazing friends. Some have been in my life for decades, like Diem Ha, Colin Dangel, David Fribush, Ty Jagerson, Caroline Egan (the real-life Baroness von Rotberg, who is definitely not a grifter), and Kate Stoia. And then there are my writing friends: Elle Cosimano, Lisa Brown, Madeleine Roux, Mindy McGinnis, Leslie Margolis, and Adele Griffin. Big shout-out to my L.A. ride or dies: Jessica Postigo, Betsy Brandt, Bonnie Zane, Anikke Fox, Claire Gordon-Harper, Matthew Raymond-Goodman, and Michael & Wendy Landes. Sending much love to the remarkable people I work with—I'm in awe of your talent and passion. Leah, Jo, Jak, Mickey, Mike, Natalie, Lindsey, Yoselene, and everyone else at the Center who puts their time, energy, and love into helping LGBTQ+ youth through their most challenging moments, it's a true honor and a pleasure to work alongside you.

Thanks as always to the amazing readers, librarians, and booksellers who have enthusiastically enjoyed and promoted my books. I'm so grateful to all of you. And thanks as well to the good folks on #bookstagram and #booktok for embracing these characters. I loved all the creative ways you showcased *Killing Me* (especially the pet pics)! I appreciate your support so much.

And of course, my family, aka my net. Thanks for being understanding when I was at my most overwhelmed, and for making my life easier in ways both large and small. My parents, for their boundless love and support. My sisters, for always being there—Kate has been one of my earliest beta readers, providing thoughtful feedback on everything I've ever written, and I trust her implicitly. I'm thankful for my kids, who are so smart and funny and charming and creative. And the final thanks will always go to Kirk, the person I've been lucky enough to pair with for this crazy little thing called life. You are my secret weapon.

As the curtain drops, I find myself wondering what life has in store for our intrepid heroines. There's a form of therapy that emphasizes narratives, positing that what makes us human is our ability to construct stories and give shape to our lives. I like to think there's an alternate universe out there where these characters we fall in love with continue on past the pages, living their lives and writing their own endings.

Anyway, thanks again for coming along for the ride. Hope you had as much fun as I did.

Best,
Michelle